DARK DIAMOND

DARK DIAMOND

Shazia Omar

BLOOMSBURY
NEW DELHI • LONDON • OXFORD • NEW YORK • SYDNEY

Bloomsbury Publishing India Pvt. Ltd
Second Floor, LSC Building No.4
DDA Complex, Pocket C – 6 & 7, Vasant Kunj
New Delhi 110070

BLOOMSBURY and the Diana logo are trademarks of Bloomsbury Publishing Plc

First published in India 2016

ISBN 978 93 85936 46 3
10 9 8 7 6 5 4 3 2 1

Typeset by Manipal Digital Systems
Printed and bound in India by Replika Press Pvt Ltd

To find out more about our authors and books visit www.bloomsbury.com.
Here you will find extracts, author interviews, details of forthcoming
events and the option to sign up for our newsletters.

For the youth of Bengal, may you love and be free.

'The Moving Finger writes; and, having writ,
Moves on: nor all thy Piety nor Wit,
Shall lure it back to cancel half a Line,
Nor all thy Tears wash out a Word of it.'

—Omar Qayyam

CHAPTER I

Legend has it, outside the city of Golconda lived a tantric devotee named Hira Lal. In youth he was dedicated to the worship of Kali but later worked in a mine to sustain his destitute family. One night before Kali puja, Hira went to bed without food, with only a glass of water to quench his thirst, yet he was grateful and thanked his goddess.

The next day, inside the jaws of a cavernous mine, Hira chipped away as if possessed, eyes unnaturally bright in the struggling flame of a candle. His pick had hit something solid and he was in a frenzy to pry it out. The foreman had blown the whistle twice. The guard on duty shouted, 'If I have to call once more, I am going to break your knees.'

Hira's body wanted to obey. He was hungry, tired and depressed. He had been working since sunrise. It was probably only a rock. His wife would chastise him for his late return. 'Ever an optimist,' she would say as she ladled cold aloo bhaji onto his plate.

He rubbed his sore elbow and hammered once more. Suddenly the rock surrendered. Rubble crumbled to the ground and from within the dry bits of earth came a promising sparkle. He dropped to his knees. The pick fell away from his hand. He lifted the pile of sediment to his lips and blew gently.

His hopeful breath scattered the dust and uncovered a gem that filled his palms with a bewitching glow. He raised it to the candle. It was a brilliant dark diamond, once midnight indigo, once stormy violet, smooth and larger than his two fists. It glowed like a star from Hell. A strange elation came over Hira. This stone would buy his liberty.

He removed the scarf from his head and tenderly polished the diamond. His wife was ill with blood cough. His children had dropped out of school. This was the touchstone that would transform their lives. He thanked Goddess Kali.

'Don't make me come in there!' shouted the guard.

Hira hid the diamond in his dhuti and walked out. He bowed, praying the guard would not search him.

Baring his fangs, the guard landed a punishing blow to Hira's ear. 'What did you find?'

Hira emptied his basket. A few of the gems were worth a trifle but the guard was not impressed.

'Is this it? You made me wait for this?' He slapped Hira across the face then cracked his knuckles. 'Go!' He spat at Hira's back as he turned to leave.

Hira could not conceal the excitement coursing through his veins as he darted home. He had heard of miracles but never dared hope for one.

'So late?' Rupa greeted him when he reached. 'The children are asleep.' She laughed when he grabbed her around the waist and lifted her to the air.

'My love, you will not believe what I have to show you!'

'What is it?' she asked. 'Did you steal fruit from the overlord's orchard? Really Hira, it is too dangerous. His wife is a witch, do not anger her. Is it a mango?'

'No, it is much grander,' he said. Kneeling before her, he kissed her palms and placed in them the diamond.

'O Gracious Kali,' cried Rupa. 'You work in mysterious ways.'

'A diamond this size must be worth half the King's treasury. I won't have to work another day in my life!'

'You won't?'

'We will live in a house.'

'We will?'

'Our children will go to school.'

'They will?'

'We will eat mutton.'

'We will?'

'Twice a day.'

'Oh Hira!'

'We will live as kings!'

Hira Lal and Rupa embraced, laughing and weeping at once.

'If others come to know, they will kill us,' said Hira at last. 'We must take it to the mine overlord right away.'

'Now?' said Rupa. 'In the middle of the night?'

'We can't keep it,' Hira reasoned. 'Too risky.'

'Let's take it to the Maharaja ourselves?' said Rupa. 'I don't trust the overlord or his wife.'

'He may be rough but he's a good man,' said Hira. 'He won't deny us our reward. We cannot betray him. It would not be right.'

Rupa sighed.

'Come with me?' suggested Hira Lal so she could enjoy the gem a while longer. They wrapped the diamond in a rough spun cloth and made their way to the home of the overlord.

A dog barked as they approached. Hira knocked on the door. A grumble and a scuffle sounded within.

The overlord received them, scratching his hairy chest, rubbing sleep out of his eyes. He saw Hira and scowled. 'You have some nerve disturbing me so late.'

'Master, look what I found.' Hira presented him with the parcel. It unravelled to reveal the diamond.

'Never seen anything like it,' said the overlord. 'Kohinoor ka behna!'

Hira cleared his throat. 'I request the honour of accompanying you to present this to the Raja.'

'You do, do you?' said the overlord.

Hira nodded. He had to ensure his due.

'Come inside,' said the overlord.

Before Hira could defend himself, the man hurtled a broad-bladed dhup down upon his arm, cleaving it in two. Hira howled in anguish.

Inside, the overlord's infant began to wail. His wife called out from her room, 'Who is it, so late?'

The overlord hissed at Hira, 'Thief, leave before I call the guards and have you thrown in the dungeon!'

Hira rushed to the door.

Rupa screamed. 'We shall inform the Raja of your brutality.'

Scarce had she finished her words, the bully grabbed her hair and threw her to the ground. 'I cannot allow news of this treasure to spread,' he said. 'I have to kill you both.'

'O Master, be merciful.' Hira bent his head to the ground. 'If you have one grain of goodness in your soul, release her. She will tell no one of the diamond. It was I who found it. Kill me, spare her. We have young children.'

The overlord turned his wanton eyes to Rupa. 'Alright. You can live. But you have to kill him. I do not want his blood on my karma.' He thrust the dhup into her hands. It was four feet long and heavy.

Rupa looked at her husband standing miserably before her and collapsed into tears.

'Do it or I shall have him kill you instead,' said the overlord.

Rupa wailed in agony.

'My love,' said Hira gently. 'You must kill me. Do it for our children. They need you.'

Rupa crawled to the feet of the overlord, sobbing, 'Have mercy, Sire.' The overlord kicked her away.

'Leave her!' bellowed Hira Lal.

With what little strength she had, Rupa lifted the dhup and stabbed it into her own heart. Hands over her wound, she sank to the ground.

'No!' Hira crumpled in grief by her side.

The overlord pinned him to the wall. 'Who else knows?'

'No one,' said Hira. Enraged, he lunged at the overlord.

The overlord wrenched the weapon out of his wife and struck at him with its cold steel, mercilessly hacking into him.

Hira Lal called out for help, 'Jaya Mata Kali, Divine Mother, hear my cries. You are the destroyer of time! You are the embodiment of terror! You are the giver of boons! Avenge my wife's death! Hrim! Srim! Krim!'

A gust of wind threw open the windows, tearing the door off its hinges. Before them appeared Kali, Goddess of Destruction, red eyes, dishevelled hair, breath like roaring waves. She wore a garland of skulls, a skirt of human arms and in her hand was a vengeful khadga.

The overlord who had a minute earlier towered in domination now quaked in fear. 'Forgive me!' he begged. 'Forgive me, Ma Kali!' He tried to hand her the diamond.

Kali turned to Hira, blood dripping from her lips. What Hira saw in her eyes was Love, a love more tender than he had ever known in his belaboured life. So sweet was her gaze, his pain disappeared. His sadness dissolved and poured out of his soul as tears of joy.

Kali cupped Hira's face in her palm and stroked his hair. She kissed him on the crown of his head and liberated him with death.

She rose to her full form, seven thousand feet tall. With the fury of the tortured and the betrayed, with the rage of the oppressed and the exiled, with the miseries of monsoons unleashed, she brought her jagged blade down on the overlord's head, smashing it in. She then hacked his wife to gory pieces and then his suckling child, then his animals: the dogs, goats and ducks. When nothing lived in the vicinity of his homestead, Kali raised the diamond to Heaven and said, 'This stone which man so adores, whosoever possesses it shall suffer. All that they cherish shall perish.'

CHAPTER 2

The night's chill clutched at her bones. Madeline could not draw her cloak tight enough to ward off the dread. Beggars huddled by gutters cursed as carriages splashed mud. Drunken rogues quarrelled on street corners. Madeline hurried past so urgently even the skilled pickpockets hadn't time to assail her.

She skirted the periphery of L'Hotel du Turannes and looked over her shoulders. It was unlikely that she had been followed. She was dressed in a man's hooded cloak and trousers, her purse carefully concealed. Still one could never be sure. She knocked three times against the wooden gate, invoking Saint Anne for protection.

A scar faced man cracked open the door wide enough for her to slip in a coin of some value. He examined the currency then allowed her in but not before itching his jaw with the edge of his chipped dagger.

The smell of stale ale and smoke accosted her. Rambunctious men drank frothy slosh and flirted with lacy bar maids. The tavern catered to a morally ambiguous and highly inebriated clientele. It still drew a crowd though it was built two years earlier, when King Louis moved to Versailles.

Madeline whispered in the doorman's ear and handed him another coin. He nodded and led her to a room with two tables and one lamp.

At the lit table were four men playing cards. At the table shrouded in shadows, a man with a tricorne hat sipped on a drink. From his outline she could make out he was narrowly built and chiselled. He wore an overcoat, breeches and pointy leather boots. She had no view of his belt to ascertain his weaponry. His tumbler was nearly drained.

'Are you Captain Costa?' she asked.

The stranger nodded.

'I was told you have a ship.' She lowered her hood. 'Is there some place private to discuss matters of delicacy?'

He motioned to the table across from them. 'Mi amigas,' he said. 'Your secrets are safe here.'

Madeline did not want to negotiate in the open. Only yesterday, Duc de la Rochefien was incarcerated for conspiring against the King. 'I have no secrets,' she replied. What did he know?

'We all have secrets,' said Costa. 'Some dirtier than others.'

'I beg your pardon, I am a natural philosopher not a creature of dirty secrets.' What was he insinuating? Had he heard? Certainly her deportment and grace had not given her away. She had spent most of her adult life studying and perfecting the tropes of nobility.

The captain shrugged.

Reluctantly, she sat down next to him. 'I require safe passage to Bengal.'

'What are you running away from?' he asked.

Madeline produced a woeful countenance. 'Alas, my father is unwell. It is for him, this expedition. Bengal's herbal solutions are renowned. I hope to find something that might cure him. I have been informed that you are familiar with the route?'

Costa nodded.

'I will pay in gold.' She produced from her leather purse a promissory note.

A gold tooth sparkled when Costa smiled. 'I'll take you to the Subedar in six months.'

Madeline shivered. She had heard of the Mughal Viceroy of Bengal, a fitful despot who lived in Dacca and killed on whim.

As if reading her fears, Costa continued, 'He's my mate. We're like this.' He crossed two fingers. His nails were untrimmed and grimy, his hand calloused.

Most sea captains Madeline had met were braggarts and liars. 'It is not Dacca I wish to travel to but the Port of Chatgaon.'

'Chatgaon?' said Costa. 'Nothing there but tigers.'

'There is a tribe in the hills of Chatgaon with ancient recipes known to cure my father's affliction.'

'Dutiful daughter,' said Captain Costa.

Madeline could not tell if he was being earnest. Her hands perspired inside her gloves. Even if he were to agree to ferry her to Hindustan, how would she possibly survive six months in his scurvied company?

She spoke authoritatively to seal the deal. 'I offer you 20,000 crowns. Half now and the remaining to be paid upon my safe return to France.'

'Double that and pay upfront,' said Costa. 'That's what Tavernier paid me.'

'Monsieur, I do not have the purse of a thief,' said Madeline.

'No, just the debts of a liar?' said Costa.

'How dare you cast such aspersions!' said Madeline, blood rising to her face.

A bar maid stepped into the room and offered them drinks. Madeline declined in a hurry to get on with business. The captain bantered with the girl who in turn laughed and lingered. Madeline glowered, waiting for the tart to leave. Patience, she told herself. She must do this for her father. At long last the bar maid stepped out.

'You can't escape your troubles,' said Costa before she could get in a word. 'You have to change your way of thinking. That's what I discovered from my years of wandering. The only escape is to reshape your attitude. Reconsider your foolish mission. The sea is no tame lover. No place for natural philosophers. Nor women.'

'Women are stronger than you think,' snapped Madeline.

'Ain't that the truth, Mother Mary.'

If this lowly buccaneer wasn't her last resort, she would have slapped him for his insolence. With icy politeness, she replied, 'Attack a kitten, its father will run, tail between its legs. Its mother will fight till her last breath.' She bit her lip. She mustn't antagonise him. 'I assure you, I shall be an entirely pleasant travel companion. My father was a sea captain.'

Costa cocked an eyebrow, 'Your blood father?'

Madeline nodded.

'Never met a sailor's gal who pretends to be above her station.'

Irritation flared at Madeline's finger tips but she faked an angelic smile. '200,000 rupees is a most generous offer.'

'You will need a cabin and constant supervision,' said Costa.

'Supervision? I am not a child!'

'Can you hold your ground against a man?'

'Indeed, I can fence,' Madeline retorted. 'I trained as a child.'

'Can you hold your ground against twenty men?' asked Costa.

Madeline hesitated. 'Should I disguise myself as a man?'

'You've been reading too many adventure books ... Hush!'

'Excuse me?' she said, annoyed.

The captain pressed his finger to her lips.

Then Madeline heard it too. The sound of footsteps: boots rushing in their direction. She hid her face under the hood of her cloak and whispered, 'I'll pay double upfront!'

In streamed a dozen policemen armed with batons.

'Where is she?' demanded the chief of party.

'She?' said Captain Costa, knocking over the oil lamp. It crashed on the floor leaving the room in near darkness.

'Scoundrel! Why did you do that?' yelled the policeman.

'Accident, Sir. Beg your pardon.'

'Have you seen her?' asked the constable.

'Who?' asked Costa.

'Madeline du Champs, the criminal?' said the constable.

Madeline held her breath, her heart was a racing stallion.

'She stole the Duchess of Bourbon's emeralds,' said the constable.

'Just me and my men here,' said the captain. 'Care for some grog?'

'Search the place,' shouted the constable to his men.

Madeline tried to control her trembling body. French police were known for burning women at the stake under false accusations of witch craft. Sick with fright, she longed to be home with Minaloushe curled in her lap.

'Go on. Get outta here. We don't want trouble,' barked the doorman at the police.

Madeline felt a rush of gratitude. He could have turned her in.

Frustrated with their search, the police were about to depart when the constable noticed Madeline's purse on the table. 'Fetch a lantern!' he ordered. He walked to the chair where Madeline had been sitting and lifted the purse to examine it.

He was so close, Madeline could smell his breath. He had only to turn his shoulder to discover her trembling behind him. Alarmed, she grabbed a pitcher and brought it smashing onto his head.

He screamed, clutched his head and turned to face her in fury. Two shots exploded.

For an instant, Madeline thought she was dead then the constable fell to the ground before her. Behind him stood Costa, a flintlock pistol in each hand, smoke streaming out of the nozzles.

What ensued was too rapid for Madeline to process. Only later did she piece it together. In a blur of action, Costa shot the constable and whistled for his crew. They swarmed in swinging cutlasses and massacred the police men to rescue her.

'Let's go!' shouted Costa. 'GO! GO! GO!'

Madeline stood stunned, sick to her stomach at the sight of the culling. She might have fainted but Costa grabbed her by the waist and ran, dragging her out of the tavern with him. He hoisted her onto a saddled horse and raced like the wind.

'Where are we going?' Madeline screamed.

The captain hollered back, 'To the wilds of Bengal!'

CHAPTER 3

C hampa knocked on the door, a cage full of mice in her hand.
'Enter,' called her grandfather. The door opened itself.

Champa stepped into the darkness. Pir Baba, holy mystic by qualification, healer by hobby, her grandfather by bloodline, chose to dwell without light. It suited his weak eyes.

'How are you Dada?' Champa asked. From his silhouette she could tell he was on a doeskin rug counting prayer beads. 'Have you eaten?'

He shook his head.

'Are you cold?' she asked. The windows were shut and a damp chill had settled in. 'The room smells musty.'

He sniffed the air and waved a hand. A fresh mist of rosewater permeated the room.

Careful not to knock over his artefacts, Champa placed the cage upon the floor. The mice scuffled, whiskers twitching in the air.

'Light?' her grandfather offered.

Champa nodded and lit a wax candle. The flame danced upwards, illuminating stacks of books, leather-bound tomes opened to yellowed pages, some folded back, some marked with indecipherable symbols. A titanic magnifying lens suspended from a tripod scattered prisms across the aged leather.

With a majestic spread of wings, the falcon flew off its perch and alighted on a beaker of ink. Its talons clutched too tight and the beaker shattered, sending the bird into an agitated frenzy. The mice ran amok, distraught and crashing into one another.

Blowing kisses on his shoulders, Pir Baba concluded his prayers and rose to calm his pet. He donned a leather glove and held out his hand. The bird flew to his glove.

'There, there Hafez,' cooed the pir. 'You mustn't let trivial matters ruffle your feathers.'

The bird cocked his head to one side.

'One might mistake you for a craven raven,' said Dada. 'Such behaviour is not becoming of a thorough-bred falcon from Isfahan.'

Though Dada had let her name the falcon after the poet her father used to love before he became orthodox, Champa had never grown fond of the creature. Its mood was foul, its talons sharp and the scar upon her left cheek served as a souvenir of its ferocity. The bird was loyal to her grandfather and no one else.

'Come child,' said Dada. 'What news has Hafez brought from the Ruby Monkeys?'

Champa was hardly a child at 25 except to her Dada who was an octogenarian. She loved him dearly but she was growing weary of his obsessive hunt for the mysterious diamond that distracted him from the ordinary demands of the day such as eating and sleeping.

Begrudgingly she removed the bamboo carrier tied to Hafez's leg and retrieved the scroll from within. She unrolled it and secured its four corners with books. Dada had taught her to read and write and ever since his eyes had grown weak, he had relied on her to do both.

She held a candle to the scroll and examined it. It was written in blue ink with carefully curled letters, small as ants. Squinting, she read.

'Kalinoor was last seen in Golconda
50 years ago
before the Mughal invasion.'

'And...?'

'That's it, Dada.'

'Confound it!' shouted the pir, his face clouded with rage. 'We know that!!!'

Everyone knew the dark diamond was stolen from Golconda in the 1630s by conquering Mughals under the command of Prince Aurangzeb but nobody knew where it had gone since. Not even the best sources could track it.

Dada had been hunting for this diamond since she was a child. Back then her father was his assistant. Champa recalled one time Dada had travelled to Taj Mahal acting on a tip that suggested the diamond was hidden there. Like many other clues, it turned out to be a red herring.

Then two years ago, Dada heard rumours that the diamond was close by, within the borders of Bengal. He redoubled his efforts to find it, this time with Champa as his reluctant assistant.

'There is also this lemon,' said Champa, reaching inside the bamboo. 'It must be a gift for you.'

The pir's face cleared. 'Ah, a coded message.'

Champa raised an eyebrow.

'Slice the lemon,' the pir instructed. 'Squeeze it on the scroll.'

Champa did as she was told, licking the tart juice off her fingers. Sure enough, as the juice splashed upon the scroll, new letters emerged. Champa read,

'Kalinoor is with the Subedar of Bengal.
Winds of Change will carry it
far from the land of the Red Tiger
in the New Year.'

The pir stroked his beard, a faint smile on his lips. 'It is closer than I thought.'

'Wonderful!' exclaimed Champa, unable to control her joy. At long last his search was yielding results.

'Silly girl. The diamond is not a trifle meant to delight,' he admonished.

She drew her face back to the lifeless canvas he preferred.

'Kalinoor will help me channel God's power to preserve Bengal.'

With age came eccentricities. Champa nodded politely though she didn't understand what her grandfather meant. 'How will you get it from the Subedar?' she asked.

'I am willing to pay amply for it,' he mused. 'But how to persuade a Mughal to part with his treasure?' His eyes drifted in thought.

Champa nodded. Subedar Khan was only the most powerful man in the Empire. Since she was a child, she had both revered and feared him. He was as vicious as he was handsome, as brutal as he was just, as likely to execute a Muslim as a Hindu, and execute he did aplenty.

She had seen him once from a distance at the Janmashtami parade where elephants carried wildly coloured canvases 40 feet long and miniature shrines of Hindu gods with musicians, dhol wallahs and dancers trailing in festivities stretched over a mile in length. Her father had forbidden her from going but she went anyway and there she discovered dance.

The dancing girls with sculpted bodies saw her mesmerized eyes and befriended her, inviting her to practice with them in secret. Her father would have been dismayed if he came to know. His disdain for the material world prevented him from seeing the body as a temple but Champa believed the mind without the body could never connect to the spirit. The experience of living, breathing, dancing were holy to her. Besides, dancing was fun.

'Perhaps I can help you retrieve the diamond?' Champa suggested. She would do anything for her grandfather.

The pir barely hid his contempt. 'You? How?'

Champa drew her brows together, desperate to find a way to help. If only ... Her brows snapped up.

'Cousin Faruk tells me his friend owns a tent in Chowk Bazaar which the Subedar frequently visits. It's called Jannat, have you heard of it?' She knew he hadn't. He never left the house.

'The Subedar would NOT take Kalinoor to a tea tent!' he exclaimed, as if she had insulted the very treasure he had dedicated his life to.

Champa smiled, stitching up a strategy in her head. Her grandfather would never agree to it but if she disguised herself as a dancer and enticed the Subedar to follow her home, she knew Dada would be pleased.

'Dada, I'm late,' she said. 'My students are waiting.'

'I have cosmic knowledge and the mantras of Vedic sages to teach you and you run off to waste your time with orphan girls? Why, like your baba, are you turning your back on ancient wisdom?'

'Those girls need me!'

'If you're so dedicated to the material world, you might as well be married by now,' snapped her grandfather. 'Have some children of your own.'

'Now *you* sound like Baba,' said Champa. 'If I were married, who would read and write for you?' She knew she had struck his weak spot.

The pir grunted.

Champa softened. She did not want to leave him feeling irritable. She owed him everything. 'Besides, I teach both: the old knowledge and the new. Shall I feed Hafez or will you?'

Dada knelt to the floor and with his ungloved hand, unlatched the cage. He caught a rodent by its pink tail and brought it out, hanging upside down, wriggling for dear life. It had toffee fur, a pink nose and white whiskers.

Dada let it loose upon the floor. Hafez observed it, eager to attack. The mouse scurried around in confusion looking for a place to hide. Its desperation made Champa cringe.

Dada snapped his finger. Hafez swooped down upon the rodent and began yanking out its intestines with his talons, toying with it, careful not to put it out of misery. Its paws scratched the floor as it tried to escape. Hafez looked at Dada as if for affirmation, pink flesh hanging from his mouth. Ruby patches of blood stained the sides of his beak, painting a diabolical smile.

'Do you know why I released the rodent before I let Hafez devour it?' said Dada, when at last the feast was over.

'To test Hafez's obedience?' she guessed.

'Hafez would not defy me. I am the hand that feeds him.'

Usually it was she who fed him but she replied, 'Then why, Dada?'

'Freedom tastes better than fear. Fear tightens muscles and makes meat stringy. One minute of freedom lulls the rodent into a false security. It dares to hope. Its blood flows, its muscles relax, its meat becomes tender and tasty.' Pir Baba gave an unhinged smile. 'Go now, child. I have work to do. Bengal is in grave danger.'

Champa eyed the mouse cage. She wanted to take it with her but her grandfather's gaze warned her not to. There was more feasting to come. She turned to leave. The door swung open to let her out.

CHAPTER 4

On the banks of the Buriganga in the heart of Chowk Bazaar was a tent known as *Jannat*, Paradise. Under its crimson canopy lounged sinister mercenaries waiting to catch whiff of a golden opportunity. Here merchants could sell stallions from Arabia, camels from Egypt, gems from the coast of Masulipatam, dark secrets, pink lies, promises and primroses by the dozens. Here one could trade in silver, copper, counterfeit coins and scabbards bejewelled in rubies of cherry red. Here one could hire cutthroats to execute with words or swords any brutality for a reasonable price.

In the midspring sun, the tent was sticky. Wafting scents of cinnamon and cloves from the neighbouring spice souk did little to mask the stench of greed. Above the rowdy din of voices floated the melodious duet of a sitar and tabla. A dozen voluptuous dancers strayed from the uthaan to mingle with the chequered crowd. A lanky waiter served almond sherbet and liquor.

Subedar Shayista Khan entered the tent incognito, the hood of his fustian cloak low over his brows. He had eluded his bodyguards and was keen to protect his rare privacy. Only in disguise could he enjoy such freedom. Passing the bulging figure of Sheikh Obaidullah, he slipped him a coin. The inn keeper recognized the Subedar and nodded to assure him discretion.

With a disdainful glance, Shayista took cognition of every person in the tent then sat on a cushion positioning his back to a stack of crates to protect it from hungry blades.

To his right, Ottoman Turks discussed the aesthetics of Mughal architecture and Bengali women. They were trained assassins, he could tell by the way they sat with their palms against their hips, hiding sheathed khanjars, ears alert.

To his left, slaves with peacock feather pankahs cooled the gluttonous flesh of their aged master, Nawab Arifullah, a regional governor known for his penchant for rape. Pudding-faced and drenched in pearls, he looked like a royal oyster with a blond slave boy massaging his feet.

Shayista had prohibited slavery in Bengal to protect people from their own greed. He considered reprimanding the nawab but did not want to draw attention to himself. He was at Jannat to meet his European spymaster. He would send Dhand later to rescue the boy.

The nawab drooled over a dancer, one Shayista had not seen before. She tapped a tambourine against her thigh. Bony and dark, she was not what one would expect. Her face was an expression of crystalline contempt. Her nose was crooked, her eyes unsymmetrical, a purple scar snaked along her left cheek. The nawab seemed helplessly under her spell.

Shayista had not lusted over a woman in twenty years. He tried to tell himself it was his age though he knew the truth was that the only woman he had ever loved was taken from him in a moment of weakness. His wounded hand served as a constant reminder of his fatal mistake.

A waiter placed a hookah encrusted with topaz before Shayista. The Subedar drew in a deep breath of saffron-flavoured smoke. It coated his tongue. His muscles relaxed. He watched the dancer. She was not performing for money. She was a devotee whirling to the rhythm of the cosmos. He admired her dharana. Only with singular focus could one achieve such finesse. They were not so different, she and him.

A dancer danced to the rhythm of song, a warrior to the pulse of enemies. Alas that was where their similarities ended. While art was elegant, dismantling false heroes and upholding the Empire's sovereignty was rather odious. Yet this task fell to him as there was no one else to take on the burden.

Shayista gulped smoke from his hookah and tried to formulate battle strategies in his head but the dancing girl was a distraction. The bells on her choli jingled. He saw the outline of her rose apple breasts, the undulating curve of her hips. The more she danced, the lighter he felt, nearer to peace, closer to freedom.

A waiter served him a glass of sharab. He let its coolness soothe his throat. From the corner of his eye, he saw two ruffians enter the tent. Dark, brooding men with thick beards, blood caked on their narrow scabbards. White shalwars, orange turbans, cummerbunds glistening gold, they looked like Marathas.

Shayista's hamstrings tightened. It had been twenty years since he last fought Maratha guerrillas. He glanced at his left hand: pinkie, index, middle finger gone, chopped off at the second knuckle.

The Marathas puffed their chests and flanked the nawab. The larger one spoke. 'Is this the fierce Subedar Khan? The one who burns Hindus at the stake? Ha! He looks like a bowl of jelly.'

Shayista's ears perked up. Even if they had gotten hold of the wrong man, even if they had mistaken his political stance (he had vehemently opposed jiziya and the destruction of Hindu temples proposed by Aurangzeb), the most pressing issue at the moment was: how on earth did they know he was in the tent? He ran his fingers over his stubble. Had someone betrayed him?

The fanning servants quailed but the nawab displayed an irreverent disregard for danger, the kind that's only possible when alarmingly inebriated. 'Do you know whooo-oo-oo I am?' he said with such force that he knocked himself over. Regaining balance, he slurred, 'I'll have you flog-g-g-ged.'

Shayista rubbed the ruby hilt of his shamsher. He didn't trust a drunkard to resolve conflict without violence. He had seen too many boys raised on golden milk, swinging from fornication to altercation, reckless and wild.

Royal history was replete with alcoholics: his father, his uncle, his cousin Daniyal whose funeral he had attended. The clammy feel of the prince's swollen cheek was forever imprinted in his memory. Blue lips, icy hands, stiff fingers.

A piercing scream ripped through the tent. The larger Maratha had yanked the slave boy by his curly hair and with one definitive swipe, severed the boy's head. Blood spilled out of the boy's neck and onto the Maratha's kurta. The child body splattered upon the Persian carpet.

'We have come for Kalinoor!' the warrior shouted. He waved the head for onlookers to see: horror frozen on the disembodied boy face, eyes bulged, tongue lolling.

Grabbing the tambourine dancer, the smaller warrior pulled out a double-bladed bichua from his cummerband. 'Give us Kalinoor or she dies,' he said to the nawab.

The wavy scorpion dagger hovered volatile below her chin. The girl shrieked. No one dared to move. Stunned, they waited for the lymphatic nawab to act.

'Kill her,' said the nawab. 'What do I care? She's only a...'

The dancer sunk her teeth into her captor's arm. He howled and recoiled. She leapt away only to be caught by the larger Maratha. He grabbed her hair and pulled her face to the boy's bodyless head, eye to dead eye. She screamed.

The smaller Maratha was livid. 'You whore of Kali!' he shouted, rubbing his bruise, eyes bloodshot. He raised the bichua to kill her.

Shayista swore under his breath. When he travelled incognito he did not wear chainmail, only his forearm guard. Neither could he carry his Damascan seif. A sword of that magnificence drew too much attention. He had only his shamsher for close combat but the dancer was across the tent.

With a volcanic battle cry, Shayista emptied his glass upon the hookah. A brilliant explosion of blue lit up the room. Shayista hurled the flaming hookah at the Maratha. Before the warrior could comprehend the danger, Shayista leapt to his side and thrust his shamsher into his heart.

The second Maratha was frightened. Never before had he seen a demon emerge from an explosion and kill a man.

Shayista turned to him. 'You have murdered an innocent boy. Your atonement can only be through your life for his.'

'Who are you?' the Maratha asked.

Before the man could receive an answer, the Subedar delivered his imperious judgement, plunging the shamsher into his throat. The man fell to the ground dead. Shayista cleaned his blade on the Maratha's turban and sheathed his shamsher. The dancer added a few kicks at the dead body for good measure.

'Y'Allah! What happened!' shouted Sheikh Obaidullah, panting and sweating from the exertion of running in, pavilion guards close behind him.

Shayista grabbed him by his kurta and drew him near. 'How did they know I was in here?' he hissed.

'Sire, I beg your pardon, I did not see them,' Obaidullah said, looking darkly suspicious. He fell to his knees and kissed Shayista's hand with his fat, wet lips. 'The troublemakers must have recognized your stallion tethered outside?'

Shayista pulled his hand away and wiped it in disgust. The inn keeper was lying. He had come without his horse. But he'd had enough killing for one day. 'If you ever betray me, I will pluck your eyes out one by one and feed you to my wolves. Now move the bodies out of my sight. And Obaidullah, the music please?'

The obliging host ordered servants to remove the bodies and instructed performers to resume the show. He then led a dazed nawab out of Jannat.

Shayista returned to his seat. A grey mongoose scurried across the carpet and slipped out from under the tent. The crowd resumed its banter but now all eyes riveted on him. The dancer had not returned. The temperature had gone up. His pipe was empty, his glass drained. He contemplated leaving when finally his secret agent arrived, looking sorely foreign despite his shalwar and chapals.

Vroomen Van Diemen's shiny bald head was white and no matter how locally he dressed, he looked like a flamboyant firingi. Timidly he scanned the room and grinned as he spotted the Subedar. He bowed in a theatrical taslim. His waist coat stretched tight across his belly, the button securing it threatened to pop.

'What's the commotion? A tussle on the way?' he asked, easing onto a cushion next to Shayista. He craned his neck to watch the dancers.

'No,' said Shayista. He motioned for a fresh hookah.

'Bengali women are the finest in the world,' said Van Diemen. He imitated a dancer's moves trying to get her attention.

'Are you drunk?' asked Shayista.

A waiter relit the hookah and served them a mixture of cashews, almonds, pine nuts, pistachios and raisins on a silver platter, followed by glasses of sharab.

Van Diemen nodded sheepishly. 'You will be pleased, Subedar,' he said, reaching for a handful of nuts. 'I have much to report.'

'Let's see if you can keep your facts straight. Really Van Diemen, you must learn to handle your alcohol. You're a disgrace to the Dutch.'

Unperturbed by the censure, Van Diemen took a sip and began. 'King Charles is dead. King James is the new king of England. Charles' bastard son was executed at Tower Hill by London's worst executioner. It took eight strikes to sever his head.'

'Were they beheading him with a butter knife? What do I care of English politics? The uncivilised lot don't even bathe. They have a long way to go.'

'There's more, dear Governor,' said Van Diemen, pausing dramatically. He clapped and whistled at a dancer shimmying by his side. Henna tattoos snaked up her slender back.

Shayista pulled on the hookah. Obaidullah had kindly laced it with opium to redress the damage done. Shayista allowed his body to relax as he released lazy smoke rings. Intimidated by his indifference, the dancer drifted to another group.

Vroomen sighed. 'Germany, Sweden and Spain are aligning against King Louis. In America, they have chartered a city called Albany.'

Shayista picked out a cashew. It was fresh, come perhaps from the southern part of the province where he had set up an orchard after Costa presented him with saplings from Portugal, cashews and pinapples.

Every variety of delicacy was available in Dacca thanks to the channels of trade he had established, channels his enemies wanted to exploit. Enemies he would crush.

'What of the farcical Company cullion in Hindustan?' he said, popping the cashew into his mouth.

'Lord James is gone. He married a Muslim noblewoman, did the full circumcision and conversion ceremony, then deserted the Company for a holy pilgrimage to Mecca.'

'If only outer excursions could promote inner evolution,' said the Subedar.

'Sir Josiah Child is the new Company Governor. Our lady spy stole this from his pocket. It is addressed to Mr. Charnock in Madras, a Company man.' Van Diemen handed him a scroll.

'A lady agent of espionage?'

'These days there's nothing a woman can't do.'

Subedar Khan scrutinized the royal insignia. 'It says it is their duty 'to lay the foundations of an English dominion in Hindustan, to acquire possession by force ... come what may.''

'Your foolish Emperor doesn't mind,' said Van Diemen.

Shayista thrust his shamsher menacingly close to the Dutchman's neck. 'Never speak of the Emperor with disrespect,' he growled.

'Alright, alright, take it easy,' said Van Diemen, sobering.

'The Emperor does not understand the implications,' explained Subedar Khan. He tucked the parchment into his cloak. Aurangzeb was making a critical mistake.

'It gets worse,' warned Van Diemen. 'Sir Child has appointed Mr. William Hedges as Chief Officer of trade in Bengal. A handsome man, I hear. A virtuouso with the women. O, I am scarce able to recount the unsavory practices of these Englishmen. They petitioned the Emperor for a spot of soil in Hooghly upon which to build a factory house. No sooner was it granted, they constructed a fort, surrounded it with a ditch and mounted a great number of guns upon its walls. How is that in return for hospitality?'

'English soldiers on Bengali soil? This cannot be true.' Subedar Khan laughed.

'The Company's Secret Committee has requested King James for permission to seize Bengal.'

'Seize Bengal? What audacity!' The Subedar laughed even harder. Bengal from Bihar to Orissa, from Assam to Arakan, was his and he had hundreds of thousands of mansabdars protecting it. 'Like mosquitoes plotting to attack an elephant.'

Van Diemen chewed thoughtfully on a handful of raisins. 'It is, isn't it? A tiny Company wants to take on the Gunpowder Empire.'

Most of the world's saltpetre was produced in Bihar, over one hundred and twenty maunds annually. Saline earth collected off mud heaps and waste grounds where saltpeter developed into thin white effervescence resembling frost was dissolved and filtered through bamboo grass mats and the remaining liquor was evaporated to a crystallizing state in earthen pots. The refined saltpetre, better known as gunpowder, was his. Though it was close to the river Ganga and could easily be transported to Hooghly, Shayista had prohibited its trade. One had to be possessive of strategic resources.

'I will warn the Emperor,' said Shayista. Aurangzeb was scheduled to arrive in Dacca within a month. If they had their way, the English would not need to engage in armoured warfare. They would simply suck out their blood through unfair trade. That could not be permitted.

'Perhaps the Emperor is already aware of the English advances but has not seen it fit to inform you as yet?'

Shayista peered into his eyes. Was Van Diemen holding something back? 'Company designs on Hindustan are a joke,' he said in disgust.

'Everyone has designs on Hindustan,' said Van Diemen. 'Just as the Mughals did when Hindustan belonged to others. Sire, you must admit the Empire is imperialism at its zenith!'

The Subedar arched an eyebrow with scorn. 'Mughals are natural leaders. The expansion of our power is a sign of our benevolence to humanity. We protect Bengali peasantry from the dominion of Afghans and Arakans. We encourage commerce and culture, education and growth. Poetry, music and art are our bastions. We nurture our people. Our sole purpose is not to loot resources.'

'Who can blame the English really?' said Vrooman. 'You've turned Bengal into the richest kingdom in the world. You're an alchemist! Now Bengal glitters like diamonds on the Peacock throne.'

Shayista frowned.

'Speaking of which,' continued Vroomen. 'Everyone knows King Louis wears a Deccani diamond as blue as the ocean. Now King James wants to wear one too.'

'Kohinoor is not for sale,' replied Shayista dryly. If he knew anything about the diamonds of Golconda, he wasn't about to reveal the details to his spy.

'There is another diamond...' Van Diemen leaned in to whisper. 'It is as black as a moonless midnight and as large as a lion's heart. Merchants say it has mysterious powers...'

Shayista was stunned. Twice in one day? He replied, 'Why would the Emperor sell such a diamond if it exists?'

Candid from his drink, Van Diemen replied, 'He doesn't have it. We hope he can find it. All European sources have failed so far. He is the last hope. Unless you happen to know something about it?'

Shayista narrowed his eyes to scrutinize Vroomen. Was he really as clueless as he seemed? 'I am not in the diamond business.'

'The Company offered Emperor Aurangzeb twenty lakh rupees to procure this diamond...' Van Diemen's words trailed. A dancer approached.

'You saved my life,' she said to Shayista, her head bowed. The margins of her nether lip quivered.

Shayista shrugged. 'Think nothing of it.'

'You might have died,' she insisted.

'I welcome death,' Shayista replied, releasing a chain of smoke rings that meandered into the shape of corpses. He noticed a spot of blood on her choli. A sapphire pendant hung between her breasts.

'I prefer dancing over death,' said Van Diemen. 'Want to see?' He fell back to his gawky moves.

The girl ignored him and studied Shayista's face. 'You are not well,' she said. 'You need help.' Her voice was soft, her eyes sharp.

Shayista was startled. This slip of a girl was intrepid. She spoke to him directly, looked him in the eye. She told him to seek help, something even his trusted Chief Commander Dhand would not have dared to do. He glanced again at her sapphire. It had a hypnotic glow.

'My grandfather can help you,' she said. 'Come with me.'

'I don't need help,' mumbled Shayista, trying to tear his eyes away from the pendant.

'You can help me,' suggested Van Diemen.

'Why do men always mask their weaknesses?' said the dancer. 'Even if a man is distraught with loneliness, wrecked by despair and tormented by guilt, he'll tell you he's alright. It is apparent from your posture, you are morose! Dada is an awliya, a direct disciple of Hazrat Shah Jalal. Let him help you.'

Shayista sat upright, intrigued. A direct disciple?

'My name is Khadija Fatima Ali but people call me Champa. I am the only grandchild of Pir Zulfiqar Ali,' she said. There was a pleading in her eyes that could not be disappointed. 'I owe you my life. Allow me to repay the debt?'

Hardly could he resist her. Shayista was ready to go with her wherever she wanted to go.

'Wait, we're not through,' said Van Diemen, acutely aware of the Subedar's intention to leave before paying him. 'The Japanese want more opium.'

Bengal's intra-Asian trade was mostly opium and its major source was Bihar. The young fruits of opium poppies were incised and their thick juices dried out and cut into cakes. The quality of the resulting opium could be ascertained by its colour. The best grade was brown and the worst nearly red. Bihar's annual output of opium was 8700 maunds, all of it brown. Shayista sold half and kept the rest.

'Holland wants to increase its order of tanna-banna silk to 6000 bales,' continued Van Diemen, trying to engage the Subedar's interest.

In addition to raw silk, opium and saltpeter, Bengal was a major supplier of cotton and silk. Bengal provided more textiles to European companies than the rest of Asia put together. Some of it was sold in Asia—Japan, Persia, Ceylon—but the bulk was for Europe where the textiles were used for clothing, bed furnishings, table covers, curtains and wall hangings, but these weren't things he felt like discussing. 'Come by the fort later,' mumbled Shayista.

Exiting the tent with Champa, he passed the double-crosser Obaidullah. Shayista knew he should probably kill him right then and there but he didn't like to spill blood before Zohr prayers.

CHAPTER 5

C hampa led the Subedar down the winding streets of *Indur Goli*, Rat's Alley, to meet her grandfather.

'Who were those men?' she asked. And why were they after Kalinoor?

The Subedar shrugged. He seemed quite cavalier.

Champa could not shake it off so easily. Never had a boy been decapitated before her very eyes. She chose the route least likely to be crowded though all paths were narrow and bustling with vendors. She tried not to think of the slave boy and instead thanked her stars that the turbaned warriors had attacked her. Had they not, she would not have recognized the Subedar cloaked incognito.

'People travel for days to visit Dada,' she said. 'He will help you.' She didn't like lying to the Subedar after he had saved her life but she couldn't tell him the truth. What would he say if he knew she had gone to Jannat to ensnare him for her grandfather who, like those warriors, was also after Kalinoor? One lie led to another and in the end she convinced herself she was doing the Subedar a favour.

She hurried him past stubborn men swatting flies with the ends of battle axes and women hardened under the weight of one hundred deaths, past snake charmers and butchers and beggars and goats, ducks, dogs, camels and elephants, taking care not to step on the colossal droppings of shit on the path.

'Puffed rice for the princess?' A moori wallah called out. 'Put some flesh on that *chikna* ass.'

Champa wasn't prepared for the Subedar's instantaneous reaction: a single hard punch to the vendor's face. She heard his nose crack. The vendor fell to the ground and whimpered in a puddle of blood.

Embarrassed, Champa hurried the Subedar on, wrapping a veil around her dancing dress. Once they were out of ear shot of those who had witnessed his behaviour, she hissed, 'Why did you do that?'

'Indecent behaviour towards women cannot be tolerated,' he said.

Champa wanted to say, 'address ignorance through education not punishment' but instead she chewed her lips. Unrestrained anger was unseemly for someone of the upper strata. Such uncouthness was generally associated with lower castes. Still she was secretly intrigued. It was in favour of women that he had lashed out. Did his ends justify the means?

A pack-horse laden with muslin trundled past. A rooster squawked out of its way and flew directly into Champa's path. She leapt back to avoid collision and found herself in the Subedar's strong arms. He was walking very close to her. He smelt of attar and smoke, an intoxicating combination.

'If you ever need to buy anything in Chowk Bazaar, let me know. I can bring any price down to one eighth. It's my unique talent,' she said, then cursed herself silently for offering her bargaining skills to the richest man in the Empire. She dropped a paisa into a street urchin's cup.

The boy thanked her.

The Subedar followed her lead and dropped a coin into his cup too. From the boy's ecstatic whoops she guessed the Subedar had been generous. Perhaps it was a coin of silver.

A paan wallah called to them. Champa feared for his safety and hurried the Subedar on. Rat's Alley had sprouted around the periphery of Chowk Bazaar and Lal Bagh fort, both of which the Subedar had built. He had also constructed Boro Katra and Choto Katra nearby to accommodate travelling merchants who came from far corners of the Empire to participate in Bengal's trade.

As they walked, Champa could not help but reflect upon the Subedar's contributions to the subha and his heroic commitment during the plague. He personally paid for doctors and medicine and levied a tax on rat-infested European ships to prevent a relapse. He had gone beyond the call of duty, though it had not been enough to save her mother.

When the plague took Champa's mother, she was only ten. Devastated, her father wanted to marry her off so he could renounce his responsibilities and drown in his only solace, the Quran. It was Dada who intervened and raised her while her father's bitterness congealed around the fragments of rituals on which he hung his heart. Now Dada was all the family she had. She hoped the diamond would bring him closer to unlocking the mysteries of the universe as he hoped.

Champa noticed the Subedar was staring at the emerald bajuband on her arm. She examined his face. He had fair skin burnt from hours under the sun and deep gashes that ran across his cheek, above his chin, through his eye brow. His broad jaw was covered with inch-long stubble and his hair was a dishevelled tangle of black but apart from that, he was delectable. He was tall, perhaps 6 feet tall, muscular as a maiden's fantasy. His lips were red as radishes, his eyes brown like soil. His age was indiscernible. She noticed his expression change. He looked petrified.

'What's the matter?' Champa asked.

'I hate cats,' the Subedar mumbled.

Champa noticed anew. Cats everywhere. Lean, scruffy, rheumy eyed cats with patches of fur clawed off. She was surprised to see a brave warrior afraid of felines but somehow his vulnerability made him human.

Suddenly he lunged at one of the cats, chopping off its head with his sword. It let out an eerie howl then died shuddering. He lifted his sword to kill another. The remaining cats scrambled to escape.

'STOP!' screamed Champa, grabbing his arm. 'What are you doing?'

'It was rabid,' explained the Subedar. 'Cats carry diseases.'

'Rats carry diseases too,' she countered. 'Haven't you heard of the plague? The best solution for rats is cats.' She was unable to comprehend how one could be so cruel. Not all problems could be solved with a sword!

The Subedar looked taken aback.

'Here we are,' she said before he could kill another cat. 'Home sweet home.'

CHAPTER 6

The roots of a primeval banyan tree crawled towards them. An eerie community had formed around its gnarled architecture. Suspended on one limb was a barber's cracked mirror, on another, a cobbler's decrepit stand. Fakir tents hung off its branches, on its bough, a murder of ravens. The temperature was cool there and thick with the smell of decay. Behind the tree, a half-hidden house, still and desolate as a coffin.

Shayista's chest tightened. A vampire bat flew over his head. Banyan roots uncoiled like arms of the buried dead, twisting and writhing to and fro, grabbing at his ankles. Feeling uneasy, he followed Champa down a path to a mildewed gate that groaned as she opened it. A black cat slipped out. Its tail curled around his ankle, making him cringe. The mossy walls seemed to watch him. There was something deviant about the place, something dismal and haunted.

Champa led him down a stairwell with a marble banister to an underground chamber with no windows.

A silver-bearded holy man sat crossed legged on a wooden charpoi, a single candle on the table. He wore black garbs and a slick black turban held together with a sapphire broach. He was counting prayer beads. His quivering lips concealed sinister secrets. By his side, a masked falcon fidgeted.

'I have been expecting you, Subedar Khan,' said Pir Zulfiqar.

'You have?' said Shayista, betraying the surprise in his voice.

'Sit down,' commanded the pir. The Subedar obeyed.

'Lion-hearted, you are,' said the pir. His eyes were a metallic green. 'Do you believe in Allah?'

Shayista nodded, though lately He had been obscured by clouds.

'If you believe in Allah then you must also believe in black magic.'

As a child, Shayista was trained by Huzur, a mystic of the highest order, so of course he believed in white magic. He had personally seen Huzur perform astonishing miracles with the power of his mind. It was black magic that Shayista was sceptical of. Ghosts, demons and djinn he had never seen but he did not care to argue with the holy man so he nodded.

The pir frowned.

'Would you like some water?' offered Champa, her demeanour altered.

Shayista nodded gratefully, welcoming any excuse to stray from the probe. He scanned the room. There were lines of shelves: moth-eaten books, a telescope, an oil lamp, a silver-hilted rapier. No human effigies, pickled snakes or overt signs of sorcery.

Zulfiqar frowned. 'You have suffered.'

'Suffering is the fate of mankind,' said Shayista. A cold blast of wind with no apparent source caressed the nape of his neck.

'There is an artefact in your possession called Kalinoor.' The pir spoke with hypnotic cadence. 'Bring it to me.'

'How do you know about Kalinoor?' asked Shayista. Why was everyone suddenly after his diamond? He had kept it hidden for so long. Now it seemed his secret was out.

'Kalinoor is cursed,' said the pir.

'Curses are for fairytales,' said Shayista.

'Whosoever possesses the dark diamond shall suffer. All that you cherish shall perish!' He grabbed Shayista's wrists and stood up. 'Bagh Khan, beware. Thrice you have been struck.'

Champa placed a tumbler by Shayista. 'Dada, you're frightening him.' Her eyes conveyed concern for her grandfather's safety. One mustn't offend the Subedar.

The pir let go of Shayista's wrists and sat down. He brought his fingers to a steeple. 'Bring me the diamond and I will undo the curse.'

Shayista grinned. The audacity of the pir amused him. 'How does one undo a curse?' he asked, sarcastically.

'I will consult the djinn,' said the sorcerer.

Shayista nearly snorted and stood up to leave.

The pir noted his reaction. 'One cannot divine Truth without conferring with the other world. Our knowledge of the universe is too shallow.'

'I suppose for these metaphysical services I must pay you materially?' said Shayista.

'What good is your money?' said the pir with contempt. 'Will it save Bengal?'

'Save Bengal?' said the Subedar. The pir had his attention.

'The stone will use YOU as its weapon of destruction.' The pir's voice rose in volume, disturbing the falcon. It unfolded its wings and beat the air. 'YOU will destroy Bengal.'

Shayista had heard enough. His mouth closed to a hard line.

'Mark my words, Subedar. Bring me the diamond before the Emperor arrives or else Bengal is doomed.'

Shayista bid the pir salaam and exited the antechamber. He climbed up the stairs and wondered how the pir knew the Emperor was coming. There had been no public announcement.

Champa came chasing after him. 'Dada's not an imposter,' she said.

'Is that so?'

'He is respected in this community. Ask anybody. No one provides better cures or exorcisms.'

'I don't need either,' said the Subedar. 'And by the way, how did he know who I am?'

'He knows many things,' said Champa. 'Can I see your hand?'

Shayista raised his brow. Such impudence on the threshold of his departure, she was asking to hold his hand? She reached for it. He yanked it away a bit too abruptly, hurting her feelings. A pout sprang to her lips. He softened, passing her his other hand, the undamaged one. She cupped it in her dainty fingers and pressed the mound on his palm. He felt a bolt of lightning shoot through his arm.

Her brows furrowed as she peered at his palm. 'Like the moon, you have a light and a dark side but you wrestle with the two. You forget, we do not stand in the light or the shade but in the twilight in between.'

She traced a line with her finger. 'Yours is the gift of eternal youth.'

Shayista frowned. Did she know he was really 84 years old, not 42 as he appeared? When he was born, as per tradition, his father took him for a blessing to Sheikh Chishti, the spiritual leader of the royal family, direct disciple of Khwaja Moinuddin Chishti himself. Sheikh Chishti poured an elixir down Shayista's baby lips, a mixture of zamzam water from Mecca and a prayer.

Years later when Shayista reached manhood, he found his aging process seemed slower than natural. He believed it was the effect of the tonic. When he thanked Sheikh Chishti, the saint said it wasn't he who had performed any miracles, it was Allah. This information Shayista hadn't shared with anyone.

Champa poked at his palm. 'As a child, you learned of battle.'

A forgotten memory flashed before Shayista. He was at Agra Palace with his sister Arjumand watching elephants fight in a ring. Jahangir's elephant was pitted against Shah Jahan's elephant, father against son. The terrified creatures had to kill or be killed. Inexplicably, the memory seemed to spring not from his mind but from the tip of Champa's finger. As she lifted her finger, the memory cleared.

Champa pointed to another line etched on his hand. 'You have known your Destiny since before it was sealed.'

A second memory appeared before him. It was June 3, 1611, the wedding of his aunt, Mehrunnisa, to Emperor Jahangir. Shayista was ten years old and known as Mirza Abu Talib. He had travelled with his family for 40 days from Lahore to Agra for the celebrations. He was miserable, drained from the marathon journey and heart-broken having had to part with his ducks. Forced to wear silk turbans that restricted blood flow to his brain, he had a continuous headache and double vision. To add insult to injury, his mother had dragged him to the public baths twice in preparation for the wedding. Twice too often.

The wedding was lavish. Scarlet shamianas fringed with gold brocade covered acres of gardens, princely pavilions as far as the eye could see. Layers of thick lamb wool padded their feet and rows of potted jasmines fragranced the air. Elaborate feasts were laid out. Ten thousand people were fed and another ten thousand received gold coins and goats. Three hundred musicians had rehearsed for five months to perform a spectacular recital of song and dance.

Emperor Jahangir spared no costs. On the day of the auspicious union, Mehr sat on a ceremonial divan plated with gold and studded with emeralds. Covered by a golden veil and decked in diamonds, she glowed, befitting the title bestowed upon her: Nur Jahan, Light of the World.

Talib grumbled as he was pushed on to the dais to bow to the Emperor and his aunt.

Lifting her golden veil to kiss him, Nur Jahan whispered in his ear, 'Everyone is here for a reason. Why are you here?'

Talib tried to wriggle free.

'What's your purpose in life, beta?'

Talib was accustomed to adults disseminating unsolicited advice but this was really too much. He had been uprooted from his home, travelled 440 miles, bathed TWICE, and now he was being asked personal questions at the party when all he wanted to do was play with his friends.

Emperor Jahangir leaned into the conversation, the ruby broach on his turban glittering, eyes aglow with uxorious euphoria. 'His purpose, your purpose, my purpose, everybody's purpose is to LOVE!' he offered gleefully.

Nur Jahan blushed. 'No, my Jahapana, everyone has a unique destiny. See how he moves, how he observes you, measuring your vulnerabilities. He has the eyes of a warrior, so serious for a little boy. His dharma is to fight battles and kill men. He will serve you well but he will never find happiness. Such men never find happiness.'

Champa lifted her finger and the memory dissipated.

Shayista had not thought of his aunt's wistful prophecy in many years. Was it true, was he destined to destroy? Would happiness elude him?

Champa pointed to a third line on his palm and said, 'You have made a choice that you regret.'

Shayista pulled his hand away before the memory sprang.

Champa nodded as though she had understood something of him. 'Your regrets haunt you?' she asked. 'I can undo regrets.'

Undo regrets? Shayista was curious but the dancer already knew too much. He bid her farewell and hurried back to the bazaar.

Despite the noisy banter of urban bustle, Shayista heard the pleasant *poo-poo-poo* of a hoopoe and the *chah-chah* cough of a blue roller. He spotted a drongo whistling, hopping from rooftop to rooftop in search of a ripe papaya, its glossy blue plumage glistening. An Indian cuckoo sang carefree, *bou-kota-kou, bou-kota-kou, bou-kota-kou.*

The natural beauty of Bengal comforted Shayista briefly till he passed Jannat and remembered his troubles. He had to tell the Emperor about the Company designs. Could it be that Aurangzeb already knew? He needed a drink and some opium.

'There you are, Sire,' said Amir Dhand, Commander of Shayista's cavalry, slapping a titanic hand on his back. 'Wandering without your bodyguards again? How many times must I tell you it isn't safe? There are forces conspiring.'

'My death is written in the stars. Nothing we do can change it,' Shayista replied.

Dhand was not impressed with this line of reasoning. 'At least allow me to accompany you on these excursions,' he insisted, falling into stride with his commander.

More ogre than man, Dhand was seven inches taller than Shayista, placing him at a giant 6'9'. He was a fierce fighter, muscles bulging on his arms, legs and neck. His head was shaven to deny enemies the advantage of yanking his hair in close combat. Tucked into his belt was his weapon of choice: a *Zaghnol*, Crow's Beak axe, with two cutting edges. This axe had never known defeat but it was not for his martial skills that Shayista made him *Amir-i-Akhur*, Commander of the Cavalry. It was his stalwart loyalty Shayista valued most.

'Look at the splendour around us,' said Shayista. 'I have built roads, ports, mosques. One rupee purchases eight maunds of rice, I feed the Empire. Cotton, silk, muslin, I clothe the world. For what? So a covetous company can invade my province and pillage its wealth? I won't allow it!'

'Sure, Sire,' Dhand mumbled through the corner of his full mouth.

'What's that you're eating?' asked Shayista.

'Shutki,' said Dhand, through clenched jaw.

'Dried fish?' said Shayista, averting his nose from the stink.

'You want some?' Dhand stuffed his massive hand into his pocket and pulled out a few brown crumbs.

What Dhand had in brawn he lacked in brain. 'Even after all these years, I haven't been able to make a gentleman of you,' said Shayista.

Amir Dhand wasn't listening. He had spotted a fish monger and was replenishing his stock of his favorite snack.

A bevy of cats moped about, judging Shayista with piercing gazes. He couldn't help but feel perhaps Dhand was right. Perhaps forces were conspiring against him.

CHAPTER 7

Her Highness Nasim Banu, the Subedar's wife, held the incriminating dupatta a careful distance from her rosewater-bathed body as she stormed across the menagerie to the zenana, silk ghagra clinging to her hips, eunuch following close behind. She was already plagued by pernicious worries: Shayista never once visited the mosque on the west side of the fort and drank himself to oblivion regularly, Emperor Aurangzeb was due to arrive within a few weeks, she was aging fast, and now this ... this dupatta?

Shayista was a considerate husband though he had no passionate attachment to her. Still, insecurity was an emotion she had not experienced, not since the death of his slutty mistress, the Hindu princess who died in the attack of 1664. Apart from that one unfortunate indiscretion, Shayista was not an amorous philanderer.

Most Mughal lords had harems full of courtesans but not Shayista. Their zenana housed only qualified kenchens, professional singers and nautch dancers. Shayista never consorted with them. His only obsession was his Imperial Duty for which he would willingly sacrifice his arms and legs.

Nasim did not care so much for the Emperor. She found him guileful and scheming, not a true supporter of his uncle Shayista. The problem with fanatics was that they got fixated on other people's purity. Who asked him to be the meddlesome vigilante of human imperfections? Religion was a private affair.

Still, he was the Emperor so he had to be kept satisfied. Shayista's epicurean habits offended him and it was up to her to keep the peace. She arranged Pari's marriage to the Emperor's son to bring their families closer together but alas the plan went horribly awry.

Prince Azam turned out to be an intolerable imbecile, disrespectful and profligate. To make matters worse, Pari died. It wouldn't have been all in vain if Shayista had managed to secure decent positions for their lazy sons but instead he had become preoccupied with the so-called 'Enemies of the Empire' and was verging on the brink of paranoia. This was clouding his judgement.

That morning, Nasim was appalled to discover just how badly his obsession had distorted his decision-making ability when she found the dupatta under the bed. It was made of fine white muslin with roses embroidered in golden thread. Never had she seen anything so exquisite.

At first, she assumed black magic. Genghis Khan was a necromancer. He conducted regular animal sacrifices and ate herbs to sire 8000 sons. Babar saved Humayan's life, circling his sickbed to lure away Death, sacrificing himself so his son would live. Djinn could be hired for all sorts of misdeeds. Dark pacts with Death and the Devil were known to all. Any amateur conjurer could command a spirit to drop a dupatta under her bed with a spell wrapped within it.

On further examination however the cloth seemed less an act of occult assault and more an act of seduction. It occurred to Nasim that her faithless husband had not only abandoned God but also his lawfully wedded wife. This made her furious rather than sad. She suspected it must have been one of the brazen dancing girls and proceeded directly to the zenana to find the slut who dared threaten her position in the Empire and in bed.

She dismissed her eunuch and entered the zenana. Rays of sun streamed in through latticed walls casting stars upon the ground. Nasim had commissioned this pattern herself from the renowned Ustad Ahmad Lahauri who had built Taj Mahal.

Not only was Ustad Lahauri talented with brick and mortar but also he was strikingly handsome despite his age. Still she hadn't flirted with him not even with an accidental slip of her veil because she valued the vows of marriage. Shayista it appeared was less meticulous with his lust. Of course, princes were permitted to be promiscuous but that didn't mean she had to sit idle and allow it.

Emperor Jahangir had proposed her marriage to Shayista 39 years ago. Shayista was forced to accept it just as he had accepted his position as a political leader of the Empire though that too he had never wanted. He believed his Imperial Duty was ordained by God so he relented. He married her with the same resignation.

She was fifteen years old then and fair as the moon. He was older and climbing the ranks at a dizzying speed. Just how much older, she would never know, for his family never kept record of his birth. After their marriage, she kept aging, as one does. Shayista distressingly did not. He remained a chiselled young man, despite his heavy drinking, while she started looking more like his mother than wife. This troubled her because her position in society was entirely and precariously dependent on her relationship with him.

Nasim had already relinquished youth and good looks. She could not bear to surrender power and wealth too. She had seen Nur Jahan displace Jahangir's first 19 wives and Shayista's coquettish sister, Arjumand Mumtaz, memorialized for eternity in the Taj while Shah Jahan's first wife lay forgotten forever. She was desperate not to suffer the same fate.

Nasim passed through the latticed corridor into a room full of kenchens. Their feathery cholis left little to the imagination. She considered ordering Amir Dhand to have them all flogged but drastic measures would draw Shayista's attention. She was not one for domestic conflict. No, she must be cunning.

The dancing girls were huddled together pleating ribbons in one another's hair. She envied their sorority. She had no close friends. She suspected everyone was out to cheat or con her. In the centre of the nauseating nautch circle was heavy-set Didi Ma, reclined on a silk cushion. A lithe young beauty massaged coconut oil into her thinning hair.

Didi Ma produced a smile as insincere as a whore's orgasm. 'To what can we attribute this gracious visit, your Highness?' She lumbered to her feat like a cow that had toppled over, waddled to Nasim's side and bowed in taslim.

'Salaam. How lovely it is to see you,' Nasim said. 'I have come to inquire about the nautch girls. Are they well?'

'Your most graciousness,' said the instructor, her tone suitably subservient. 'Your generous patronage keeps us in the peak of summer throughout the year.'

Nasim frowned.

Didi Ma bowed even deeper.

Nasim scanned the girls. The singers, comely faces, buxom buttocks, thighs like overripe squash, were dressed in silk, not muslin. The dancers sat on the far side of the room, applying henna to their hands and feet, wearing gaudy coloured chiffon. No one was wearing a virgin white muslin choli that matched the incriminating dupatta. She needed another clue.

Perhaps if she saw Shayista watching a performance, she would know from his face which of the dancers he fancied. She decided to test her theory. 'Didi Ma, on the eve of the full moon, the dancers will perform the Dance of Seven Veils.'

'Next week?' Didi Ma wrung her hands. 'Your Excellency, allow us more time to prepare?'

'You will have to manage,' said Nasim curtly. She liked to make the lazy cow squirm. With that, she excused herself from the zenana.

Shayista was so concerned with running the Empire that he barely gave a thought to the future of his family. He had five living sons to look out for but all he worried about were the *enemies*. She would not be his victim. Didn't she deserve some security in her evening years? With Shayista gambling fast and loose with their fortune, she felt nervous to say the least.

They had almost lost it all last time Shayista failed the Emperor, twenty years ago. Luckily the Emperor was lenient and only reassigned him to the backwaters of Bengal. It could have been worse. They were able to recover. She had turned Lal Bagh fort into a symbol of Mughal taste, while he had turned Bengal into the richest province in the Empire. Now, if Shayista kept up with his shenanigans, they might really lose it all, the treasury, the fort, the province, everything.

She had to trap the harlot and silence her so the subha's prestige, and her own, remained intact. The Emperor was scheduled to arrive in time for the Nauraz and she wanted everything to be perfect.

CHAPTER 8

Aboard the ship, there were two challenges Madeline faced first. Rats. Fat, ebony rodents that darted about the ship, fell under boots, screeched and scurried to death. Rats under beds, over ceilings, inside closets, on her clothes. Then there were the waves. The endless rocking motion of the ship was not easy to adjust to. Much of the first day was spent teetering about until Madeline finally succumbed to a rebellion of her stomach and a bout of torturous retching that lasted a week.

Next Madeline was beset by fear. Her travel companions were a band of runaway sociopaths. The ship was named Belo Diabo and its sails were blood red. Its flag was black with the face of an angry red tiger on it. The crew of about 200, from Portugal, Spain, Italy, Germany, Belgium, Greece and England, were all men. Everywhere she went, lecherous eyes followed her. She mentioned her concern to Costa but he paid little heed to her complaint.

Across her bosom Madeline wrapped a cotton shawl, a gift from the old kitchen hand, Abdul, who had an unnaturally red beard and could cook the tastiest sea turtle. He was a Firingi-dosha, a bastard son of a Portuguese pirate and a Bengali peasant woman. He had been a cook aboard Costa's ship for some twenty years and could speak French fluently. He quickly became Madeline's best friend aboard the Diabo.

Of the sailors, the grisliest were two beasts by the name of Um Olho and Perna de Pau. Um Ohlo, which meant One Eye, was Costa's first mate. He treated Costa with utmost respect but at Madeline he cast devouring glances with his one roving eye. Perna de Pau, thus named for his wooden leg, looked at her in the same way, and additionally, was misogynistic, a trait she noticed common among the sailors. Consequently, Madeline stole a robust kitchen boti, one used for scaling man-sized fish, and hid it under her pillow. Costa gave her the room next to his so he could keep an eye on her and mostly, she kept to herself.

They had only been sailing three weeks and a day when they anchored by a quiet coastal town. The captain had some business and Madeline took the opportunity to purchase new vestments and accessories so she could present herself in full resplendence when they arrived in Bengal.

When they set sail again, the crew was giddy. Costa had by some unprincipled means secured a valuable treasure map. He promptly arranged to sell it for a hefty sum to another ship captain who would be arriving soon.

'You might want to stay in your room?' suggested Costa. 'Our guests are a slippery lot.' He had laid out the lambskin map on his table and was copying its contents somewhat carelessly onto a papyrus canvas.

'Mais pourquoi?' replied Madeline, peeking over his shoulder with disguised curiosity. Her father had taught her to read maps before she learned to write. This was a French map of Bengal.

'Unscrupulous pirates. Sea scavengers!' said Costa over his shoulder as he burnt the edges of the map he had drawn to make it look older. He rolled up the original lambskin map and tucked it into his coat.

Madeline bit her lip. She had heard of seafaring thieves who would rape, pillage and plunder anyone in their path, for a few coins of gold. Though she knew she should be afraid of men with shallow morals, but they were coming to buy a map from Captain Costa and the most common currency at sea was diamond.

'I may be of help. I am a student of mineralogy,' said Madeline.

'Suit yourself,' said Captain Costa.

At midday, the ship was a speck of dust in the spy-glass. By afternoon it was the size of a duck. By night, it anchored some hundred yards away from their vessel. A party of four approached in a skiff, rowing with broad strokes. Costa's men were on deck, singing, cheering, watching as fortune approached.

'Throw them a rope,' shouted Costa. 'Reel them in.'

As a child, Madeline inherited her father's love of adventure, accompanying him on all his excursions till the fateful night when she was nine and her mother died of a heart attack. Soon after, her father lost two of his ships to storms off the coast of Africa and retired to his room with a bottle. Her upbringing was left to her very strict and very deaf maternal grandmother.

Madeline occupied her loneliness with books. Voraciously she devoured the travelogues, nautical manuals and atlases in her father's library. She then moved on to books of astronomy, biology and the flora and fauna of diverse climates. Her keen interest in the natural philosophies soon found its focus in the study of earth minerals and precious metals, especially those that glittered.

Over time, her obsession distilled into a detailed study on the material properties of diamonds: classifying, categorizing and chronicling specimens by colour, cut and cost. Her research paper was published and heralded by nobility as the first inquiry of its calibre. Increasingly enamoured by diamonds, particularly polished ones, the elite called upon her to value their purchases and paid her generously for her services.

Madeline wondered if Costa's guests would be trading in diamonds. She pushed through the crowd to obtain a view. The men who alighted were dressed in so similar a fashion as their own crew, the same skull tattoos on their arms and letch expression in their eyes that a realization dawned belatedly on Madeline: Captain Costa's men were probably pirates too. Panic struck in her head but was drowned out by the ensuing events.

Perna de Pau led the four visiting pirates to the captain's cabin. Um Olho and Madeline followed them in, the rest of the crew waited by the door. The visitors took seats around Costa's table, sharing stories in Portuguese. Their black-bearded captain introduced himself as Silveria. With a crooked nose and greasy head of curls, he offered Madeline a lascivious smile. From his pocket, he retrieved a pouch of velvet and emptied its contents onto the table: two dazzling, egg-sized diamonds.

Um Olho lifted the artefacts to his good eye. A silent excitement rippled through the air. Costa's face flushed but he refrained from an obvious display of thrill.

Silveria asked to see the map of the hidden treasure. Costa passed him the papyrus replica. Silveria unrolled it with utmost tenderness. His eyes shimmered as he drank in the details.

Silveria and Captain Costa exchanged a few words in hushed tones. Madeline heard the mention of an Emerald Tablet. She wondered what it was, a Mughal treasure? Silveria thanked Costa and rerolled the map, placing it in his satchel. They embraced and slapped each other's backs heartily. Both parties seemed satisfied with the trade.

Costa passed around a bottle of flip, a concoction of rum, beer and sugar. They took noisy sips and smacked their lips. The smell was so strong it made Madeline nauseous. She lifted one of the diamonds to the light of the lantern to examine. It was luminescent but something was not right ...

The bulk of France's diamond supply came from English networks. East India Company was a large supplier and had tried to establish a monopoly over the lucrative trade but independent merchants such as Thomas Pitt and Jean-Baptiste Tavernier were often more ready in supply. Madeline rubbed the diamond in her hands. It felt cool, not drawing heat from her as a diamond was meant to do.

The captains shook hands, about to part, when suddenly Madeline announced, 'These are fake.'

The merriment froze.

'Now just a minute, wench, are ye suggestin I'm a cheater?' fumed Silveria, his eyes bulbously enraged.

Um Olho glowered and unsheathed his cutlass.

'Will you believe this rumour mongering slander?' demanded Silveria. 'By the honour of Alfonso, I swear these diamonds are ...''

Madeline threw the egg-shaped diamond to the floor. It shattered into fragments of glass.

'Do you take me for a chuckle-headed fool?' yelled Costa.

Um Olho grabbed Silveria's collar and lifted him clear off the ground.

Costa whistled and a dozen men stormed in, armed with pikes, arquebuses and spears. They dragged the prisoners to the plank.

Costa pressed his blade against Silveria's throat. 'Have you bilge rats no Code of Honour? You come to my ship as my guest and you try to cheat me? I will feed you to sharks!'

Madeline squeezed her eyes shut, unable to stand the sight of a man being killed. Instead of a scream she heard a splash. She opened her eyes to see Captain Costa had merely sliced off Silveria's nose and pushed him overboard. Silveria's men were also made noseless and thrown into the water. Costa's crew lobbed bottles at them as they swam back to their ship.

That evening the mood aboard Belo Diabo was one of felicity. They had not been hoodwinked thanks to Madeline. She was hailed as hero of the hour. What had been lust and hostility in their eyes transformed into admiration and gratitude.

The drunken wastrels continued their revelry late into the night with off-key violins and tambourines. At one point, Costa thanked her and for a moment, she thought he was quite cute, even charming, with his carefree ways and his love for life. It wasn't till he passed out several hours later that finally the noise subsided and Madeline had a chance to reflect on her experience.

More often than not, women in 1685 accepted their fate without a fight. Not Madeline. She was determined to design her own destiny. She had raised the finances for an epic odessy. She had convinced a captain to ferry her across the world. She had held her ground against pirates. She had tolerated months at sea without salons or stylists, without friends or admirers, without even her cat. Now if she could just pull off the final stunt, she could secure for herself a position in the upper echelons of Parisian society.

CHAPTER 9

The next day, Shayista was in no mood for domestic or administrative duties. He would much rather be outside, armed incognito, hunting down enemies but there was no easy way to slip out of the fortress without being seen. He was trapped between Charybdis and Scylla: across the latticed fountains was his wife's zenana window, beside the pebbled pathway was the *Diwan-i-am*, Durbar Hall.

The Diwan-i-am was a classic piece of Mughal architecture: serene, spacious and splendid from the outside. Inside was a hornet's nest of hassles for Shayista to deal with. Citizens from across the province came to the daily darshan to seek his assistance. The hall could contain an assembly of two hundred people and during public hours, it was always filled to capacity. From a plinth covered with Persian rugs, Shayista dictated his verdicts to his *Diwan-i-ala*, Chief Revenue Officer, Bhopal Singh.

Bhopal was a capable man, practical and reliable. He had served Shayista's father till he died and then he served Shayista with the same ferocious loyalty. A dwarf by birth, taunted and bullied in youth, he took distinct pleasure in his position of power, upholding equality and protecting the underdogs. Bhopal would gladly die for the royal family but despite all this, Shayista wanted to avoid him. He had too much on his mind.

The Subedar grounded his gaze and crunched his body low, moving in the shadows of bushes to escape the Diwan's punctilious surveillance. He made it past the entrance and the orchard of mango trees but as he crossed the central water channel, the *ghu-ghu-ghuk* of a collared dove interrupted his concentrated escape. He glanced at the bird, then back at the durbar, and saw Bhopal at the doorway gazing at him imploringly. Bhopal's face lit up when their eyes met. Shayista could not in good conscience ignore him. He sulked back to make an expedient appearance at court.

Just then, Nasim Banu glided out of her zenana. She saw her Lord husband and blushed, hiding something behind her back.

'I see your Highness received the gift from Zamindar Singh?' said Bhopal, trying to recover the moment from awkwardness. 'It is from his karkhana in Midnapur.'

Shayista scowled. The bushy-browed aristocrat was a trained warrior known for his ruthlessness both on and off the battle field. What did he want from Nasim?

Nasim Banu seemed flustered. 'This ... this is a gift for me?'

Bhopal nodded.

'Please convey my gratitude,' said Nasim, wrapping the scarf around her neck. She bowed and retired to her room.

Shayista followed Bhopal to the durbar.

'The Amir ul-Umra, Mughal Viceroy of Emperor Aurangzeb, Governor of Bengal, Subedar Shayista Khan cometh,' announced Bhopal, his voice booming out of his small body despite his age.

Citizens and guards fell to their knees, heads bowed in respect. Subedar Khan entered the hall. He despised talking about taxes. Nothing could be more tedious.

'Arise,' said the Subedar, taking position on the plinth.

Ceremoniously Bhopal brought forth Akbar's sapphire encrusted khanda, holding it upright in a velvet wrapping, laying it on the pillow next to Shayista. The broad-bladed straight sword was heavy and as tall as Bhopal himself, still he insisted on its presence as an emblem of sovereignty during darshans.

The first supplicant was a shy peasant. Bhopal led him to the stand.

The citizen, crisply dressed in his best kurta, cleared his throat but before he could muster his feeble plea, a voice from behind interrupted, 'Your Excellency, the Zamindar awaits your counsel.'

Shayista saw him then. Not only were his brows as bushy as before, his mustachio stretched to a curl on his cheeks. With a vainglorious swagger, Shobha approached the stand. His sense of entitlement was irritating. He expected preferential treatment.

'Wait your turn,' said Shayista.

The zamindar's nostrils flared, blood rushed to his face. Never in his buttermilk life had he been subject to such humiliation.

Unable to contain his glee, a grin burst upon Bhopal's face.

The zamindar would have drawn his sirohi and minced the midget to a thousand pieces if it weren't for the Subedar's stern gaze. He twisted the tip of his moustache into a sharp self-aggrandized point.

'Subedar Khan, Salaam. How are you?' he said with false intimacy. 'You have not recognized me. I am your humble servant Zamindar Shobha Singh. I have come to ...'

'Wait your turn.' Shayista cut him off.

Shobha smouldered. His left eye twitched. His moustache quivered. 'Do you mean to say ... Could you be ...' Seeing no change in Shayista's apathy, he ended with, 'Subedar Khan, you will regret this.' Without taslim, he stormed out.

Shayista signalled for the peasant to speak.

Distressed, the peasant uttered, 'I weave in a karkhana but we haven't been paid in months. When we ask for our dues, he threatens to chop off our thumbs.'

'Who?' asked Shayista.

'Zamindar Singh,' he whispered.

Shayista was not surprised. The muslin weavers of the North were the finest in the world. Fashionable men and women in Europe wanted to wear nothing else but Shobha's enterprise was based on unfair trade not sustainable local economy. He was selling muslin to the East India Company who then rolled it in hollow bamboos and shipped it to Europe for vast profits without paying tax.

Shayista called Bhopal to the plinth. 'Execute the zamindar,' he ordered.

'Sire, I hate to contradict you but as your Diwan-i-ala, it is my duty to advise against this,' Bhopal cautioned. 'Hindus will revolt.'

Only Bhopal who had known him since he was a child would dare counsel him thus. Shayista gnashed his teeth and slammed his fist into the dais. He had to protect the Empire. He would have to find another way to curb the zamindar. Perhaps he could strike Shobha and the

Company together. He had banned the trade of saltpetre, why not take that one step further?

'Ban trade with the English,' he said. 'They are a company of foul dealers.'

'Muslin trade?' asked Bhopal.

'Yes.'

'Indigo?'

'Yes.'

'Cotton?'

'ALL trade!' said Shayista.

'Are you sure, Sire?' said Bhopal.

'Yes,' said Shayista. The Emperor would not approve of this but Shayista had to prioritise the wellbeing of his people.

'Free merchants or company wallas?' asked Bhopal.

'Both.'

'Hookum.'

Shayista noticed the weaver looking lost in the stand, despair etched on his brows.

'You ... Do you make fine cloth?' Shayista asked the weaver.

'Yes Sire, I believe I do.'

'I want my army outfitted in local textiles. You are hereby commissioned to produce the cloth needed to dress my army for the next ten years!'

'Your Highness, that's impossible ...'

'Quiet! I will pay double the market. Fail to deliver and I will have your head!'

The weaver's eyes flashed as he tried to grasp the possibilities. After a moment of bedazzlement, he bowed and left.

In an aside, Bhopal said to Shayista, 'Sire, that's impossible, unless ...' A new understanding washed over his face. 'Ah, you want him to set up a karkhana and take on apprentices so that the art is not lost?'

Shayista said only, 'See to it that he faces no obstacles.'

'Consider it done, Sire,' said Bhopal, beaming.

'Now Bhopal, I leave the darshan in your capable hands. I have other matters to tend to,' he concluded.

'Hookum,' said the dwarf. 'And the Nauraz, Sire. We will have ten thousand soldiers here to greet the Emperor.'

Shayista thanked him and stepped out. In the garden, a grey-capped woodpecker called *tit-tirr, tit-tirr, tit-tirr* ... like a mechanical clock. Shayista recalled the pir's eerie warning. Was Bengal running out of time?

CHAPTER 10

The madrasa premise was delineated by a masterpiece of botany, a garden elegantly laid out to fulfil the needs of the children living there. Coconut trees stretched up to the sky heavy with milk, jackfruit provided shade against wind, cilantro protected from pests. On one side of the property was a pond of delightfully edible fish. By the gates, a pair of mango trees with wooden swings and a nest of flying squirrels. A banana grove with a thin pathway running through it demarcated the classrooms from the hostel.

Champa pushed her finger into the soil bed of a hasna hena to check the moisture. The flowers had blossomed. At night, their scent would fill the air. She would water them then and feed the fish. It was almost time to harvest the tilapia. How quickly one year had gone by.

The first day she met Guru Ma, she was singing under her breath at the spice bazaar, a song she had learned from the dancers. Guru Ma heard her and invited her back to the madrasa to teach the girls. One song led to another and Champa found herself falling in love with the girls. Saraswati, or Guru Ma as she was called, needed assistance to run the madrasa since Pari Bibi, her principal supporter, had just died. The death had blown a hole in the heart of the madrasa, a hole Champa tried to fill with light.

Champa strolled towards the sound of children, pausing for a gaggle of goslings crossing her path. One gosling strayed to inspect a yellow butterfly.

'Champa Miss!' shouted Rezina. 'Come inside quickly!' Her voice was pitched with panic.

Inside, a dismal scene: the girls were huddled around Guru Ma, crying.

'What happened?' exclaimed Champa.

Guru Ma's silvery hair framed her angular face, dark kajol outlined her sad eyes. She had no words, only tear-streaked cheeks. In her palms she cradled their puppy, Kukur Mia, mangled and bloody.

Champa couldn't believe her eyes. 'Is he ... is he ..?'

Guru Ma nodded. Wooden beads hung from her neck. Though she was sixty, she carried herself with the style and grace of a vivacious young woman, except when she was worried. Then the lines showed on her face.

'Who did this?' Champa asked. It was hard to see Guru Ma pained and the girls upset.

'The mullahs,' Rezina whimpered. 'I had just finished my fazr prayers when I saw two men call Kukur Mia to the gate. He went to them, wagging his little tail. They caught him, killed him with a boti. Threw his body back in.'

Champa shuddered. What beasts dwelt in the guise of men? Her mind flashed to the Subedar killing cats that morning. Tears of rage burned in her eyes but she subdued her feelings for the sake of the girls, assuming a calm and purposeful demeanour.

Tenderly she lifted the puppy from Guru Ma's hands. 'Girls, let's clean him before we bury him,' she said. 'Rezina, a bucket of water. Alina, my white orna. Popi and Parvin, a grave by the mango trees. Little ones, how about some flowers? We will bury him properly.'

'Is there a heaven for dogs?' asked Marium.

Champa nodded, though she wasn't sure. Sweet Kukur Mia's fur was caked in blood. He was warm still but stiff. Champa had found him a week earlier, yelping by the roadside, less than a week old, separated from his mother. She brought him to the madrasa and fed him. The girls loved him. Coming from Muslim families, they had never played with a puppy. Quickly he became the central joy of their days. And now this.

Champa began the sombre ritual of cleansing the pup. He was barely larger than her two fists. She had washed many dead bodies. Dada performed funeral rites for the folks in their community and she sometimes helped with the ablutions and bath before the burial, if the deceased was a woman. There was something about washing a corpse that was very grounding. It helped her accept the inevitability of death.

But senseless violence and premature endings were not part of the natural order.

Once his fur was clean, Champa wrapped him in her orna. Outside, a grave the size of a jackfruit was ready and the girls had gathered around.

'Allahu Akbar,' began Champa. 'Dear God, we return to you your beloved creation. Thank you for sharing him with us, though only for a brief while. He brought us much happiness and he will shine on in our hearts. Ameen.'

'Ameen,' the girls repeated.

Champa placed the puppy in the grave and filled it with earth. When the ceremony was over, she asked the girls to write a poem to commemorate Kukur Mia. The kagaji walla had delivered sheets of paper the day before and by dipping their quills in grief and sharing it with one another, Champa hoped they would find some comfort. She and Guru Ma retired to their office.

'What happened?' said Champa. 'Was it the ulema?'

Guru Ma nodded faintly and laid her head upon the desk.

Champa's blood churned. 'Why are they obsessed with doctrines of hatred?'

Guru Ma sighed. 'They're looking for an excuse to fight us.'

'Should we fight back?'

Guru Ma said feebly, 'We must survive. The girls need us.'

Champa hugged her frail shoulders then walked to the library to reflect. Though their school facility was meagre, their library was a treasure trove. A gift from the Subedar, it was a collection of masterpieces. Calligraphy from the Safavids, miniaturist illustrations from the Ottomans, manuscripts from Mongolia, volumes from Venice, portraiture from Portugal, epistles from England and astronomy charts from Arabia competed for space on the shelves with books by Ibn Arabi, Ibn Sina and Ibn Battuta.

A few girls were quietly reading in the library when Champa arrived. Marium, hair in braids, was absorbed in an illustrated copy of *The Travels of Ibn Battuta*. Champa cleared her throat.

'Miss, there you are! Will you tell us more about the world today?' said Marium.

'Darling one, may you grow up to be a wanderer! But there are other topics we must also explore,' said Champa. 'Laws of motion and universal gravitation. The dichotomy of mind and body. The theory of tides.'

'Planets?' said Rezina, who was sitting not far. 'Chachu didn't believe me when I told him that there are stars as large as our world!' She handed Champa a leather bound book titled *The Compendium of Stars*. The humidity had caused the leather to grow musty but the pages were still intact.

'Ah yes, al-Farghani,' said Champa. She opened the book and was about to begin reading when the sound of muffled voices drew her attention.

She glanced out the window. A crowd of bearded men in white robes and prayer caps had gathered by the gate. She recognized one face in the crowd and turned red.

'It's the mullahs again,' said Guru Ma, rushing into the library. 'Stay inside with the girls.' Drawing an orna over her, she stepped out.

Champa ushered all the girls into a classroom and gave them a writing assignment to keep them occupied. Only snippets from the conversation outside were audible. Guru Ma was asking the mullahs why they were on the madrasa premises.

'Madrasas are for boys,' said a gangly mullah with an unkempt beard.

'What's happening?' asked Marium, tugging at Champa's sleeve.

'Hush, little one,' said Champa, straining to hear Guru Ma speak.

'Heed our warning,' said another mullah. 'Or Allah will destroy your madrasa.'

'They want to destroy our madrasa?' wailed Marium.

'You think I'd let that happen?' said Champa.

'This orphanage was established for girls under the auspices of Princess Pari,' she heard Guru Ma say. 'The Subedar will not allow you to shut it down.'

'Bagh Khan is busy with his monopolies. He doesn't care about the girls. Only we have their interest at heart. Close the school. Send them to the mosque.'

'God is not confined within a mosque. God is everywhere! God is within us,' said Guru Ma.

'Blasphemy!' yelled the cleric.

Marium started crying. 'First they killed our puppy, now they will kill us!'

'No one's going to kill you,' said Champa, dragging herself away from the window to comfort the child.

'What do they want?' asked Rezina.

'Men want to oppress women,' explained Champa. 'But we won't let them!'

Marium nodded but she did not look entirely convinced.

'My uncle says it's because you teach music,' said Rezina. 'He says music is the instrument of the Devil.'

Champa frowned. Creative expression was the purest way to connect with the Divine.

Champa believed there were as many shades of worship as there were colours in a rainbow. Her grandfather searching for mystic truth, her father following the five pillar routine, she dancing, it was all for the love of God. What did it matter how one chose to express love? Why put rules around that?

Misguided ideologies were infiltrating the collective conscience and impinging upon the liberty of thought and being. Furious, unable to hold back any longer, Champa grabbed her orna and ran outside. The mullahs were already leaving. 'Don't come back!' she yelled.

A particularly spiteful mullah grabbed a goose by its neck on his way out. The creature squawked and flapped frantically, feathers flew in all directions. With one menacing swipe, the mullah cut off its head and chucked its bleeding body into the well, contaminating their water source.

When they were gone, Guru Ma and Champa peered into the well. A swarm of flies buzzed about the goose. It had not been easy to raise the money to build the well. Now the girls would have no drinking water. The goose's mate wept by the side of the well.

'O Princess Pari, what will happen to your school?' cried Guru Ma.

'What about the Subedar?' said Champa. 'Will he help us?'

Guru Ma shook her head sadly. 'He was never pleased with Pari's involvement here. He felt it was risky and did not encourage it.'

'Monster,' Champa muttered, remembering the Subedar striking the cat. Were all men boorish? 'Then we must sort this out ourselves.'

She wouldn't sit idle while insidious dogma penetrated the public psyche. Women had been sorting out girls' schooling for centuries without men. Emperor Humayun's wife founded a college near her husband's tomb. Emperor Akbar's foster mother established a madarasa in Delhi. Jahanara Begum founded a madrasa in Agra.

The madrasa was only minutes from Champa's home but she chose the slightly longer route by Lal Bagh fort. She skirted the walls of the fortress, past the Chowk Bazaar and a congregation of stray cats by a fish monger's stall. After her father abandoned her for his faith, all she had left was the orphanage. Now the mullahs wanted to destroy it too. She would have to be clever and resourceful. She would not let the mullahs discourage her. She would find a way to raise money to fix the well herself.

CHAPTER 11

Dressed in a lavender silk frock with a peach stomacher and petticoat, Madeline studied the books she purchased at the Port of Masulipatam. Costa, it turned out, was a metropolitan merchant whose strange intelligence allowed him to make money wherever he went. He sailed from port to port, trading goods: weapons, nautical equipment, jewels and other random booty. He conducted the exchanges in so swift and exact a manner, Madeline marvelled that he could have been a true bred merchant if he had not become a pirate. His interest gave her ample opportunity to delve into research for her mission.

The first book she picked up was about diamonds. It contained fascinating facts about the colour of diamonds and the light they refracted. Black diamonds absorbed the most light and pink diamonds the least, while blue and yellow were somewhere in between. The illustrations were of sensational diamonds set in the Peacock Throne.

The throne of the Mughal Emperor was made of rubies and emeralds and Kohinoor, the brightest diamond in the world. The canopy above it was fringed with pearls and above that was a golden peacock with a tail of blue sapphires and a ruby breast. Madeline dipped her quill in ink and drew the throne in her moleskin diary, replicating the exquisite details as best she could. She wondered what sort of people the bejewelled Mughals were, with their lavish lifestyles and their dazzling gems. She imagined how it would feel to wear a strand of first water diamonds from the coveted Kollur mines.

The second book she purchased was a collection of recipes of concoctions that could make a man forget a night, confess a secret, fall out of love, sedate or even kill him. Such potions might prove useful so she copied them into her notebook and hoped for a chance to test them.

Armed with a spy-glass she had assembled herself, she gazed at the distant shoreline of Bengal. Orchards, water wheels, prosperous villages and manicured gardens dotted the riverside. Brown-bodied children splashed in the water. Beyond the banks, lush jungle foliage spread out like an emerald carpet. A seagull flew overhead. The sky was a brilliant sapphire, unlike the grey canvas suspended perpetually over Versailles. The aquatic voyage had fatigued her both physically and psychologically but with the end in sight, an inexplicable hope sprouted in her heart.

'Can you see it?' asked Abdul. His voice conveyed the eagerness of homecoming. 'The Emperor's Paradise?'

Madeline passed Abdul her spy-glass and helped him adjust it to his eye. From his squeals of delight, she knew when it came into focus.

'There it is!' said Abdul. 'Lal Bagh Fortress.'

'What does Lal Bagh mean?' asked Madeline.

'Lal is red,' explained Abdul. 'And Bagh means garden but it also means tiger.'

'So ... the fortress is full of flowers?'

'Indeed it is brimming with impeccable gardens. The Subedar relishes his roses but he is as ferocious as a beast. Bagh Khan is what the simple folk call him. Tiger Khan, Subedar of Bengal.'

Madeline had grown fond of Abdul's apocryphal stories. Many afternoons she spent by his side, learning about the countries he had visited: their histories, politics, cultures and beliefs. He seemed to know something about everything though she suspected he embellished the truth and sometimes indulged in outright confabulation.

'Tell me more about the Subedar,' she asked. 'What sort of weapon does he wield?'

'Subedar Khan is a master warrior,' began Abdul. 'He is adept with most forms of martial arts but predominantly he fights with a sword called Azdahar which means Dragon. It was a gift. It belonged to Emperor Akbar.'

'Akbar's sword?' Madeline was awestruck. 'But how did he get Akbar's sword?'

'The Subedar is no country bumpkin. He is of high pedigree. His father was Shah Jahan's vizier. His grandfather was Jahangir's vizier. Aurangzeb is his nephew.'

'Is it true he was trained by a Sufi?'

Abdul nodded. 'I met a man, a chowkidar from Agra palace, who told me a wondrous tale of the Subedar when he was a boy. Would you like to hear it?'

Madeline nodded.

'As a child, the Subedar was known as Talib. He was a reserved and serious boy. His father was a political strategist who threw lavish parties and had a cold demeanour. His mother was occupied with her younger children. Talib was raised mostly by a Kashmiri aseel whom he loved dearly.

'One afternoon, his father berated the aseel and Talib, though merely a boy of six, drew a dagger to defend her honour. He was given a thrashing and sent to bed without dinner but in the morning he did not relent and eventually his father apologized to the maid.

'After his aunt married Emperor Jahangir, Talib found himself free to explore the wonderland of Agra. He drifted around the palace, among stable keepers and guards, in and out of school with a handful of friends, mostly princes. There were endless games of hide and seek to play in the intriguing passageways of the fort and delightfully vulgar stories to eavesdrop on in the tents of burly soldiers drunk on sharab.

'Warriors from around the Empire travelled to the Mughal court to teach the princes their skills in exchange for rewards. Among them were wrestlers from Panjab, yogis from Bundelkhand, slingers from Gujarat, archers from Assam and stone-throwers from Bihar. Talib was trained alongside Dara and Aurangzeb, under the guidance of the Emperor's personal tutor, Huzur Seif Khan.

'Huzur was a Sufi of the highest order and a formidable warrior, honoured with the title *Seif Khan*, Sword Master, for his valiant service in the Mughal army. He taught Talib mathematics, Arabic, Persian and self-defence. He read passages by Jalal ad-Din Rumi off exquisite manuscripts from Tabriz. He explained to Talib: the purpose of life is to love and the truest lover is God.

'At first Master Huzur was impatient with Talib who, though athletic and adept with weaponry, was more interested in horses and elephants than studies. Huzur would say, 'Your father, the Itiqad al-Daula, your grandfather, the Intimad al-Daula, and you? The Idiot al-Daula?'

'Then something happened that made the Sufi scholar realize the potential of his new protégé. It was along the course of a routine training. Huzur had taken Talib, Dara and Aurangzeb to a moss-covered boulder in a forest nearby. He asked the boys to hit the rock with their bare hands' knife edge while chanting 'Al-Haq' which meant 'Truth'.

"Perform each strike with perfect precision one thousand times and Universal Truth shall be revealed to you. Allah is al-Haq,' he said, then went to the mosque to pray.

'The moment he disappeared, Dara stopped his practice. He had no interest in fighting and while the pursuit of Universal Truth tickled his fancy, he was distracted by a gazelle. Nimble and quick, he scampered off behind it in search of a water hole.

'Aurangzeb looked to see if his young uncle would follow but Talib had the ethos of a warrior and continued industriously. Soon Aurangzeb grew bored. 'I already know the Truth,' he said. 'The Truth is that we shall never fight with our hands when we have canons and steel.' He pulled a Damascan katara out from under his kurta and held it before Talib. Together they admired the ripples of folded metal that ran along the length of the short blade.

'Aurangzeb brought the dagger hurtling down on the rock. The impact left no injuries on the blade or the rock, only a ringing pain in his shoulder. 'One cannot use Truth to rule, one must use deception.' With that, Aurangzeb ran into the thicket to play too.

'Hands bruised and pulpy like an overripe plum, Talib persevered not because he was afraid of Huzur's wrath but because he wanted to see Allah. Minutes rolled into hours. Sun set and with darkness a fresh horde of challenges. Night expanded and contracted in waves. Talib lost count as he slipped in and out of sleep. In the midst of the delirium, between crickets, frogs, foxes and owls, Talib heard a tune. It was a melancholic melody coming from no discernible direction, everywhere all at once. At that moment, Talib's hand sliced through the rock as if it were made of wet mud.'

'Splitting the rock in two?' asked Madeline.

Abdul nodded. 'When Master Huzur returned to the glade the next morning, he found Talib asleep on the grass, hands bloody, rock split in two. Talib could not recall how he had done it, only that at one stage he had heard Bageshri, the raga of Dawn. Huzur said it was possible because Talib had experienced Truth in his heart.'

'He sliced through the rock?' asked Madeline, incredulous.

'With meditation, anything is possible,' replied Abdul. 'Wizards can rearrange the very structure of matter. From then on Huzur treated the boy not as a disciple but a prodigy, initiated him into the realm of the metaphysical, primed him to one day protect the Empire from its enemies.'

'The Subedar is a wizard?' asked Madeline.

'Some say that is how he amassed his vast wealth and influence. Alas, he gave up his mysticism to become a warrior when he took on the title Amir-ul-Umra Shayista Khan.'

Madeline marvelled, a man with wealth, power and magic! She wondered if the Subedar could be of help to her. If only she could find a way to win his favour. She leafed through her book of spells in search of ideas.

CHAPTER 12

Nasim Banu climbed out of the steamed hammam and lay naked upon a cool marble slab as her chambermaid lathered coconut oil onto her skin. They massaged the curves under her breasts and tops of her shoulders where she was most sensitive then rolled her onto her stomach to rub her back. If there was one thing Nasim loved most in life, it was the hammamkhana. Shayista built it with a room below for heating water. There was something about being pampered in steam that melted away her aches and worries.

She was lucky to live in the plush cocoon of Lal Bagh but this luck was hazardously poised on the whims of the Emperor. If his distaste for Shayista grew, he could easily relieve him of his duties and then what would become of them?

Nasim donned a silk robe and while maids brushed her hair with golden combs, she planned the final details of the Nauraz. It was only weeks away and she was determined to host the most memorable party of the year. Shayista was still cheerless since the death of his baseborn daughter a year earlier. A celebration with music was just what he needed. Softened by the tunes, he was more likely to do as she asked. The Emperor would be visiting and she wanted Shayista to request a promotion for their son. Fortunately the scarf was not a sign of Shayista's infidelity but still she needed to secure a safety net.

Iradat was not much to brag about but what choice did she have? Buzurg had married below them, a grisly woman who would treat her as a chambermaid if she were to depend on them. Aqidat shirked all responsibilities. Jafar and Abu Nasr were indolent whiners. Alas, if only Abul Fateh were alive.

The maids plucked her grey hairs then combed in traces of amloke berries to create a shine. She sucked in her cheeks as they brushed crushed rubies onto her high cheek bones.

The kajol around her eyes she applied herself. She liked to draw the ends out elaborately. In her jewelled looking glass, she noticed on her forehead, a fresh wrinkle. If she was going to rule the Empire she couldn't look like an aging goose. This would not do.

She chose a muslin choli, an elegant strand of diamonds and an Arabian attar to dab onto her décolletage. While men with money and power were respected and obeyed, women needed beauty to command. In her youth, she was accustomed to having things just as she liked, her stunning features ensured that. She envied women who were unattractive to begin with. They would never suffer the pain of fading beauty. O, how she yearned for youth.

Nasim met a witchdoctor once who claimed he could slow the aging process but for this he required the blood of a virgin. She would happily have sacrificed one of the dancing girls but they were far from virginal so Nasim gave up on that venture.

Recently Nasim came to know of a pir in Lal Bagh whose elixirs were highly recommended by her friends. Perhaps she would visit him, see what he could offer. Nasim suspected Shayista dabbled in the dark arts. How else could he stay perpetually youthful? Occupied with such thoughts, she stepped out of her chamber to find Eunuch Khajah Ambar waiting.

'Good morning, your Highness,' he said, bowing low.

'Ambar, there you are. The distribution of golap jamuns may begin today,' she instructed. 'The full moon is twenty one days away. We mustn't offend the djinn.'

A wide and fiendish grin spread across Ambar's face. 'Have I ever failed you, your Highness?'

'No, that you haven't Khajah. Not in the twenty years you've been with me,' she replied sincerely. He came just when she'd needed him most, in the aftermath of losing Abul Fateh, a wound that she seemed to carry alone.

She blamed Shayista for failing to save their son. If Abul Fateh were still alive she would not have to worry about her future. He would have taken care of her. He was the best of her six boys, her youngest, her most cherished.

Nasim dismissed her eunuch and made her way to the durbar hall. She found Shayista there, the public hearing had just finished. He was frowning, frothing at the mouth, dictating instructions vehemently to the Diwan.

Nasim waited at the doors and when he finally stepped out, she greeted him formally. 'Your Highness, salaam.'

'Nasim, how are you?' he asked, his mind elsewhere.

'Preparations for the Emperor are underway,' she said.

'Fine, take what you need from Bhopal. How are our sons?'

'Aqidat sent a messenger dove: his wife is expecting. Buzurg has fever but he assures me it is not too bad. Jafar and Abu Nasr are fine. Sire, I worry about Iradat. Is it not time to give him responsibilities, perhaps a subha of his own?'

'He has the brain of a banana bat,' said Shayista, not disguising his disinterest. 'He cannot manage his own room. How will he manage a subha?' His eyes wandered to the immaculately tended rose bush by the edge of his garden.

Nasim jumped to another topic, one more likely to keep him engaged. 'Pari's mausoleum is progressing but the stone cutters have asked for a lakh! A hefty fee, don't you think?'

'So cancel it,' said Shayista dismissively. 'I must exercise.' With that he took leave.

People were forbidden to interrupt him when he was exercising in his garden. This was his way of ending their conversation with nothing resolved. Nasim sighed. If only Abul Fateh were alive.

'Your Highness looks distressed,' remarked Ambar as she returned to her quarters.

'I don't know why I put in all this effort: stone carvers, calligraphers, carpenters, for what? Shayista doesn't even appreciate it.' She vented her emotions though it was unbecoming of a noble lady.

'The height of Mughal pretension, these mausoleums and never before have I seen one built for a bastard. When I worked for the mighty Emperor Aurangzeb, I learned the beauty of austerity. One ought not waste.'

'Yes, yes,' said Nasim, irritated by his insolence. 'And *you* ought not preach.'

What Nasim did not need was a lecture from her eunuch. What she did need was a spell that would make Shayista susceptible to her charms so he would do as she requested when the Emperor arrived. Perhaps the pir could help her. It was worth a try. With the Nauraz almost upon them, she needed a prompt solution.

CHAPTER 13

A spring breeze carried cool air from the fountains and water ways to the rest of the garden. Vines climbed brick walls and within them nested singing yellow napes, cuckoos and koels. Ashy wood swallows flirted under the canopy of mango trees while squirrels and chipmunks played hide and seek.

Shayista hurried to his 'exercise place'. Cloistered behind the high hedges of his charbagh, he felt safe. Here, no one could disturb him. Between three bougainvilleas, was a floral tile, upon which he rested his forehead in prostration. The bougainvilleas he had planted, one for Ellora, one for Miri, and the smallest one, most recently, for Pari. The tile, an intricately designed marble slab, was where he offered his penitence.

Shayista closed his eyes to meditate as Huzur had taught him but mental silence proved elusive. The blasted joint stock company gnawed at his skull. Why would Aurangzeb support the Company? How could Aurangzeb be so different from Arjumand and Dara? The beauty of the Mughal Empire lay in its harmonious plurality of faith and culture. Aurangzeb was compromising the syncretic Empire which Akbar worked so hard to build, the essence of which was liberty.

If only Shayista had acted in time to secure the throne for Dara. The mutinous thought startled him. He had successfully repressed it for years. After Dara was killed, he swore to uphold the interest of the Emperor and the Empire as one and the same. Divisive politics would lead to trouble. It was better that he stand by Aurangzeb. Wasn't it?

A peacock strolled past. Shayista had not thought of Dara in a while but the words of the palm reader tore open old wounds. He could not dislodge her promise. She said she could undo his regrets. Then perhaps he could set things right.

CHAPTER 14

Champa poured water onto her wrists, ears, neck, scalp, arms, elbows and feet to activate the energy meridians. Ablution was a perfect prescription to awaken the astral plane of the body for meditation. She was grateful to Dada for teaching her the deeper purpose of these rituals. Her father had chosen a narrow interpretation of religion. To him, ablution was merely a process of hygiene.

'Look carefully,' Dada said to her when she was a girl. He bought a piece of ice from a burly ice seller who chiselled it off a huge block, tick-ting, tick-ting, tick-ting. Vah! A sparkling diamond, freezing cold. She popped it into her mouth. It trickled down her throat, melting horizons, cooling her inside out. He splashed a chunk of ice into a glass of water. 'One tenth of it is visible. The rest we cannot see but it is there,' he said.

He taught her that the Quran was a book with many layers. Readers could access stratums of meaning based on their own depth of understanding, which in most cases was fairly shallow. The deeper meanings of the Quran lay submerged within the text and at its core was a hidden secret. If you could discern this secret, all your wishes would come true.

While Champa's father was satisfied with the literal meaning of the holy book, Dada yearned for the wish-fulfilling secret. This clash between literal and esoteric was not only a philosophical debate, it bled into her real life.

Dada encouraged Champa to pursue education through reading and observation rather than rote learning. He taught her English, Persian, Bengali and Arabic and also how to listen to flowers and gaze at clouds to understand the Divine.

Her father, obsessed with her purity, did not care about her education, only her chastity. He tried to arrange her marriage before she reached puberty and insisted this was for her own good. Champa refused to marry and her grandfather sided with her. Her father moved out to join the mullahs and she became Dada's new assistant in the hunt for the diamond. Since then, she and her father very rarely met.

Champa climbed down the stairwell with a broom and entered the antechamber. She lit a candle. The flame illuminated a spider on its web by the window. She held the candle close to admire the craftsmanship of the spider. The web was delicate yet strong, woven with admirable skill. The masterful spider, black with a white stripe, rested nearby. God's creatures were born to be creative. Nothing could be godlier and yet the mullahs pursued destruction.

Champa rolled out a Persian rug and lit three sticks of frankincense, chanting the glorious names of Allah. She drew her legs into a lotus and tried to meditate. The image of Kukur Mia's fleshy pulp invaded her serenity. She abandoned the mission and instead got to work. She stacked the firewood, washed the black cauldron and swept the room, then went to call her grandfather.

Trailing her hand on the marble banister, she climbed the stairwell and wondered what would happen to her once her grandfather found the diamond. He would probably discontinue his practice and then he would no longer need her services. What then, would he pressure her to get married?

The empowerment of women was doomed by the institution of marriage. Wedlock was a form of imprisonment. She would much rather teach girls and be the apprentice of a spiritual master than cook and clean for a lazy husband but such choices did not fit the conservative framework of patriarchy. It was only her maverick grandfather who allowed her the space to be independent, that too because she helped him with his hunt and his practice.

Dada's practice was thriving. He treated patients all morning, prescribing ointments, unguents and spells which she helped him prepare. People came from across the city and waited for hours to see him. Very rarely did anyone leave disappointed. Champa respected her grandfather's work though she did not always agree with his methodology.

She put away the broom and walked to Dada's audience chamber. A pregnant lady stood outside waiting to meet him. Champa wondered what he would prescribe: a prayer written upon a piece of paper folded a thousand times and pushed into a metallic amulet to be worn around her waist for nine months or a grain of rice dipped in holy water to be consumed with breakfast on the night of a full moon. Both methods would ensure safe birthing.

Dada was no conventional grandfather. He believed if he could remove the seven veils of his ego, he would discover the secret to divine alignment. Enlightenment was of course of universal benefit and she did not want to hold him back, it was just that his pace of pursuit was objectionable. Neglecting both health and domestic duties, he chased knowledge with such fevered urgency, one could mistake him for an addict.

Champa poked her head inside the chamber. Dada motioned her to enter. Though he was a wizard of the highest order, a Master of Celestial Energy, an Astral Alchemist, he still made time to treat patients. Champa was convinced it was not the money that drove him but the wellbeing of his community.

The patient inside was a farmer. His hands were rough, his face burned from toil in the sun. 'Pir Baba, I lent my land to my brother for a season,' he was saying. 'The season is over. He will not return my land nor will he pay me for it. My wife is pregnant.'

'What do you want?' prompted the pir.

'Pir Baba, I ask for justice,' replied the farmer.

'Did you bring the chilli peppers?' said the pir.

The farmer produced two red chilli peppers from his pocket.

'Once I burn these, the spell cannot be reversed,' warned the pir.

The farmer grinned with a hint of malice.

Dada whispered a prayer upon the peppers then closed his fist around them. The aroma of spice and sin floated out of his fist into the room. The chilli peppers cackled in his palms as if on a flame.

'You will be at his funeral within three weeks,' said the pir.

Champa could not believe the wicked farmer was plotting to kill his own brother and her Dada was actually helping him but she bit her tongue. She knew better than to interrupt his consultation.

Dada dropped the burnt pepper seeds into the man's hand. 'Place these under his pillow.'

'Thank you, Pir Baba,' said the farmer, bowing deep, seeds burning his clenched fist.

'That will be thirty rupees,' said the pir.

The farmer stammered. 'Thir-thir-thirty rupees?'

Dada nodded.

The price of rice was eight mounds a rupee. Thirty rupees was enough to feed a family for fifteen years! Champa wondered how her grandfather could ask for such an outrageous sum.

'O, gracious Pir Baba, I cannot pay so much even if I sell the recovered land along with everything else I own!'

'Be warned,' said the pir. 'If you fail to pay within three weeks, you may find yourself suffering the same symptoms as your brother.'

The farmer nodded, terror stricken, and exited the room.

'Dismiss the patients,' commanded the pir. 'I am done for today.'

Champa conveyed the message to the dismayed patients waiting in the corridor. As the last of the patients departed, she turned to face her grandfather. Back against the door, hands on hips, she challenged, 'Dada, was that right, what you did?'

'What child?' he asked, kindly.

'The death spell you embedded in those seeds. Isn't that an ... *evil* use of power?'

'There is no good or evil. Just one less nuisance to worry about.'

Champa puzzled over his words. Did the ends justify the means?

'Have you prepared the room?' asked Pir Zulfiqar.

Champa nodded. 'Yes Dada. The room is ready for the séance.' She wondered what secrets they would discover.

CHAPTER 15

Two days had passed since his meeting with the clairvoyant dancer but Shayista could not shake the idea of undoing his regrets. He donned his cloak, slipped past Dhand and galloped out on his stallion in search of Champa to see if she could alter history.

Shayista dismounted his warhorse, Bageshri, tousled his mane and offered him a handful of amloke. The horse nuzzled his muzzle into Shayista's shoulder. Shayista handed the reins to a stable urchin at the Imperial post by the gates and entered the Chowk.

Children dressed in colourful weaves loitered on the streets. A beggar girl with two braids sat on a withered stump, tattered clothes, something precious cupped in her hand.

'What's that?' Shayista asked her.

She held it up, chest swollen with pride: a dead butterfly with delicate iridescent wings. Her eyes shimmered with awe.

Shayista longed for child-eyes and youth unencumbered by ego. He wanted to experience life afresh, without the burden of regrets. The sky was awash in weeping blues and watery greys. He handed the butterfly girl a gold coin, grateful for the fresh perspective.

Misunderstanding his intentions, she shouted, 'Not for sale!' She clutched the dead butterfly to her heart and ran off.

An essential wretchedness spread over Shayista. No matter how hard he worked, there were always more enemies conspiring, more hungry children to feed. He felt responsible for the little girl and guilty.

A flitting memory of his sister materialized. Fifty five years ago when he was still Talib, he had led a troop of fifty thousand men into a stormy battle. It was 1630, the monarch's third Deccan campaign, and he was a young but hardened man of 29. Their mandate was simple: abolish the rebel Khan-Jahan who threatened to usher in an age of darkness if he took over.

Shayista's army grossly outnumbered the rebels but they were fighting for their homeland with a ferocious disregard for their own lives. What followed was an epic clash.

Granite clouds blitzed a furious deluge of torrential rain. His soldiers slogged through slippery mud and charged as best they could. Heads flew off necks, bodies slipped off mountains, lives were blown asunder. The air trembled in grief. The river was stained crimson.

Talib obliterated the enemy and confiscated their treasury of spectacular jewels but lost half his men in the battle. It was grief he felt, not pride. Harrowed by months of fighting, the conquering hero travelled to Agra to recover in the comfort of kin, reading poetry with Dara, playing with his sister's children. He presented to his sister one of the jewels he had acquired, a dark diamond of extraordinary brilliance.

Arjumand had thirteen children, all of whom he doted on. A demanding and opinionated lot, they forced him to endure endless rounds of questions and games, and called upon him to whistle. Arjumand herself had grown into the role of mother and knew how to shower affection like healing rain. She was heavily pregnant and happy to hand off children and chores to Talib who savoured every minute of it but these domestic joys did not last long.

Three days after Shayista arrived, Arjumand was in bed giving birth to her fourteenth child when something went terribly wrong. Physicians, scholarly doctors, nurses and maids stood terrified on one side of her bed. Charm-writers and holy men with sacred books stood on the other, calling upon spirits for help. Emperor Shah Jahan sat gripped in misery by her side.

'Talib,' said Arjumand, gazing at the dark diamond. 'Give this gift to a woman who loves you as much as I do. And whenever you see it, remember my love for you. Love is everything.' She had scarcely finished saying this when they heard the wail of the baby in her womb, a sign they recognised all too well.

'Promise me, bhaiya,' she said, her face tense with pain. 'Promise you will nurture peace in our family. Promise?' Behind her words loomed the gruesome shadow of their fratricidal history. 'So we do part.' With her last breath, she bid farewell to Talib and died in the Emperor's arms.

The hurt of losing his sister was eclipsed by dark political clouds and the question of succession. Talib tried to remain neutral to prolong peace but Sa'di was right:

> *'Ten dervishes can sleep on one rug,*
> *but two princes cannot rest in one climate'.*

As Emperor Shah Jahan fell ill with grief and dedicated his time to building a mausoleum worthy of his beloved wife, his sons each eyed the throne. To Talib, the writing was clear: it would come down to a tussle between Dara, the heir apparent, and Aurangzeb, the ambitious. No two contestants could have been more different. Aurangzeb was a disciplined soldier and cunning statesman. Dara was a poet and philosopher who loved knowledge.

When the dreaded infighting began, it was a polarization of liberal and conservative forces. It fell upon Talib to choose between the princes just as it had fallen upon his father to choose between Talib's cousins, Khurram and Khosru, when Emperor Jahangir died. It was his father chosen to protect Arjumand's interest and promoted her husband, Khurram.

For Khosru, the decision was fatal. Talib was infuriated but his father simply said, 'Kill or be killed.' The irony of Fate weighed upon Talib as the Empire waited for his decision.

Then one day Dara called upon him. 'Uncle, Aurangzeb is ambitious and cunning. He will not stop at anything. You have always given good counsel. Tell me, should I step aside, join a monastery, let Aurangzeb rule Hindustan?'

Talib was touched by Dara's genuine love for his family and Empire. 'Stay on and rule with Truth in your heart, with the help of trusted advisors and our Huzur. Let the Empire be expansive with light, not narrow with dogma.'

Dara said wistfully. 'I fear for Murad and Shah Shuja. These are dark times.' He handed his uncle a gift wrapped in muslin.

Talib immediately recognized it as the jewel he had presented to Arjumand on her deathbed. He had not expected Dara to return it. Something so valuable could easily have assured him political success. It was enough to make a pauper a king, and it certainly would have secured an eldest son an Empire.

'It was on Ma when she died,' Dara explained. 'Such a gift could only come from someone who loved her so purely.'

But these words were exchanged in private and Talib did not act.

Within months, through a series of treacherous manoeuvres, Aurangzeb seized the throne. He used the Deccan campaign as evidence of Talib's loyalty to him and tricked the key counsel into believing that he had his uncle's blessings to slaughter his father's advisors and their revered Huzur.

He convinced Murad to help him capture and kill Dara and served his severed head upon a silver platter to their father. He prodded the head with his sword and demanded, 'What choice did you leave me? Kill or be killed.' He imprisoned his father in Agra Fort where the once celebrated Emperor spent the rest of his days shuffling through corridors alone.

Aurangzeb then went for Murad. He bribed a courtesan to inebriate him and relieved him of his sword during their love making, then incarcerated him and had him executed. He would have killed Shah Shuja too but the latter escaped to Bengal, where he met a bloody end a few months later at the hands of the Maghs of Arakan.

For his victory, Shah Jahan bitterly presented him a sword called 'World-Seizer' Alamgir.

Aurangzeb in turn awarded Talib with the honoured title, Amir ul-Umra, Chief of the Nobles, Shayista Khan. He showered him with gifts: a khilat of four brocaded cloaks, a Damascan sword and gold katara that belonged to Akbar, two Andulisian horses with jewelled saddles, a Mansabdar of 10,000 horsemen and huge portions of land. He even requested Talib to beat the drums at his coronation ceremony, as his father and grandfather had done for the emperors preceding him.

Talib saw that ruling with emotions led to disaster. Love did not conquer all. Decisive brutality did. If he did not act with tyranny, the people he cared about died. From that day on, Talib swore he would never make another decision with his heart. Only with totalitarian authority could loved ones be protected. He had to rule with cruelty to protect the innocent.

The advisors and Huzur were dead and Shah Jahan removed. There was no one else left to guide his nephew. Talib put aside his personal convictions and swore to assist Aurangzeb for the sake of the Empire. With a cold appreciation for violence, he would rule for the rest of his days. So Talib became the ruthless warrior Aurangzeb wanted, Amir-ul-Umra Shayista Khan.

Being an Emperor's warlord comes with certain burdens. Aurangzeb could not afford to wear the shame of Dara's dirty murder. His subjects would hate him and revolt. Instead, the crime was pinned on Shayista. He became the Beast, the object of fear and hatred among enemies and citizens alike. With Aurangzeb's ascent began Shayista's descent.

Shayista hid Kalinoor for thirty five years, never once suspecting it had played a role in his downward spiral which began with Arjumand's death. Now he wondered if her death was the dark diamond's doing, the first of its three strikes? Was he its improbable champion, its vehicle of destruction, its means to an end? With doubt creeping in, Shayista found himself standing in front of a ghastly banyan tree at the doorsteps of the dancer's house.

Chapter 16

Champa entered the antechamber and was surprised to find Dada pacing the room.

'Couldn't sleep?' she asked.

'The usual aches and pains. Nothing to worry about.'

'Dehydrated, Dada?' cooed Champa. She poured him some water. He drank it gratefully.

'Would you like anything else?' she offered.

'Nothing, thank you my child.' He was lost in thought.

She needed his full attention. She offered him some honeyed words. 'You are so wise, Dada, your knowledge knows no bounds.'

'The knowledge is within you too,' he replied. 'Tap into it.'

'Show me the way!' She saw her opening. 'You raised me to be a seeker. You helped me reject rote learning and the conditioning of society which anchors us in worldly desires. You encouraged me to keep the lamp burning through self-inquiry and books. There is only one thing you haven't taught me yet.'

'What's that?'

'It's something I would love to learn.'

'Tell me, my child, what is it?'

'Could you please teach me how to summon the djinn?'

'Don't be ridiculous,' Dada rebuked. 'Summoning is not for the uninitiated.'

'The ulema want to destroy our madrasa. Please help me use the Dark Arts to stop them!'

'The ulema are insignificant imbeciles. Their archaic vestiges of ignorance will never cast a shadow on Enlightenment, have no fear. Can a man snuff out the moon? Child, we will NOT waste our time on such trivial matters.'

'Then at least lend me some money to fix the well?'

'Allah can only be experienced through expanded awareness. The only school you need is here with me, nurturing the omnipotent force of Allah through intuitive comprehension. I cannot give you money—money procured from clients in the name of Allah—for your inferior pursuits.' He closed his eyes to indicate the end of the discussion.

Champa clenched her teeth. He was as stubborn as her father.

'Hush child, we have some important work,' he said. 'I need that diamond to save Bengal. Without further ado, let us begin ... Bismillah-irahman-irahim.'

Champa paid close attention.

He pir chanted Allah-Hu and Al-Haq three times to awaken his kundalini and then he raised the energy up his spine to his heart using his breath. He recited Sura Noor three times in reverse and blew a prayer upon each shoulder. He rubbed his palms together to create heat which he washed over his face before settling into a meditative trance.

Champa followed. She was careful to keep her tongue rolled back: a necessary precaution when communing with spirits. Not adhering to these simple rules could result in consequences of unfathomable magnitude. She certainly did not want to spend eternity trapped in a parallel dimension.

Zulfiqar began performing the powerful cat breath from the depths of his gut. He sounded like a howling feline on opium. No sooner had he started, the cats in the alley began baying in chorus. They meowed, moaned and hissed, creating a vortex of negative energy.

Champa had seen her Dada summon the djinn only a few times before. Every time, it gave her the chills.

'Arise Shopno,' called Zulfiqar in a sonorous voice. He whispered something under his breath and a sulphurous gust of wind drifted in. The windows rattled. The falcon fidgeted. 'Show us the diamond,' said the pir.

Tele-transportation and telepathy were easy for djinn who existed in a dimension where time and space had no meaning. Djinn could travel to any part of the world and hypnotically project what it saw upon the minds of those engaged with it in séance.

Champa closed her eyes and prepared for the ride. Before an image could form, a knock at the gate disturbed her concentration. She scrambled to her feet. Up the stairs she climbed, wondering what Dada muttered under his breath to open the porthole to summon the djinn.

At the gate she was astonished to find the Subedar, cloaked in rough cloth. He looked as if he had seen a ghost.

'I have come for what you offered to do. Undo my regrets,' he said. 'That is, if you really can.'

'Of course I can,' said Champa defensively.

His piercing brown eyes begged for salvation. His desperation resonated with her. She caught herself feeling sorry for him till she remembered he was the richest, most powerful man in the world, and yet, not willing to help their madrasa. The last thing he deserved was her sympathy. Rather, perhaps he could be useful to her. She needed to raise money to fix the well. Why not charge him for her services? He could be her first client. She was not technically allowed to treat patients but it was for a noble cause and anyway, she was angry at Dada.

'It will cost you thirty rupees,' she said professionally. It was a steep price but his face expressed no concern.

He tossed her his coin purse. 'Keep it all. I don't care.'

'Follow me,' she said, leading him to the back garden rather than the antechamber where her grandfather was rollicking with djinn.

There was a sheet laid out where she liked to meditate. She seated the Subedar upon it, and she across from him. She bowed, touching her third eye to the ground and began to concentrate.

'Breathe,' she instructed. Perhaps she could not summon the djinn but there were other things she could do. She started her séance with chants.

Allah-Hu. Allah-Hu. Allah-Hu.

Al-Haq. Al-Haq. Al-Haq.

When the energy in her body was sufficiently activated, she recited Sura Noor backwards, then closed her eyes and steadied her mind for meditation.

Soon she was in a labyrinth where only the conscience exists. She had followed Dada into this zone before but she had never done it alone. Separate from her mind and body, separate from her ego, she merged with the energy around her client. She began to synchronize her breath with his. Magic tingled inside her arms and legs, especially at her joints and under her navel, tickling her like a rush of cool water.

When finally the Subedar became psychically open to her, his aura was not what she had expected. He was not an arrogant despot. He was a tortured soul ... and tortured souls were the best conduits of the Dark Arts.

'Inhale,' she instructed. 'Exhale.'

As he exhaled, she captured his breath in her cupped hands. She held it to her ear. What she heard surprised her again. 'The source of your regret is not what you think,' she said.

He growled. 'Are you saying I don't know the source of my regret?'

'Grief and regret are not the same,' she remarked. 'I can show you the source of your regret, if you like.'

She opened her fingers and in her hand, his breath had transformed into a joba petal. The Subedar gasped in disbelief. She placed the dainty petal in his large, calloused hand. Choked up with emotion, he thanked her and left hastily.

Champa could not help but notice he was very strong, both physically and spiritually. Perhaps Guru Ma was wrong. Perhaps he would help her if she asked. His troubled expression engraved itself in her mind. She wondered what the joba meant to him.

CHAPTER 17

As Belo Diabo sailed towards Bengal, Madeline sat on a stool in the kitchen. A ship's kitchen is not a place of pleasant odours or posh company nor is it suitable for haute couture silk taffeta gowns of mauve like the one she was wearing, but alas, there were no other places to go or people to meet. Madeline wore her gown with dignity to keep it from growing mouldy in her trunk as she grilled Abdul for clues.

'Tell me about Chatgaon?' she asked. A manufactured dispassion rested on her lips concealing her true machinations.

Abdul was peeling potatoes. 'Chatgaon is uninhabitable jungle,' he replied. 'Home of the Maghs.'

'The Maghs?' asked Madeline.

'Ferocious slave traders,' said Abdul.

This was alarming.

'Not to worry,' said Abdul chuckling. 'Subedar Khan cleaned up Chatgaon twenty years ago. It was his first assignment in Bengal. In one year, he did what Shah Shuja failed to do in a lifetime. He liberated the island of Sandip from Magh warriors, stopped the Portuguese pirates from plundering the rivers of Bengal and established complete order and peace.'

Abdul paused to select a potato, stalling long enough to elicit a prompt from Madeline.

'How?' she asked.

Abdul wiped his brow with the chequered cloth slung around his neck. His eyes took on the special glow reserved for storytelling.

'It was 1665. The Subedar arrived as Mughal Viceroy to Bengal and began building a covert fleet of 200 ships in the dock yards of Tanti Bazaar. He won the support of the Dutch and with his own wealth, he armed his men.'

'His own wealth?' Madeline asked. 'Is he very wealthy?'

Abdul snorted. 'Only the wealthiest man in Hindustan. Perhaps the world?'

'How much wealth exactly is that?' asked Madeline, notebook ready.

'He lives an ostentatious life, dresses in grandeur, throws fantastical parties, and the rest. And why not? He has a monopoly over all trade,' explained Abdul. 'They say, his daily income is 2 lakh rupees of which he spends half and distributes half to the needy.'

'Sacred bleu!' exclaimed Madeline, scribbling furiously. 'Is he a philanthropist?'

Abdul laughed, bearing his discoloured teeth. 'I don't think anyone has ever referred to him as that. His temper is as fierce as a monsoon. Those who enter his durbar know not if they will leave dead or alive. He is a skilled statesman, a cunning warlord and a shrewd entrepreneur. He can anticipate the enemy's next move before it has been conceived. How else did we win Chatgaon?'

'How?'

'Strategic acumen,' said Abdul. 'He sent his son, Aqidat, with a flotilla of ships along Karnafuli river, and his other son, Buzurg Umid, with an expedition of 6,500 foot soldiers through the steamy jungles of the coastal corridor. They hacked with axes through the desolate wilderness from Feni to the Chatgaon hinterlands, braving tigers and rain!'

'Tigers?' A shiver ran down Madeline's spine.

Abdul yanked on his red beard. 'The Subedar's mansabdars were old men, not fearsome savages like the Maghs. The night before the battle, the Subedar made them dye their white beards with henna and this little trick worked. The flaming red beards frightened the Maghs. From a distance, they thought demons with fire on their chins were attacking them. I've been dyeing ever since.'

Madeline jotted the peculiar fact into her notebook. Perhaps the women in France would like this style. She would talk to the Compagnie des Indes Orientales. Perhaps she could supply them with henna for a profit.

'Did you meet the Subedar?' she asked.

Abdul nodded. 'My father was a Portuguese pirate. I have lived my whole life on a ship. The Portuguese historically hated Mughals but a month before the battle of Sandip, in an astounding reversal of fate, the Subedar won the friendship of a gun-toting Portuguese sea captain and changed the course of history!'

'Captain Costa?'

'Indeed!' Abdul wet his lips and the story spilled out. 'The Portuguese were a menace: sailing up the Ganges raiding Jessore, Hooghly and Bhushna, sailing down Brahmaputra, raping and pillaging Bikrampur, Sonargaon and Dacca, buying kidnapped people from Maghs to sell as slaves in Europe.

'Captain Costa was one of them, the terror of Bengal Bay. He preyed on merchant ships sailing in or out. One such ship belonged to the East India Company, laden with treasures for Europe. Captain Costa smelt the opportunity and navigated an ambush. He moved in close and launched three cannon balls onto the stern.

'He did not know that the ship was protected. An English Man-of-War armed with 24 canons suddenly rounded a bend in the river and blasted canons at him. One struck the deck and his crew were left bailing out buckets to keep from sinking. Just when they thought it was over, Subedar Khan came to their rescue with a 48 cannon Man-of-War.

'On the prowl to rid his waters of thieves, he had been tracking the English warship unbeknownst to them. The English found themselves outmanoeuvred. In hours, their warship was sunk and the merchant vessel captured. Imperial soldiers and pirates fought side by side, killing English sailors, confiscating the booty: diamonds, pearls, spices and silks. The Subedar split the spoils with the pirates, sealing a solid friendship. Nothing brings two men closer together than a common enemy.

'Weeks later, when the Subedar attacked Sandip, Captain Costa joined the battle, leading the fight from the Bay. In three days, the Arakanese Maghs were massacred and the citadel was conquered. Chatgaon was declared a Mughal sarkar and the Subedar released thousands of Bengali peasants who had been enslaved.'

'What happened to the Maghs?'

'He decapitated them. Impaled their heads on bamboo. You could smell it for miles, an unbroken coastline dotted with thousands of crucified Maghs rotting in the sun. Boys and men alike. I remember it as though it were yesterday.' He shuddered.

The Subedar sounded as barbaric as the Maghs. 'And Captain Costa?' she asked, quaking.

'He became the most pampered pirate in the Empire. The Subedar had navy ships escort him in and out of the Bay, even fought off other pirates from Arabia and Africa on his behalf! Captain Costa traded with Bengal for a full ten years before he grew bored of the merchant life and went back to hunting for treasure around the world. He has sixteen ships, you know?'

Madeline rotated the quill in her fingers, amused. So Costa was not only a firebrand thief but also an affluent merchant and his friend, the Subedar, was not only a cruel warlord but also a millionaire. This presented new opportunities. Perhaps she could seduce one of them, or at least get introduced to one of their friends, a minor Raja of some small subha. How nice that would be? Wealthy people were never lonely.

CHAPTER 18

Shayista left the palmist's house feeling more alone than ever. It was as if Champa with eyes as deep as Ganga had peered into his soul and seen his cracks. Disguised in his fustian cloak, Shayista walked through the bazaar not stopping till he reached the elephant haat.

The pungent stench of wet fodder and dung soothed him. There were a dozen studs in the haat and one heavily pregnant female. Her mahut, a scrawny boy with a hint of fuzz on his chin, ogled women passersby while shooing flies with a branch of neem. He was so engrossed in his view that he didn't notice Shayista approach.

Shayista stroked the pregnant elephant, assessing her age and health. She would deliver within a week. As a young man, Shayista had been a prodigious breeder of war elephants. He would pay handsomely for breeder bulls and had a fleet of six hundred trained to fight with swords and javelins in their trunks. It wasn't for naught that the lake north of Lal Bagh was named *Hatir Jheel*, Elephant Lake. Every day mahuts would guide hundreds of elephants to the lake to bathe.

Drawing his hood low over his brows, altering his posh accent, Shayista asked, 'Where is this elephant from?'

'Be off,' replied the mahut. 'You're scaring my clients with your stench, fakir. They'll think this place is haunted by djinn.'

The hierarchies of the bazaar amused Shayista. There were no 'clients' around but still the mahut had to assert his superiority.

Shayista patted the elephant. 'What do djinn smell like?' he asked.

When the mahut was sure there were no witnesses to catch him cavorting with a baseborn beggar, he replied, 'Like rotten eggs of course, goat-wit.'

Shayista had heard many tales about djinn. They were taller than humans and had hairy faces. Their feet were attached backwards to their ankles so when tracking them it was best to trace their footsteps in reverse. Best of all, they had a sweet tooth so if ever attacked by djinn, one could offer a sugary chom chom or gooey golap jamun to negotiate a truce. But rotten eggs he had not heard before.

As a man of faith, Shayista was compelled to accept the existence of djinn. The Quran stated that God made humans out of earth and djinn out of fire but with no first hand evidence, Shayista found it difficult to believe. He preferred to consider 'djinn' a metaphor for one's inner demons: representations of darkness, depression and separation: the wisps of smoke that lurk in the wilderness of one's mind, beasts to battle along the spiritual journey of life.

'There is a mango tree beside my house,' said the mahut, lowering his voice. 'One night my father made love to the washerwoman under that tree. Their dalliance disturbed a djinn in slumber. Oh boy oh boy, take it from me fakir, an angry djinn is a horrific ordeal.'

'What did it do?' probed Shayista.

'It slipped into the washerwoman's ear and possessed her, shook her like a banana leaf in a cyclone. She screamed like a banshee.' The mahut paused to twiddle his tooth. 'Really, what was she thinking, traipsing under the moon during menstruation? Everyone knows djinn only enter ladies during their impure days. Baba had to invoke the name of you-know-who to scare the djinn away.'

'Who?'

'You don't know? You good-for-nothing fakir. Why don't you educate yourself once in a while? Let me tell you a few important things. There are many saints in Bengal but the most powerful of all, the only one who can punish djinn when they misbehave, is Pir Saheb ...' The mahut lowered his voice in veneration or fear. 'Abdul Quader Jilani,' he said. He touched his fingertips to his forehead then his lips then the floor in an elaborate taslim.

'Abdul Qua ...'

'Shhh!' said the mahut, pressing his finger against the beggar's lips. 'You must never say his name without the utmost of reverence.'

'What happened to the washerwoman?' asked Shayista.

'She went mad,' said the mahut. 'Now be gone. I have animals to care for.'

'I hear the Subedar is a fan of elephants. Perhaps he will be interested in this one?' said Shayista.

'The Subedar, eh?' said the mahut, eyes narrowing. 'That man is a wizard not an elephant farmer!'

'Wizard?' asked Shayista, intrigued.

'Do you know nothing? He has powers. Super sensory powers. He can hear thoughts. He can smell fear. He can...' A pair of merchants approached.

'Hati? Hati for sale!' the mahut offered. They walked off, taking no notice of him. 'Go on then,' he said to Shayista, irritated. 'I am losing customers. Shoo!'

Shayista gave the elephant a pat on her bristled forehead and looked deep into her watery eyes. The beast wrapped her trunk around his arm. He would send Bhopal to purchase the beauty.

At the Imperial post by the gates, Shayista unfettered his stallion. As he rode home, he mulled over the mahut's story. While it was amusing, it did not prove anything. The washerwoman perhaps suffered from a nutrient deficiency which caused her convulsions and damaged her brain. Let others blame improbable events on superstition, djinn and curses, enabling pirs to make happy profits off their naivety. Shayista hadn't time for such skulduggery.

The sentries at the Lal Bagh fort gate were slouched over a game of shatranji.

'White triumphs over black,' jeered a bald guard. With his white knight he flicked the black queen off the board. It ricocheted off the side onto the cobbled road. He cracked his knuckles, stretched his interlaced hands above his head, cleared his throat and spat at the wall.

'Not so fast,' said his adversary, a hirsute guard shouldering a musket. 'Without darkness, we could not know light!' His black bishop knocked off the white horse.

Brows knit, the bald guard scratched his head and peered at the board.

'Upon this chequerboard of nights and days, the two governing forces are fear and love,' said Shayista uncloaking himself. 'But is it safer to be loved or feared?' His royal colours brought the guards snapping to attention, knocking over the chess board. They fell to taslim, quaking in his presence.

'At ease,' said Shayista.

Beneath his rough spun cloak he was dressed like Mughal aristocracy. He wore a silk kurta and white pyjamas, a relic from the days of Genghis Khan. He had pearls around his neck and a tight white turban, tied with a band of brocaded gold. Though it cost a fortune, his attire did not conceal the disarray of his inner world. He neglected to groom his royal stubble which was now a beard. His hair was an unkempt nest of tangles. Dark circles outlined his sunken eyes.

Shayista moved unhurriedly through the cobbled passageway under the mosaic arched gate, letting the melancholy in his heart surface. He crossed the mosque and the stables and the field where the Imperial Tir-Andaz were practicing with bows and arrows. He entered the menagerie and seated upon a cushion of velvet, he summoned his attendants to fetch some sharab and opium.

For the second instance that day, he slipped into reminiscence, this time triggered by the joba petal. His mind freed by the charash revealed in lucid detail a vision of Ellora atop a howdah twenty two years ago.

CHAPTER 19

Dark clouds heckled the fair moon and warring winds stirred up restlessness in Ellora's heart. She longed to see the world, to have adventures that would thrill and exalt her, to meet a tall man, with muscles and a sword, who would sweep her off her feet and win her heart with chivalry and kindness but then, she sighed, dreams and desires were just that, dreams and desires.

She leaned upon a silk cushion with a joba flower tucked behind her ear and tried to obstruct intruding odours with her dupatta. Her howdah was ornately decorated and fringed with muslin curtains so plush that one could almost forget one was atop an elephant but for the smells: the stink of dung, the wafts of soldier sweat and worst of all, the oppressive stench of her despicable husband, inching closer by the minute.

It was a political union. Her father, having just lost all his territory to a Mughal invasion, made the match without once asking her how she felt about it. The entire town was fed spiced mutton and musicians were paid to perform for weeks. Everyone seemed to be celebrating, except her.

Ellora was raised to be fiercely independent so the prospect of marrying an unattractive bore was intolerable for her. She begged her father to take pity but years of warfare had left him detached and insensitive to her emotions. She could not oblige him to call off the wedding.

With a small retinue of thirty soldiers and a dozen horses and elephants, her husband carried her and her hand maids off from her father's home towards his small kingdom in Maharastra. Two trumpeters accompanied them, waving the Mondol dynasty banner over their heads. Behind them followed baggage camels and wagons of food.

From a howdah atop an elephant, Ellora drank in the beauty of the land and nurtured her melancholy. Was this to be her destiny, a loveless marriage to an asinine man? By the second day of their voyage, she lost interest in her broken heart and abandoned herself to an intense appreciation of life around her.

The unfamiliar landscape danced outside her window: moist Mother Earth succulent with fruits blooming in shades of pistachio, olive and parakeet green. Sun-kissed fields ripe with spring. Ruby-faced gibbons and saffron foxes. She realized there was much of Hindustan she had never seen and at least marrying Mondol Raja had won her a journey beyond the walls of her father's fortress.

On the third day, they reached the gaping mouth of a ghostly forest where the road was so narrow that foot soldiers had to clear space so the elephants could enter without knocking the howdahs off. A thick fog enveloped them, obscuring all visibility. It became apparent they would not make it to the next village by nightfall. Owls howled, cicadas lamented and bullfrogs wailed. They skulked forward invoking the Gods. 'Ram nam satya hai,' sounded from a hundred throats. Their skittish steeds were difficult to rein.

Ellora could sense her husband's fear as he rubbed the jade ring on his pudgy finger, appealing to a deity for protection. She offered him a caustic smile. The pusillanimous pig she had married was timid and superstitious.

Outside, a drizzle. Their howdah was built by the best carpenters in town with artistic images of the Mahabharatha etched into it but though aesthetically pleasing, it was not practical for the monsoon season. Ellora crouched under her veil to stay dry.

With the rain, their progression slowed even further then sputtered to a halt. She could see her husband eyeing her to gauge her reaction. Her face was stolid, a trick she had learned from her father.

Mondol Raja called out to the captain of his soldiers, 'Boy, why are we stopping?'

'Raja saheb,' replied the captain, drawing his horse to their howdah. 'The men are frightened. This forest is haunted. Perhaps we should stop for the night?'

'What? A bit of wilderness and my men are unnerved? I'll execute every last one of them if they do not pick up pace this instant!'

'As you command,' said the captain, off to deliver his orders.

Ellora smiled. How brave he pretended to be from atop his howdah.

Mondol Raja scrutinized her expression then cleared his throat. 'Do you know the duties of a respectable wife?' he asked.

Ellora was about to deliver a derisive reply when the rain began to beat like battle drums on their wooden roof. Ellora wondered if the forest was really haunted as the rumours claimed. She had no weapon on her apart from a small khanjar with a steel blade and an ivory handle in the shape of a horse. The Raja shuffled in poorly concealed discomfort, jumping at every noise.

Only a complacent fool would set out on an expedition on such a night. A shiver crept up the young bride's spine as she stared at the fresh henna on her hands. How could she live with this geriatric who smelt like coconut grease and cowered at every sound?.

The path was treacherous and in the distance, a hungry wolf howled. Mondol Raja snivelled and tried to nestle into her but she pushed him away as nausea threatened to overcome her. The elephant bearing Ellora's howdah stumbled into a muddy pothole and lost balance. The carriage lurched forward, sending her crashing into its wooden frame.

A scream from outside launched an uproar. Mondol Raja cautiously parted the curtains of their palanquin for a peak. Ellora caught sight of his captain approaching, white as a ghost. The news he gibbered was bad.

A tiger had taken one of the men. The unfortunate sepoy had stepped off the clearing to urinate. The others witnessed the beast dragging him away but no one had the courage to rescue him.

Ellora parted the festoons to catch a glimpse of the tiger. Foot soldiers banged pots and shouted mantras to frighten it away though it was nowhere to be seen. Drenched in fear and rain, the entourage inched forward in a tight huddle, no one wanted to be the last man.

They soon arrived upon a river they would have to cross. The men sang with joy, relieved to be clear of the dense forest. They once again requested the Raja for permission to camp out the storm and darkness, promising faster progress come dawn. This time the Raja had no choice but to agree.

No sooner had they put down their weapons and tethered their horses, the forest started charging towards them. Whooping cries surrounded them and suddenly they were ambushed by a dozen horsemen with swords and muskets, pale-skinned pirates riding upon steeds with small cannons tied to the saddles, camoflauged in twigs and branches.

The pirates leapt out of the bushes so quickly, the Raja's outer layer of guards died before they could unsheathe their weapons. A handful of loyal soldiers attempted to form a blockade around the royal howdah. The rest fled, choosing to brave the tigers rather than the white devils.

Mondol Raja drew the curtains of the howdah shut and muttered prayers. Pandemonium continued outside: gun shots, screams of agony, galloping hooves and unfamiliar battle cries. Ellora reached for the curtain.

'Don't!' the Raja snapped. 'Hiding is our best chance.' His lips drew tight in fear.

'What about your men?' said Ellora. He pretended not to hear.

As the attackers came closer, they fired their canons. Two elephants came crashing down, including Ellora's. The beast fell onto its belly, spilling the howdah onto the floor. Mondol Raja ran off into the forest, a stench of shit trailing him.

Ellora whispered a prayer then cursed her husband under her breath. She swore she would kill him and renounce her religion rather than burn at a widow's pyre after.

Ellora had never encountered bandits before but if the cries outside were any indicator, these men were vicious, molesting women, killing children. She weighed her options. She was decked in gold, dressed in a flimsy choli that barely covered her bosoms. Her brocaded ghagra was covered in gems and she wore heavy gold anklets on her feet. Any attempt to escape would be futile. Ivory handled blade in hand, she crawled out of the howdah.

Men on steeds gathered around the fallen carriages, collecting loot. One pirate towered above her, bearded and masked, a silver hoop in his ear.

'I don't need any treasure. I'll take the jewel of Hindustan,' he yelled. With a raucous laugh, he dismounted his steed and approached her, musket in hand.

Ellora's heart pounded. She jabbed her khanjar at him. He caught her wrist and twisted it till the weapon dropped. She screamed and kicked. Her choli, snagged by a bush, tore, leaving her breasts exposed. He slapped her across the face with the back of his hand and threw her over his horse.

Slumped over her captor's horse, Ellora saw a hooded man approaching them like a fierce gust of wind. The pirates tried to stop him but he razed through them.

Her captor turned to face him but before he could spark his weapon, Ellora saw the silver gleam of a sword shimmer in the moonlight. Her captor's head fell at the horse's feet.

The pirates frightened by the sight of their beheaded captain fled into the forest with whatever booty they had grabbed. Ellora wondered who her cloaked saviour was: an apparition, a god, a demon? As quickly as he arrived, he turned to depart.

Ellora slid down from the horse swiftly. 'Wait,' she called. 'Don't leave me. There are tigers and Ishvar knows what.'

'Who are you?' asked her mysterious hero.

'I'm a princess,' she said. 'I was on my way to my husband's kingdom.'

'Where is your husband?' he asked, coming closer. He smelt of attar and smoke.

'The coward fled!' she said indignantly.

'Do you want me to take you to him?' the man asked.

'No!' said Ellora. 'I will never go back to him. He left me to die!' She scanned the carnage. Her retinue and soldiers were either dead or had fled.

'Shall I take you to your father?' asked her champion.

'No,' said Ellora. 'I shall never return to him either.' He had cast her off to the Raja as if she were cattle.

The hooded man was bewildered. 'What shall I do with you?'

'Take me with you, wherever you are going.' She held her hands up for him unaware of her bare bosom gleaming in the moonlight.

Her knight looked at her and could no more deny her than he could stop the sun from sinking in the west. He lifted her from the ground with an arm around her waist and placed her on his stallion behind him.

As they galloped off, she wrapped her arms around his barrel-chest tightly, as much to ensure she did not fall off as to still her wildly thumping heart. She could feel his steely muscles and that created strange sensations of excitement she had never experienced before. The bravery of this man, the ferocity with which he had fought, his total disregard for his own safety, and the way he treated her ... this man had to be Arjun. She fell headlong in love with him.

Ellora was stunned when they arrived at a manicured garden and a luxurious haveli guarded by at least a hundred armed men on the periphery of Lal Mahal, a fort she knew well.

The hooded rider helped her dismount, holding his hand for her to step on. Despite his immense muscles, she could barely feel him when he touched her. He led her to the entrance of the chateau and ordered the woman who answered the door to look after her. She looked at her with eyes like saucers and threw a shawl over her nakedness.

'You'll be safe here,' said her hero. 'Tomorrow, we will take you home.'

'But I am already home,' said Ellora. 'Who are you?'

The man just smiled.

'You saved my life,' she said.

'Think nothing of it,' he replied and left.

The matron of the house was a compassionate lady known as Didi Ma, both the dance instructor and the governess of the dancing girls. Didi Ma fussed over Ellora like a mother hen. She bathed Ellora herself, cleaning the blood off her with heated water, admiring her with glowing eyes.

Over a spicy rabbit stew, Ellora learned from the girls that it was the Subedar Shayista Khan, the Mughal viceroy of Maharastra, who had saved her. This was the man Ellora's father was fighting, the man to whom they had lost their fort. How sad, she thought, that her father never knew his chivalry.

The girls were both in awe and fear of the Subedar. They claimed he patrolled the roads of his subha late into the night with a sword and side-dagger tucked into his belt, killing criminals by the dozens. He was irascible and tempestuous but he believed in justice and he loved music. He was not the type to dally with promiscuous princesses. He did not bed his dancers. These details seemed to be common knowledge. The fact he himself had brought Ellora bare-breasted on his horse inspired many more sessions of gossip.

That night, Ellora could not sleep. She had grown up on tales of the Subedar too: Kinslayer, Hindu-hater, taxing the poor to indulge the rich. This did not match what she had seen, the gentleness she had experienced. Reality, she remembered, was a selective act of interpretation. Perhaps the stories she had heard were lies. Perhaps everything she had known was a lie, and only now, she was rising from the illusion.

When Shayista returned to the chalet the next morning and offered to take her home, she refused to leave. She swore she would rather slit her throat than return to either her father who had forced her to marry or her husband who had abandoned her to pirates. She went so far as to challenge Shayista to a duel for her freedom. In the end, he made the mistake of letting her stay.

Shayista extricated himself from the memory. He stared at the joba petal in his palm. An overwhelming loneliness washed over him. The red had dried up into a dark brown. Ellora was dead. What hope was there for happiness?

For Shayista, Ellora was everything Nasim was not. She was dark and sultry where Nasim was fair and frigid. She was a monsoon of passion, mighty Ganga gushing with love, beauty set loose upon a cyclone, while Nasim was calculating and ambitious. Nasim was obsessed with the past while Ellora had revealed no details of her history but bore instead her heart and soul and luscious body.

Most intoxicating of all was Ellora's scent: a mixture of sandalwood and attar that she learned from the pages of the Kama Sutra. She studied the manual of love with earnest vigour and applied what she learned upon Shayista. To her, sex was a spiritual act of a natural order. She approached it shamelessly, as an art to be explored and mastered, not a sin to shy away from. With coy enthusiasm, she stretched Shayista's body and imagination to new lengths.

Shayista had been living a cold and cruel life for decades. For the first time since the death of his sister and Dara, he felt his soul dance. He found sublime joy in ordinary things. But then, joy and grief are never far apart. His fate was soon to be disrupted by destiny, so what use was it remembering it now, twenty two years later?

Shayista wiped his eyes with his kerchief and headed towards the Diwan-i-am. Two steps in, he felt the cold edge of a steel blade against the soft skin of his throat.

CHAPTER 20

Nasim Banu peeked out of the curtained howdah as her trusted eunuch led the elephant through the winding alleys behind the bazaar. They were going to meet the Pir of Lal Bagh and the roads were narrow with vendors on either side.

Nasim meditated on her predicament. She needed to maintain Shayista's interest so he did not marry a second wife. She needed to tone down his enthusiasm for unorthodox pleasures such as alcohol and music to appease the Emperor. She needed to convince him to ask the Emperor to promote their son. She needed to ...

'We have arrived, your Highness,' announced Eunuch Ambar.

Following the mahut's prodding ankus, the elephant sat down. Nasim Banu gingerly dismounted. She noticed a bevy of cats surveying her. There was something haunting about the place. Questioning her decision to come, Nasim knocked on the door.

A bony young lady with a purple scar on her cheek greeted her. From the confidence in her demeanour, Nasim could make out that the lady was a family member not a servant. She was dressed in a simple cotton kamiz but comported herself with dignity. She led Nasim down a corridor to a chamber.

'Come in,' said a voice from inside.

Nasim entered. Eunuch Ambar waited outside. The room was lit dimly with a single candle. She could vaguely make out a large desk with many books and a caged falcon.

'Sit down,' said the pir, dressed in black garbs, a black turban, a sapphire broach. 'You are unhappy.'

Nasim nodded.

'You yearn for youth,' said the pir.

Nasim nodded though he was not asking so much as proclaiming.

'Is it so important?' the pir asked.

Nasim mused for a moment. No, perhaps it was not.

Pir Baba stroked his beard thoughtfully then handed Nasim a silver mirror. 'Are you beautiful?'

Nasim blenched at her haggard reflection. 'I was once.'

The pir frowned. 'Every woman is a creature of divine beauty.'

'Perhaps it was my destiny to marry a man blind to my beauty.' She regretted her petulance but her words had already slipped out and not unnoticed. The pir pulled the loose thread.

'If he cannot see the beauty in you, it is because his vision is obstructed by his ego,' said the pir. 'The ego divides. Love unites.'

Nasim nodded. The Empire could only be run properly if she and her husband were united in their aims. He needed her to guide him, to manage his ego, and it would be much easier to do so if he loved her deeply rather than passively.

'I can help you,' said the pir. He gathered three jars from the shelf behind his table and from each took a pinch of its contents to place in a mortar. With a wooden pestle he ground the mixture and decanted it into a glass.

'Drink this,' he commanded.

Nasim Banu took one sip and gagged. It was the foulest concoction she had ever tasted, grey and globular. The pir urged her on. Pinching her nose, she slurped it up.

At last, she asked. 'What was it?'

'The placenta of a black cat, dried stool from a pig and ashes from a Hindu crematorium.'

Nasim gagged and might have vomited but for the strange sensation of tingling on her skin.

'Behold,' said the magician.

She gazed into the mirror and saw to her immense wonderment, her face metamorphosed. Was it her imagination or were her wrinkles less visible? One by one, the age marks, the dark circles and the tired lines dissolved leaving her reflection that of her younger self, some twenty years younger. Nasim could not believe it. She touched her face tentatively, the texture was altered. Shayista would love her now!

'Take this cream,' said the pir, handing her a jar. 'Rub it on your face daily.'

Delighted, she offered to pay the pir.

'Anything more I can do for you?' he asked.

Nasim was confused. What more?

'I have astral powers,' said the holy man. 'My prayers can manifest your deepest desire. There must be something you wish for, your Highness?'

Nasim was stunned. 'How do you know who I am?' Was he clairvoyant?

The pir laughed and pointed to the royal insignia on her cloak.

She blushed.

'Look deep within, your Highness. What do you love most?'

Nasim Banu scrunched her brows together. Love most? She loved her palace, the hammam, her jewellery, fancy parties, her sons. What else could she ask for? 'Pir Baba, there is nothing more I desire.'

'Look deeper,' said the pir. 'Close your eyes.'

Nasim did as she was told.

The pir began chanting Al-Haq, Al-Haq, Al-Haq with such energy, Nasim felt the table shake. Her heart beat began to race. She peeked and saw the pir turning red in the face from the exertion.

'Look with your third eye,' he instructed. 'Awaken your intuition. There, your Highness, look deep within. What do you see?'

Nasim Banu saw a modest boy sitting quietly on a swing, a boy she loved even more than life itself, his feathery hair ruffled by the wind.

Nasim opened her eyes.

'What did you see?' urged the holy man.

'My youngest son.'

'Then he is your deepest love.'

She nodded. Abul Fateh she loved beyond all the riches in the kingdom, alas ... 'But he's dead,' exclaimed Nasim, wringing her hands. O how his eyes beamed when he saw her, how he wrapped his fingers around her hair when he slept.

'I see.' The pir nodded slowly.

'What is it?' asked Nasim, a tremor in her voice.

'More challenging than I anticipated,' said the magician. 'But not impossible. I cannot resurrect him but I can summon his departed spirit. To do so, I need to channel his energy through a jewel. If you want to speak to your son, bring me the biggest jewel you can find.'

Nasim did not know what to think. She had heard pirs claim they could channel spirits but they had all turned out to be tricksters. Was this also a hoax?

She thanked the pir for his time and left feeling bleak. Outside, Ambar helped her into the decorated howdah.

On their way back to the fort, two thugs in orange turbans accosted their elephant with wide-bladed gauntlet rapiers. Nasim Banu trembled from behind the chintz curtains as Khajah Ambar spoke to them in hushed tones. When they left, she demanded, 'Who were they? What did they want?'

'No need to worry, your Highness. I have taken care of it.'

Thank God for her trusted Ambar. It was Shayista's fault that she was out on the streets in the first place, sneaking off to meet the pir. Nasim wondered if the holy man was genuine. The youth serum had worked but could he really call upon her son? It was too good to be true. She prayed to God for a miracle.

CHAPTER 21

Champa walked to the madrasa feeling jubilant, jingling coins in her purse. She couldn't wait to see Guru Ma's face light up. She had a new song to teach the girls. She felt light as a kite. As she neared the premise, Champa heard shouting.

The mullahs had returned. 'Are you dancing in the madrasa?' she heard one of them yell. Why were they poking their prayer caps in her business?

'We teach dance, science, philosophy, art,' she heard Guru Ma reply.

'Idol-worshipper, your head shall be dancing its way off your body if you do not desist,' yelled a mullah.

Champa could not believe her ears. This is what the mullahs were shouting about? Her dance class?

'These books,' bellowed a mullah, pointing to the library. 'Will fill their minds with rubbish! You need only the Holy Quran!'

They were condemning books? Words were what separated man from beast. The social experience of reality was possible only because of words. To destroy books was akin to an attack on the collective conscience, a war on knowledge, an impingement on progress. What sort of nation could they be without poets to nurture the expanse of the imagination and philosophers to challenge the borderlines of thought? Champa shuddered.

'Women must be veiled,' said a mullah. 'So they do not tempt men.'

'Why don't you wear a patch on your eyes if you find the sight of women so irresistible?' Guru Ma retorted.

The mullah slapped Guru Ma across the cheek with his sandal. The blow was so forceful it knocked her to the ground. Another mullah followed up with a kick to her stomach. Yet another man grabbed her by a fistful of hair and yanked out a chunk.

Champa pushed through the crowd. 'Stop!' she shouted. 'Stop, you monsters!'

The mullahs turned to face her.

'Baba, I teach at this school!' she yelled, addressing the leader.

Alim Al-Ali fidgeted uncomfortably with his walking stick. The mullahs stared at him in undisguised shock, waiting for an explanation.

'You are leading the girls astray,' he said, his voice stern and nasal.

'By educating them?'

'Women should stay home.' Alim scowled. A film of sweat gathered on his brow. His kurta was stained with gravy.

'Will you not discipline your own daughter?' demanded his associate.

Pressured to take a stand, Alim cleared his throat. 'What pagan idols do you worship? Have you lost all sense of propriety? I forbid you from teaching here!'

'Why should I listen to you?' said Champa.

'Because I am your father!' he thundered.

'So? You abandoned your father!' she yelled.

Alim looked hurt. 'I had to leave, Champa. Your Dada was obsessed with his search for Kalinoor. His mission lured him away from the only Black Stone that matters, the Kabaa of Mecca. Kalinoor is a symbol of the flawed human condition: the lust for Duniya! How could I stay with him after that?'

'You abandoned me too,' she said softly.

'You were under his wing. I had no choice. Join me now. I will find you a husband. God is merciful. Renounce this blasphemous sin.'

'No,' said Champa.

'Close your madrasa,' he urged. 'Don't pollute the minds of innocent girls with the dirt of worldly knowledge. The public sphere is a man's space. I'm only trying to protect you. Women are emotional, easily perturbed, weak of constitution. This is how Allah made us. Accept it.'

'No!' shouted Champa. 'Your boundaries are not for me!'

Alim Al-Ali raised his hand to hit her but she saw it coming. She grabbed his wrist and brought it down with sufficient pressure to cause his eyes to bulge out.

Bewildered, he began to scream. 'Stop it! Stop it right now!'

Champa stood tall and strong, dishevelled hair, eyes enraged.

A dust tornado blew at the mullahs, knocking off their prayer caps. They shouted, running to catch their caps, rubbing their sand attacked eyes. Suddenly the geese and crows were incensed, flapping their wings, swooping vengeance down upon the mullahs with their beaks. The bearded men scattered, afraid now of Champa. Only Alim held his ground, swatting at the birds with his walking stick.

'I have learned a lot from Dada,' said Champa. 'Should I show you my powers?'

Alim's eyes were wide with fright. He turned to make a hasty retreat but called over his shoulder, 'This is not over, Champa. Power corrupts. You have invited the wrath of Allah into your life.'

Champa watched as the billowing robes of the ulema flapped around their skinny ankles as they ran. She allowed a triumphant smile to spread across her face. They would think twice before calling a woman weak again.

CHAPTER 22

When the keen edge of watered steel meets your skin, there is no mistaking its lethal potential. This particular blade, Shayista noted, was beautifully crafted and possibly from Damascas.

A seasoned warrior, despite being high, Shayista's mind instinctively raced through a checklist of things he could do to overpower his opponent. He could apply Huzur's technique: move with the assailant's energy, draw him forward and off-balance, roll with him and turn his blade to his throat. It was no wonder Huzur was called *Seif Khan*, Sword Master. Or he could emit a deafening yogic battle whistle followed by a garudasana to the groin. Or he could strike a sharp jab to the lower gut followed by a swipe to the jugular.

The choices danced before him but Shayista decided not to execute any. A lethargic melancholia had settled upon him and he wanted everything to be over with. He had broken his promise to his dying sister. He had failed to save Ellora, Abul Fateh and Miri. All that he cherished had perished. He closed his eyes and prayed not for redemption but a swift end.

'Kill me,' he said, relieved not angry. 'I am ready to meet my Maker.'

The blade shifted. Its razor-sharp edge pressed up against the swell in Shayista's throat ... then slipped away. The attacker burst into a peal of hilarity.

'Costa? Is that you?' asked Shayista, turning to face his erstwhile enemy.

The man doubled over in laughter. 'You shudda heard your voice shiver!'

'Costa, it is you!' Shayista shouted in glee. 'You scoundrel. I might have killed you.'

'You can't kill a kitty when you're in your mellow mood.'

'You know me too well.'

'Fearless as ever, Subedar, and you never seem to age!' Costa wiped a felicitous tear from the corner of his eye.

'How did you sneak in?' asked Shayista.

'Ha ha! I'm a pirate, remember?' Costa's triangular hat tilted over his long hair. He hadn't changed much apart from a handful of grey whiskers and some wrinkles by the sides of his ocean blue eyes.

Shayista embraced his friend. 'Where have you been so long? It's been ten years!'

'Has it?' said Costa with a gap-toothed grin. 'Then that is how long it takes to circumnavigate the world.'

Costa was a true adventurer, thirsty for experiences, not wealth, not titles. Shayista wondered how it would feel to renounce his responsibilities and join his friend. 'What did you see?'

'I saw the loveliest of lands,' said Costa.

'Mecca?' asked Shayista.

'No! America!' said Costa.

'What have they there?'

'A city called Albany where shamans have an herb of knowledge that connects your mind to Mother Earth and reveals to you your inner purpose.'

'And what did you discover is your purpose, dear friend?'

'I had a vision. I saw myself as my spirit animal, a rugged bear three times the size of ol' Dhand, claws bigger than this cutlass.'

Shayista raised a brow. 'Spirit animal?'

'I was in a dream-like trance, wrapped in violet smoke. I dipped my paws in golden honey and licked it up. I could taste the sticky sweet on my tongue. Then it all made sense. I just love gold.' Costa grinned, his golden tooth iridescent. 'My purpose is to hunt for treasure.'

'Ha! You didn't need a herb to tell you that,' teased Shayista.

'But wait, as I was licking up the honey, a realization washed over me. The honey did not represent gold in the literal sense but nectar … the nectar of immortality! Mother Earth was telling me, what good is gold when you're OLD?'

'What?'

'Yes, that's what she said. And Jesu, it turned my head around. I got to thinking: here I am wasting time chasing material wealth when nothing is more precious than time itself! So I've refined my hunt.'

'You're searching for the Fountain of Youth?' suggested Shayista.

'Or the Holy Grail,' said Costa

'Or the Emerald Tablet?' asked Shayista.

'There's a map I want to show you,' said Costa. 'You have time? I'll get it.'

'I'll go with you,' said Shayista, eager to distract himself from the joba petal and his regrets. He noticed the blade in Costa's hand, the one he had held beneath his chin. His smile fell. 'Where did you get that?'

Costa swelled with pride. 'You recognized it! I hoped you would. I got it off a scurvy dreg. 'Lucky katara of the Subedar,' he said, 'brings tiger strength to he who wields it.' Well, if it really were yours, I knew you'd never sell it. I knew it was pinched so I filched it back.'

'You stole it? How unlike you,' said Shayista sarcastically.

'To return it to its rightful owner,' said Costa, handing it over.

It was a push dagger. The handle had two parallel bars with a cross-piece to grip onto. It fit Shayista's mutilated hand like a glove.

'Tavernier will never set foot in my ship again,' chuckled Costa.

'Tavernier?' said Shayista. 'You stole it from him? Where did he find it?'

'Claims he bought it from an amir in your army,' said Costa.

'Amir Jaswant Singh,' growled Shayista, recalling the traitor with the lazy eye. O how he hoped he would someday have the chance to kill him brutally.

Shayista ran his fingers over the horizontal hand grip. It was made of gold, inlaid with floral koftgari designs. He admired the watered steel. Only select sword smiths in Damascas knew the ancient technique of mixing metals. These blades were impure but more difficult to break than the purer, brittle counterparts from Toledo or Japan. Others tried to copy the wavy patterns through a process of heating and folding metal but none achieved the flexibility or stability of the true Damascan steel. It was a rare weapon, a gift from Aurangzeb on his coronation.

The gold katara could have made all the difference if it had been where he had left it, when he needed it. He suspected it was removed by none other than Amir Jaswant.

Donning his fustian cloak, Shayista led Costa past the mosque to his stables, hoping to slip out unnoticed. His plan was thwarted by Dhand who rested nearby.

'Salaam, Sire,' Dhand mumbled, his mouth full. 'I thought you might try to sneak out again. Is that you, Captain? Hello, Captain Costa!' He embraced the pirate, lifting him off the ground as though he were a ragdoll.

Costa chuckled and straightened his coat. 'Good to see you, you big scallywag. You are even bigger than before!'

Dhand laughed. 'God has been kind.' He turned to Shayista. 'Diwan Bhopal is looking for you. It is a matter of urgency.'

'Alas, the Captain has invited me to his floating fortress,' said Shayista. 'I leave the matter in your fairly capable hands.'

'May I accompany you, Sire?' said Dhand. 'I have news.'

'Dhand, is it bad news? It's always bad news. Am I cursed?'

'Cursed? Not a chance, Sire,' said Dhand. 'Her Excellency has stationed a Quran-reciting maulana in each corner of the fortress to ward off evil. They pray eight hours a day. Nothing can penetrate this force field. Inside the fortress, we're safe.'

'Then we must go outside!' said Shayista with a wink. 'But try to be discreet. I don't want an entourage trailing me like the tail of a peacock.'

'I don't approve of your covert missions,' complained Dhand. 'It is not fitting for a Governor to travel without guards.'

Ignoring the advice, Shayista commanded his stable hands to prepare the horses. Three superior stallions with caparisons of green lace were brought forth. His scientist, Adl Fahad, had raised these experimental thoroughbreds on a regimen of vitamins that made them prodigious. They stood seven feet tall and could outrun cheetahs. Fitted with jewelled saddles and vermillion face masks bearing the Mughal insignia, they were an impressive sight.

Shayista mounted his stallion, Bageshri, and galloped to the gates. The gold katara was so familiar to him it felt like a limb. It had a chiselled medallion at the top of the blade with the inscription: Godspeed. He held the crossbar clenched in his fist. Even without three fingers, he could hold it steady, though it would take months of practice before he would be able to fight with it again.

Shayista swiped the blade at a low-hanging branch and cut off a bunch of amloke berries. He offered them to his friends. Dhand shook his head.

'They're good for your gums.' Shayista took a bite into the green fruit and winced. Piquant juice jolted his senses like a shot of whiskey.

Dhand looked like he had seen a ghost. 'Where did you get that?' he asked, pointing to the katara.

Shayista replied, 'Costa picked it up in Europe.'

Dhand's face reflected that he understood what Shayista must be feeling, even as Costa bubbled happily in front of them. No words needed to be spoken.

As they approached the southern parapet of the fortress, they saw the Buriganga. The monsoons hadn't arrived yet so the water was low. From their vantage point, the river looked tranquil, its madness hidden.

Anchored along the dock were rows of vessels: sea ships, noukas and dinghies. On the banks, crowds of people: hawkers, merchants, sailors, pirates and artisans. They looked like ants swarming around the sweets of the sea. A kingfisher flew overhead. Its bright colours drew Shayista's attention.

Bageshri slowed his gait, ears pricked, and resisted Shayista's signal to move forth. He stomped his hooves on the ground. Shayista knew he should pay heed. Bageshri's intuition was never wrong but whatever it was out there, he had to face it. He patted the stallion on its rump and urged him on.

The guards at the watchtower saluted as Shayista passed.

'What's the news, Dhand?' said Shayista.

'There is a traitor among us,' said Dhand. 'We intercepted a carrier dove not far from the fortress with a message addressed to the Emperor.'

'What did it say?'

'It said Kalinoor resides in Lal Bagh fort,' said Dhand.

'Did it say where?' asked Shayista. Only he and Dhand knew where it was hidden.

'No.'

'Why all this talk of the diamond?' asked Shayista.

'There must be a plan to steal it,' said Dhand.

Shayista recalled how Shah Jahan dealt with turncoats: sewed them into the freshly flayed skin of slaughtered livestock. The carcasses dried up in the summer heat, suffocating the men within. Jahangir threw apostates into a ring with lions. He too ought to administer a few memorable executions to drive fear into the hearts of extremists.

The gates of the fortress were thick, studded with iron spikes to prevent elephants from battering them down. The guards unlatched the heavy bolts of the southern gate.

Shayista eyed them with paranoid distrust, wondering who among them would stab him in the back. Every one of them looked like conspirators now.

The cobbled road beyond the gates was sloped down to the riverbank, another strategic design to prevent enemies from ramming in. Such care he had taken to obstruct intruders but what of the enemies within? He would have to deal with them severely before the Emperor arrived. Shayista dug his heels into Bageshri and raced towards Costa's treasure ship.

CHAPTER 23

Nasim Banu stepped out of her zenana later that day and was greeted by her eunuch.

'The zamindar awaits you,' he announced.

Nasim had heard from her sources that the Emperor was not pleased with Shayista and sought to undermine his enterprise. This was unfortunate. She knew how sincere Shayista was. He could not help it that he was an avatar of freedom while Aurangzeb was a radical puritan. They were bound to clash ideologically and it was up to her to keep things civil. The future of her sons, and herself, depended on it. And now others were starting to complain.

'Bring him in,' she commanded. As she marched to the private guest chamber, bangles jangling on her arms.

Zamindar Shobha Singh had come with a dozen armed men who waited outside. 'Greetings your Highness,' he said with utmost politeness, bowing. His muscles bulged with power.

'Greetings zamindar, how do you do?' she asked, without removing her veil.

'What a vision of beauty you are, your Highness!' he said, effortlessly slipping into insincerity. He was a kingly display of vanity, sporting all the trappings of royalty: a fine kurta draped with pearls, a turban of white silk striped with gold, a shoulder strap embroidered with gems, around his waist a tasselled silk sash with a bejewelled scimitar, upon his lips, the complacent smile of easy aristocracy. He even wore red chamars, pointed leather shoes.

'You are generous,' said Nasim, accepting the compliment. Shobha was considered one of the fiercest warriors in the province, some said maybe even be fiercer than Shayista. She had last seen him sixteen years ago when Shayista granted him governance of his ancestral home in

Midnapore, maintaining equal opportunities for Hindus though this had gone out of fashion.

'Did you like the gift?' said Shobha.

'Indeed, the scarf was exquisite. How can I thank you?'

He bowed again and offered Nasim Banu another dupatta. This one was lilac, even softer than the last.

Nasim rubbed the delicate cloth. It floated off her fingers like a butterfly. 'My, my. This is lovely.'

'A humble show of gratitude. There is more where it came from, unless I am forced to shut down my karkhana.' He hung his head.

'Heavens no, don't close your factory,' exclaimed Nasim. 'Muslin trade is booming.'

Shobha looked hurt. 'Alas, your Highness, just yesterday the Subedar ordered an embargo on trade with the English. Now I can't sell my muslin or my saltpetre!'

'There must be some mistake. The Subedar is an ardent supporter of trade and commerce. Why half of Europe's imports come from Bengal,' said Nasim.

Shobha Singh lowered his voice to a conspiratorial whisper. 'Merchants in Hooghly requested a firman exempting the Company from custom duties. The Emperor will not be pleased to learn that Subedar Khan has opposed this firman and thrown the English officer out of his court.'

'Now, now. No need to go tattling on the Subedar,' said Nasim, quick to defend her husband. 'We have been friends for many years, have we not? Before you disturb the peace, why not have another word with the Subedar? Clear the misunderstanding?'

Shobha looked uncertain. Khajah Ambar whispered something in Nasim's ears.

'Please join us on the eve of the full moon for dinner and a dance,' she said. 'You can speak to my husband then.'

Shobha accepted the invitation and bowed deep, leaving respectfully without turning his back.

What would Shayista do without her? Endlessly she crusaded for him without any gratitude or acknowledgement. Still it would be well worth it if she could impress the Emperor and secure a promotion for Iradat. From her latticed window, she watched the sun set into the Buriganga, the sky a shade of murky pink.

CHAPTER 24

A s they galloped along the banks of the Buriganga, Shayista recalled the last time he'd seen the gold katara. It was the night of Vikram's son's wedding, the night he was betrayed. The twins were barely two months old. He remembered it clearly though it seemed like another lifetime, back when he was a different man.

Servants scurried across the lawn of Lal Mahal Fort preparing for the wedding. Shayista had been in occupation of the fort for over a year and his staff were familiar with the routine of hosting elaborate parties. A crimson shamiana draped over a lattice of gold-plated bamboo created a majestic pavilion on the lawn of the fortress. Diyas lit the walkways. Musicians tuned instruments. The tantalizing scent of kebabs made his mouth water.

'Vikram, I hope the decor is to your liking?' Shayista had said, slapping his friend on the back.

'Subedar, you have been too kind. Flowers from Islamabad? They must have cost a fortune,' replied the zamindar. A hundred bouquets dotted the periphery. Each had a dozen white irises in full bloom.

'No expense is too extravagant for you my dear friend,' said Shayista. 'I was thrilled you asked to use my lawn for your son's wedding. At last I have the opportunity to show you my gratitude.' He placed his arm around his friend.

'No, no, I have done nothing,' said Vikram.

'If it weren't for you, Pune, Kalyan, North Konkan might all be Maratha strangleholds. I could never have annexed those states without your support.'

Vikram's mouth twitched. 'It was you, your Excellency. All you.'

'No need to be modest, Vikram,' said Shayista. 'Of course, it was I who threw out the Mountain Rat but without you there would have been an uprising. The Hindu peasants would not have agreed to my terms. You saved a great many lives.'

'I abhor blood, your Excellency.'

They gazed out at the immense lawn of the castle. Nasim Banu was approaching, dressed in a satin choli with a dupatta carefully placed to reveal a cascade of emeralds around her neck. Her nose pin was a scintillating diamond the size of a grape. 'My Lord, the priest has not arrived,' she said to Shayista.

'The Mir-e-Tuzuk is perfectly capable of orchestrating the event,' said Shayista. 'Everything will be fine.' He paid their master-of-ceremonies handsomely. The man had organized at least seven hundred galas of this nature.

'I fear that overzealous Amir Jaswant may give our guests a hard time at the gates,' she said, her alabaster skin rouged with exertion.

'I will look into it, my Lady.' Shayista waited till Nasim left before resuming his conversation with Vikram. 'Is marriage not a strange institution? It is driven from fear not love, fear constricts while love frees. You see, marriage is from the mind, love from the heart. Surely there can be nothing unholy about loving more than one person intimately?'

Vikram nodded, sweating profusely.

'Vikram, where is your wife?'

'She is ill at home. I have asked her to rest.'

'And miss her youngest son's wedding?'

'I insisted,' replied Vikram.

'My friend, you have better command over your ladyship than I have over mine. Nasim would never have consented to miss the wedding of our youngest son. I believe he is her favourite.'

Vikram looked away and forced a fake laugh.

'Come now, Vikram. What's the matter?' said Shayista. 'The father of the groom is nervous? Let us hope for the maiden's sake that your son is not of the same temperament tonight. I have married off five of my six and not once was I this nervous. Have a drink and please excuse me as I have a word with Amir Singh.'

Shayista left his friend and headed up to the watchtower mulling over the nature of relationships. Marriage corrupts love by removing mystery and gratitude, he thought, replacing it with duty and expectation. Nasim was raised to be a prince's wife yet for all the convenience their marriage offered the Empire, it offered Shayista no warmth. For years he tried to light the spark but eventually resigned himself to a dull conjugal existence. Then he met Ellora.

The sentries fell to taslim as he entered the watchtower.

'Report,' Shaiysta commanded.

Amir Jaswant replied, 'Sire, sentinels at the North Gate sent word of brigands. Three caravans were waylaid and several villages near Kalyan were raided. Casualties are high. The brigands came armed with swords and spears. Some had battle axes I am told. We tried to arrest them but they retreated to underground hideouts.'

'You were to obliterate the base camp last week!' said Shayista.

'Subedar, I do not agree with your annexation tactics,' Jaswant stated. His left eye drooped, a lazy eye he had since birth. 'These are rebels, not petty thieves. We must negotiate.'

Shayista could not believe his impertinence. Concealing the disgust curdling within him, he said, 'Guards, leave us.'

The guards exited the room in haste.

'Amir Jaswant, don't EVER contradict me in front of others,' Shayista warned.

'Forgive me, Sire.'

'I will not tolerate rape and plunder by anti-Imperial forces. We will have peace at all cost! Tomorrow you will assemble a team to kill them. Depopulate the entire town if you have to. Burn them out of their hovels. Wipe out those rogues. AND their sons! If a few innocent lives are lost, so be it.'

'Yes, Sire.'

'The wedding party will be here soon. Raise the drawbridge at the South Gate.'

'No need for that,' said Jaswant, pointing down.

Distant torches showed the wedding procession making its way up the hill with drummers and musicians leading the way. Shayista could see about 400 people on foot, thirty horses and three elephants with decorated howdahs.

'Maintain strict vigilance,' said Shayista. 'We don't want miscreants disturbing the wedding. There will be women and children.'

'Yes, Sire.'

Shayista's eyes tunnelled into him.

'It shall be as my Subedar commands,' he said, bowing.

Under ordinary circumstances Shayista might have reprimanded the commander but tonight he had Ellora on his mind. He knew Nasim would be busy with the wedding and he wanted to spend some time with Ellora and the girls whom he had given a room in the Southern part of the fortress. He had finally found the love that poets wrote about and he wanted to celebrate every moment. He remembered the words of Hafez...

'I have no use for divine patience -
My lips are now burning and everywhere.
I am running from every corner of this earth and sky
Wanting to kiss you.'

Distant dhols and kettle drums pounded, announcing the wedding party. Oblivious to the agitated night life, the howling owl, the uneasy bull frogs, Shayista hurried to Ellora's quarters. He found Dhand guarding the door.

'Nasim is concerned about the priest. Please see to it?' asked Shayista.

'Hookum, Sire!' Dhand lumbered off.

Shayista entered the palatial room. It was lit with a chandelier of candles and scented with rose water.

Waiting on their four-poster bed, draped in a dazzling white choli, was the love of his life. Ellora, love-bitten and yearning. Ellora, tender for their reunion.

Shayista had the dark diamond in his pocket, the one Arjumand had asked him to give to a woman he loved. He had hidden it for thirty five years never thinking he would have to dig it up. Life was kinder than he had expected. Shayista paused a moment to lap up the euphoria.

Ellora's cheeks were aglow, candlelight wove in her hair. Shayista lifted her in his arms and buried his head in her bosom. She pulled his face to her lips and kissed him. 'Not here,' she said in a lusty whisper, though she was the one kissing. 'The girls might wake up.'

Shayista said, 'Let them.' He glanced fondly at the twin bassinets by the side of the bed. In one was Pari Bibi, sweet tempered and plump. In the other was Miri Bibi, feisty and stubborn. He blew a silent kiss to each of his beauties.

He grabbed Ellora with the full ardour of love. She didn't resist. He licked her shoulder and kissed her neck. She melted in his arms. His hand went to her blouse, tearing open the hooks so her breasts spilled free. He pinched her nipple between his fingers.

She drew his finger to her lips. The cosmos circled on the pink tip of her tongue, a microcosm of the universe upon his wet finger. His soul broke free and cascaded out of his flesh, connecting with hers, in a plunge of sweetness.

He knelt on one knee and said, 'Ellora, never before have I felt so certain of my purpose.'

'Your purpose?' she asked, batting eye lashes.

'My purpose is to love you! You are a perfect expression of Allah's divinity.'

'You are too kind.' Ellora blushed.

He began to unwrap the ghagra from her slender chocolate brown waist, slowly, bit by bit. She moaned in anticipation. When she was naked before him, he placed on her neck the dark diamond. It hung from her like an icy anchor. He noticed goose bumps on her chiselled collarbone. From the valley between her breasts, the diamond beckoned.

Ellora's eyes sparkled in awe. Without a word, she dropped to her knees and began to lick Shayista loins. She had prepared a pair of potent aphrodisiac ointments which she rubbed on both his manhood and his nipples. It created a tingling sensation of cold above and hot below, sharp and gentle, Krishna, Radha, black, white, good, evil. When he felt he would be torn asunder by the contrast of pain and pleasure, she led him to ecstasy. It was the closest he ever came to bliss but the jealous night stole away the moment.

She had only replaced the first wrap of her ghagra when shouts rang through the night. Distraught screams announced chaos in the distance. Then suddenly blaring musical instruments drowned out the shouts, a grating cacophony that made it difficult to ascertain the real danger.

Shayista fumbled with his pyjamas, shaking off the droopy stupor of love. There was a ramming of wood against their door. Shayista had stationed 10,000 soldiers around the boundary walls with Commander Jawant in charge at the watchtower. Where was Jaswant? What was this music?

He hadn't time to register the nature of the trouble. The door began to splinter. Ellora wrapped herself in a bed sheet. Shayista pushed her behind him for protection.

In leapt a ferocious brigand with two of his men. It was Shivaji the Mountain Rat. The Maratha King had terrorized the Mughal army with guerrilla warfare for years. Only a year earlier, Shayista defeated him and drove him out of his home.

'This time I will finish YOU!' Shivaji shouted. 'Jai Hind!' He was an immense figure with a callous sneer smeared across his gaunt face. The Maratha leapt furiously slashing a double-edged talwar at Shayista's face.

Unarmed, Shayista ducked, missing the powerful blow by a whisper. He reached under the bed for his trusted katara but it was not there where he had left it. In the confused moment, Shivaji took advantage and swung his talwar. Shayista leapt aside and retaliated with a cobra coiled kick to Shivaji's shoulder.

Shivaji staggered and roared in pain. He launched a counter-attack: swinging his shield at Shayista's head but the kick to his shoulder weakened the force of his blow.

Shayista stumbled off balance but survived. He cursed himself for sending Dhand on a stupid errand.

Ellora jumped in front of him, her arms spread wide to protect him. 'Pitaji, you can't kill my husband,' she cried.

For an instant, time stood still. Both Shayista and Shivaji were stunned.

'Ellora?' said Shivaji at last. 'What are you doing here?'

It dawned on Shayista that he was in love with the daughter of his mortal enemy.

'You are alive?' Shivaji's voice choked with emotion. 'And you are ...' His grief was replaced by a berserk anger. 'Step aside, Ellora!' Shivaji yelled. 'I will kill the swine who dishonoured you.'

'Pitaji, I am his wife,' said Ellora. The bed sheet fell from her shoulder revealing her nipple. She quickly pulled it back up.

Shayista jumped to the side of the bed where he had dumped his clothes and as he dressed, Ellora pleaded with her father.

'The Mughal weasel kidnapped you. I'll kill him!' Shivaji raged. He pushed Ellora aside and leapt across the room, talwar drawn, knocking over the chandelier. Flames engulfed the curtains and tapestries. The twins wailed.

Shayista made the fatal mistake of glancing at Ellora as the chandelier fell almost upon her. He saw the Maratha king's talwar swing at him and raised his hand in reflex. Searing pain shot through him as Shivaji's sword severed three of his fingers. The force of the thrust threw him off balance. He fell to the ground.

'Jai Bhavani!' Shivaji shouted, raising his lethal weapon.

With the strength born of desperation, Shayista twisted sideways and thrust a round-house kick at the Rat, despite the agonising pain in his hand.

Shivaji fell back then somersaulted in mid-air and landed with a kick to Shayista's temple. He brought his blade whistling towards Shayista's head for a killing strike.

In the concluding moment of his life, Shayista shut his eyes. Burning cinders assaulted his face. The room smelt of ash. The smoke made it difficult to breathe. He prayed and braced himself but the anticipated death blow never struck.

'Allahuakbar!' shouted Abul Fateh, Shayista's youngest son, charging into the room. He valourously thrust his sword into the Mountain Rat's thigh.

Shivaji recoiled like a nimble panther and snarled at the boy. He swung his talwar at the boy's left leg then his right, smashing his knees.

Pain didn't deter Abul. He put forth a valiant but short-lived effort. He was no match for the seasoned guerrilla warrior.

Shayista crawled towards his son, his hand throbbing.

Ellora was next to him, eyes wide with fright. 'He will kill you!'

'Baba!' A scream of despair from the far side of the room.

Shivaji had plunged his sword into the boy's ribs. They heard the sound of skin tearing as he pulled his blade out and then the crashing sound of Abul Fateh Khan falling to the ground.

Shayista screamed. His body failed to move and time slowed down. His heart shattered into infinite fragments as he stared at his blood-drenched son. Reality disintegrated into a series of surreal events unfolding before him but he couldn't make sense of it. He heard the babies howling. He saw Ellora pushing him frantically. 'Run. You cannot fight him in this condition.' Her words seemed distant. 'Run. Run!'

He stared dazed as Shivaji lunged forward. Suddenly Ellora flung herself upon him. He felt her body slam into his. Her lips touched his cheek. She shuddered as the heavy sword withdrew from her pierced back. He heard Shivaji's anguished caterwaul, 'O Bhagavan, what have I done?'

A rush of footsteps and Maratha soldiers barged in. Behind them, Dhand and some of his own men, armed with spears and lanterns. Smouldering curtains caught onto the rugs. Fire and smoke engulfed them. The sheet wrapped around Ellora was soaked in hibiscus red. The world went dark as Shayista lost consciousness.

When he awoke two days later he found his world altered. The Mountain Rat had escaped. Dhand had managed to save him and Pari. Kalinoor was found tucked in her bassinette where Ellora must have slipped it. Miri, Abul and Ellora, were dead.

Vikram's son's wedding had been a farce. The marriage procession consisted of 400 Maratha warriors in full armour hidden under wedding finery. Shivaji himself walked in as a drummer. He led the party into Lal Mahal and strangled the servants before they could ring the alarms. He forced the palace musicians to play merry tunes as loud as possible to add to the chaos and drown out warning calls. He stormed into the fortress to claim what was his. Amir Jaswant Singh was in on the plan. It was treachery of the highest order. Not even the English would be so dishonourable as to turn on their host.

Shayista could not forgive himself. He had missed the signs and failed to protect his family. The Emperor was the first to offer condolences but this was followed by an urgent request, or rather, an order. He needed Shayista to quell a Magh uprising. No one else could do the job. Shayista moved to the rebellious state of Bengal and there doused his burning heart with battle blood.

Shayista gazed upon his injured hand. For twenty years it had served as a constant reminder of what happened when he let his emotions rule. He wondered now, was it Kalinoor that had caused Ellora's death? He had placed it around her neck that very night. Was that the diamond's second strike?

Chapter 25

Under the flapping scarlet sails of the twin-masted outrigger, Madeline watched the docks through her spy-glass waiting for Captain Costa to return. Waves crashed iridescent foam. By the ghats, washermen in white dhotis carried baskets of rainbow laundry on their heads. Vendors sold sea goods along the path.

She had grown to love the buzz aboard the ship when docked after months at sea. To mark the occasion, she was dressed in a white satin bodice and an overskirt pinned back to reveal a decidedly fussy pink petticoat with bows and trimmings. She was eager to explore but dared not venture out alone.

She spotted Costa's wide-rim hat as he returned to the ship with two friends riding upon dazzlingly decorated horses. They tethered their steeds and were rowed to the ship in a skiff. She greeted them on the deck.

Costa introduced his companions as dear old friends: Viceroy, Subedar Shayista Khan and Chief of Cavalry, Amir-i-akhur Dhand.

Madeline was surprised to find the Subedar as handsome as the legends claimed but his face was ravaged by scars. 'Salaam,' she said.

'Enchante,' said the Subedar.

Amir Dhand gazed at her with a goofy grin. He was a colossal man. His muscles spoke of inhuman strength but his eyes were gentle.

Madeline blushed, smoothing down her dress. Perhaps he had never seen a European damsel before. Indeed, she had made an effort to primp that day. Her pale skin was powdered to perfection. Her wig was arranged in a towering mass of tight curls. She wore an elegant string of pearls and her fanciest gown. Even Costa eyed her curiously.

'It's a pleasure to meet you,' she said to them. She had studied Persian aboard the ship but it seemed they could both speak French.

'You are brave to have made this arduous journey,' said the Subedar. 'What brings you to Bengal?'

Costa jumped in, 'She is going to Chatgaon for a tribal cure.'

Madeline was momentarily baffled. She had forgotten her lie.

Costa prompted her, 'Your father's affliction?'

'Yes, my father is ill,' she said hastily. 'The witchdoctors of Chatgaon are renowned for their healing herbs.'

The Subedar nodded empathetically. 'Hindustan has many ancient healing practices. Herbal medicine is just one. There is also Ayurveda, unani, chakra cleansing, Sufi chants, pranayama, yoga chikitsa, vipasana, crystal therapy.'

'She's a natural philosopher,' Costa cut in.

'What's that?' asked Amir Dhand.

'She studies diamonds,' explained Costa.

'What is it with the French and diamonds?' said Amir Dhand frowning.

Piqued, Madeline asked, 'What do you mean?'

'Tavernier,' he mumbled. 'If I ever get my hands on him ...'

Madeline blanched. Could she not escape him even here?

'Fascinating,' said the Subedar. 'Sacred Hindu lapidary texts speak of the mystical healing properties of diamonds.'

'C'est vraiment?' asked Madeline. 'Where do these healing diamonds come from?' She smiled innocuously.

'Have you heard of the Kollur mines?' said the Subedar.

Madeline pretended she had not. The conversation was going as she had intended.

'Kollur is every pirate's fantasy,' said Costa. 'The most jealously guarded secret. When it rains, diamonds float in the mud and trickle down streams.'

'The mine is protected by Mother Nature herself,' added Amir Dhand. 'Surrounded by treacherous terrain infested with venomous serpents nine feet long. Men used to slaughter sheep at the top of hills and cast bleeding fragments down to the valley for vultures. When the birds swooped to feast on the meat, the diamonds would stick to their feathers. Later men would climb the trees at the top of the mountain to collect the booty from their nests.'

'The finest diamonds never make it to Europe,' said Costa. 'Armenian merchants ship them off to Ispahan. Any stone over twenty carats goes straight to the Mughal Treasury itself. And rarely then can others aquire them.'

'Nor should they,' said Amir Dhand, getting agitated. 'The diamonds are of our soil and belong to our people.'

'The Company is after our Deccani diamonds,' said Shayista. 'And so it seems, are the Marathas.'

'Don't let them pompous gasbags tangle your turban,' said Costa, placing a hand on his shoulder. 'Tell her how you dealt with them hen-hearted Company boys last time.'

'That's nothing to brag about,' said the Subedar.

'Go on,' urged Costa.

'Yes, do,' urged Madeline.

'The Company sent a mission to negotiate with me some years ago,' explained the Subedar. 'Their terms were as disgusting as their attitudes so I did not grant them the firman they wanted.'

'Tell her how they tried to poison you!' said Costa.

'Warrington offered me contaminated wine,' shrugged the Subedar. 'I didn't drink it.'

'How did you know it was poison?' asked Madeline, recalling Abdul's tales about the Subedar's supernatural powers. Had he smelt the ingredients?

The Subedar simply smiled.

'He made the English whelp drink the poison himself. The man died writhing in pain,' said Costa, grinning.

'They are crazy if they think I'm going to give Bengal's treasures to the Europeans without a fight,' added the Subedar. 'No offense.'

Madeline winced.

'Tomorrow you may visit the Meena Bazaar if you like?' Amir Dhand suggested. 'To see our treasures?'

Madeline expressed her interest and they agreed to collect her the following morning for an outing.

'I have another treasure to offer you,' said Costa, as Abdul arrived with mugs of aromatic black liquid, steaming hot. 'Drink!'

'What's this?' asked Subedar Khan. 'Never have I tasted anything so bitterly divine.'

Madeline savoured a few jolting sips which set her heart a-pounding.

'Coffee!' said Captain Costa. 'From Constantinople.'

'The universe is bountiful in gifts,' said Subedar Khan.

Abdul threw himself in taslim at the Subedar's feet. The Subedar patted him on the back fondly. Abdul's eyes glazed over in awe.

The Subedar, the Amir and the Captain retired to the cabin, old friends reunited. Madeline did not follow them down. Instead she reflected over what she would wear the following morning and how she would get on with her mission. The Subedar was not what she had expected but then nobody was who they appeared to be.

CHAPTER 26

Shaiysta returned home after a strenuous day with Maratha warriors, clairvoyant dancers, prophesising pirs, near death and reunions to find Nasim waiting for him.

'Sire, I must inform you,' she said. 'I was almost killed in the Chowk today.' Courtly formalism suited her well. She was raised to be unfailingly polite.

'How?' asked Shayista, surprised their paths hadn't crossed.

'Malefactors in orange turbans ambushed my elephant.'

Shayista cringed. The Marathas.

'If it weren't for Khajah Ambar, I would be dead,' said Nasim petulantly. Her eyes pinned him to the wall.

'What were you doing in the bazaar without the Imperial guards?' he challenged, feeling uncomfortable. He had jeopardized his household. How had the Marathas traced Kalinoor to him?

'I had some ... work,' she said.

Shayista swore he would eradicate the thugs and summoned Dhand to give the command, when Bhopal came running to him.

'Sire, I must speak to you at once!' panted the dwarf.

'What is it, Diwan Bhopal?' asked Shayista, casting a quick glance at Nasim. Nasim understood, bowed and excused herself.

'I'm sorry to inform you, Sire,' said Bhopal. 'Resistance is coalescing. Last night in their khutba, the ulema asked followers to impose strict vigilance on their morality lest they fall into the dark ocean of temptation. They said girls should not be allowed in the public sphere and foreign attitudes are a threat to Islam. They openly said you are too liberal!'

Shayista shook his head dismayed. A mullah mutiny? After all he had done to promote progress in Bengal, men of the cloth were whining about liberty? They would always find something to criticize. 'Freedom of thought is fundamental to evolution,' said Shayista. 'Summon the ulema.'

'Sire, I must warn you, the Emperor arrives in less than a month.' Deep concern was etched on his face.

Shayista frowned. The Emperor was the least of his worries. He thanked Bhopal for his concern then quickly proceeded to the gajashala for space to speculate.

The smell of dung tickled his nose. The stable boys fell to taslims. He asked for the grooming equipment and waved them away. A sturdy elephant cub reached her trunk out to feel him. He patted her and brushed her with a long-handled broom of coconut husk. Grooming required a combination of massage techniques: up and down then circular motions. Shayista enjoyed the moving meditation.

He spared no cost when it came to the upkeep of his beloved pets. He owned 600 elephants and provided them with the best quality food, regular baths and two mahuts each to look after them. Elephants, he found, would stand their ground in battle while even your bravest commanders would desert you. This human cowardice, once he became wise to it, made Shayista deeply unsatisfied with the values of mankind. To his wife he would say, 'You are as stalwart as an elephant.' It was a compliment on his part, the sincerest he could give her.

His relationship with Nasim had always been formal and when Ellora and the twins came to his life, Nasim was further estranged. The final blow as she saw it was when Ellora and Miri were killed and she was compelled to raise Pari as her own. To Nasim, Pari was a manifestation of their relationship gone wrong.

To Shayista, Pari was an angel sent to rescue him from solitude. For the first time, Shayista truly experienced fatherhood. He had raised his sons with a sense of duty and an iron fist of discipline while Pari had him wrapped around her little finger. If he wasn't in the durbar, he was in the nursery narrating stories to her or in the forest teaching her to ride horses, trying to compensate for her lack of mother love.

Shayista dipped a wash cloth in a bucket of soapy oil water and began rubbing the cub down. Of course, she loved water. All elephants did! She tried to upturn the bucket with her trunk but Shayista caught the vessel in time. The cub settled for a stick of sugarcane and swatted at flies with her tail.

It had not been easy to raise Pari. There was Nasim's palpable envy and also Pari was a sickly child. Most forms of coughs and fevers plagued her. She was asthmatic and allergic to dust, frail and susceptible to injuries, weak and tormented by bouts of dysentery. Though it wasn't customary for fathers to participate in the nursing of sick children, he was there helping the aseels place cool cloth on her forehead during fevers, coaxing her to drink warm basil and honey water.

Despite the trials of fatherhood, Shayista felt infinitely blessed and grateful for her love. When he moved to the jungles of Bengal, he was a damaged man. Pari was the little girl-shaped miracle that saved him. Her laughter blew apart grey clouds and made space for resplendent sunshine. She inspired him to love again.

'Baba, look at me,' Pari called. She was grinning, front teeth missing, cheeks dimpled, crown of jasmines in her hair.

'Pari, my fairy queen?' said Shayista. He reached out for her.

Pari laughed with such heart-felt joy, anyone who heard her couldn't help but experience delight. 'Catch me if you can, Lal Bagh!' she said, then dashed off.

He clambered to his feet to follow her, growling like a tiger. 'Where are you, Pari?' He called. She ran out of the stable and towards the garden.

'Catch me if you can, Baba,' her voice called between giggles.

'Pari, where are you?' he called, running after her.

'Over here, Baba,' she beckoned.

Shayista paused to catch his breath. 'Where Pari?'

'Here Baba,' came a reply from the menagerie.

The weather was torrid. Sweat trickled down his face and back. He arrived in the garden to find it dry and parched. Leaves and branches had withered. The sun was ten thousand times brighter. Pari stood in its radiance and danced.

Watching her silhouette against the blazing sun hurt Shayista's eyes. He tried to squint. His eyes watered. Before him, Pari began to shimmer then shrank and shrivelled into a bougainvillea petal that drifted into his palm.

Shayista raised the petal to the sky and implored, 'Is this all you have left for me, God?' Lifted from his palm by a breeze, the petal floated off.

'You have left me nothing,' sobbed Shayista.

The sound of canons from a neighboring battlement throbbed in his ears, louder by the minute till it was unbearable. A deafening clash of swords, blitz of bullets, anguished soldiers calling his name. 'Subedar Khan. Subedar Khan?'

Shayista shook his head and blinked. He was standing in a cloud of dust at the edge of the construction site. The chief engineer was kissing the hems of his robe.

'Subedar Khan, this un-un- unannounced visit?' he stammered, nervous beads of sweat on his face. He had to shout to be heard above the din: grinding of stones, polishing of marble, carving of mahogany, driving of ox carts loaded with bricks.

Shayista had walked across the garden to Pari's tomb with the elephant washcloth in his hand. Ever since her death a year ago, strange trances had frequented him. He accepted that the fortress was haunted, and he loved it, because it was haunted by her. Somnambulating inevitably led him to the mouth of her tomb.

'Carry on,' said Shayista, much to the engineer's relief. 'As you were.'

Workers pushed heavy boulders in bullock-carts. Stone-cutters inscribed glorious names of Allah on white marble from Jaipur. Abd-al-Ahmad Shirazi, son of the master calligrapher who adorned Taj Mahal half a century earlier, supervised. The mausoleum was Nasim's chief hobby and she was spending a fortune on it, as his father had done for his sister.

Shayista's life seemed inextricably woven into the karmic cycles of his father. His father killed Khurram to make a king of Khosru, just as his inaction led to Dara's death and the ascension of Aurangzeb. Kinslayer, Kingmaker. Were sons destined to repeat their fathers' mistakes?

Asaf Khan was a bombastic man, larger than life, his ambitions eclipsed only by his ego. He accomplished dizzying feats of commerce and architecture for the Mughals as vizier to the Emperor and he ruled with cold violence. Shayista never wanted to be like his father but here he was, perpetuating the Empire.

Shayista recalled Pari's 16th birthday, he had presented her with Kalinoor, placed it on her neck himself. The same evening, he revealed to her the truth about her long lost mother and twin sister. She wept but she understood, wise beyond her years.

Shayista found himself thinking of Saraswati, the most learned woman in Hindustan, who became Pari's tutor and guide and later also the guardian of the madrasa. Pari loved the madrasa and the girls. They were kindred spirits in many ways since she too was a motherless child.

Then one dreadful day, just as the construction of Lal Bagh fort was complete, a mysterious illness stole Pari's life. What might have been a time to jubilate instead became the gravest hours of his life: a tragedy from which there could be no recovery.

He thought of the words of the Sufi poet, Hafez,

> 'Love is the funeral pyre
> where the heart must lay its body.'

Shayista slipped under the shadow of a guava tree and buried his head in his palms. He longed for his daughter to dote on. He felt bitter. God had granted him a precious gift only to snatch her away again. He wished it had been him and not her who had died.

He had worked so hard to build a subha with schools and hospitals and gardens, with roads from Hindustan to China and ports full of ships carrying riches from Europe, with magnificent mosques so people could revel in God's luminosity. And in return? His best laid plans had been waylaid by Fate. He was left with nothing to cherish.

An itchy doubt spread in Shayista's mind. Could it have been Kalinoor that caused Pari's death? Hadn't she died with the diamond around her neck? Strike three? Suddenly Shayista knew the pir was right: the diamond was cursed!

Kalinoor was meddling with his destiny, destroying all that he cherished. Like a magnet, it drew enemies: Marathas, Englishmen, mullahs, zamindars, all infected with material lust for which they were willing to kill. Bengal was heading towards an apocalypse. But how could he counterpoise the curse? Perhaps the dancing girl would know.

CHAPTER 27

The next day Madeline dressed in lilac and sat on the docks poring over her books. She distinctly preferred pastels to bold colours and she liked especially to wear heavily brocaded dresses though the underskirt made them somewhat cumbersome in the ship.

Her research was disrupted by the rowdy cheers of Costa and the crew who were huddled around a cockfight. They had pitted their cockerel from Portugal against a scrawny red-breasted jungle fowl half its size.

On closer inspection, Madeline saw that the local fowl's owner was an anguished local boy who was as scrawny as his bird. His pleas to release his pet from the ring fell on unrelenting pirate ears pierced with golden hoops.

The cockerel had a natural skull cap of white feathers that stood erect like a helm on its head making it even more enormous than it already was.

The fight had barely begun when a retinue of soldiers approached the boat, a strange grey beast in their tow.

The captain's face lit up. 'Hold the game, it's the Subedar!' he shouted. 'I'll bet he will wager three gold coins on the local cock. He's a patriot!'

The pirates snickered. The birds were seized. The Bengali boy looked momentarily relieved. Um Olho held the monstrous cockerel to his hairy chest.

The Subedar and the Imperial guards arrived. It turned out the grey beast was called an elephant. Madeline had never seen a creature so majestic.

'Governor, would you wager three gold coins against my crew in favour of your local bird?' said Costa.

The pirates greeted this challenge with whoops of joy. The Subedar appeared to ponder the proposition. Madeline did not expect the Subedar to agree. The gamble was clearly in the pirates' favour. The local fowl would be pulverized.

'Alright,' said the Subedar.

'I advise against it, Sire,' said Amir Dhand, glaring at the pirates. 'Chances of winning are slim.' He toyed with his battle axe in a display of menace.

'Shall we raise the stakes? Double that, boys?' Costa instigated.

Madeline couldn't believe it. Was Costa trying to swindle the Subedar? Amir Dhand fidgeted uncomfortably. He cracked his knuckles and wiped his sweaty palms on his kurta.

'Aye, Captain,' said Perna de Pau, egging him on. 'Double it!'

'Six golden coins?' A Cheshire grin appeared on Costa's face.

Dhand smouldered at the pirates.

'Unless ye be a lily-livered loon?' urged Perna de Pau.

'Are you calling me a coward?' Subedar Khan demanded. 'The last man who called me that left his slanderous tongue hanging at the tip of my blade. I ACCEPT your challenge.'

Amir Dhand grimaced, unable to tolerate the shame of his Subedar being bamboozled. 'Captain, our fowl is dying already. Allow us a replacement.'

'I'm sorry Amir-i-Akhur,' said Costa. 'This is the bird you bet on.'

'Now look here,' said the Amir, puffing his formidable chest. He was easily double the size of the European seafarers. He outsized even most Moors. His muscles were massive and hard. His fingers tightened around the heavy wooden handle of his battle axe.

Madeline flinched but the pirates stood their ground.

'Six gold coins,' said the Subedar, agreeing to double the stakes. 'Go!'

'What? No, Sire,' argued the Amir.

'The Guv'ner said go!' said Um Olho. He patted his prized possession and spat off to the side of the ship.

Costa signalled. The birds were released into the ring. There was no circle dance. The cockerel wasted no time. It dove straight for the jungle fowl's brain. Little fowl was on the run, fleeing from the monster as fast as its little legs could carry it. It tried to escape the enclosure but tattered pirate boots kicked it back in. The louder it squawked, the louder the pirates cheered in joyful anticipation of six gold coins.

'God Almighty,' said the Subedar. 'Is that a rooster or a dragon?'

'Aye, he's a rare cock. A white-crested Polish cockerel. I call him Bobo.' Um Olho's eye sparkled with affection. He took a bite out of a red apple and threw it at the fowl's head, knocking it off its feet. It reeled, red crown quivering, trying to regain balance. Bobo, the cockerel, pounced on its emaciated neck.

Amir Dhand shouted, 'Foul on fowl!'

Subedar Khan snatched the fowl away from enemy beaks. The pirates hollered threats and vulgar insults. Ignoring the uproar, Subedar Khan whispered a prayer and blew it upon the jungle fowl's head then released it back in the circle.

From the moment it landed, it went ballistic. It charged like a demon and rammed its beak directly into Bobo's eye. Victory swung like a pendulum. Within a minute, the battle was over. Bobo was minced meat.

White featheres lay in a pool of garnet blood. Bobo's headless body ran in a frantic search for Eden, colliding into a dispersing wall of disappointed pirate boots till it was yanked up by Um Olho.

The pirate groaned, cradling the limp headless bloody cockerel to his hairy chest.

The local boy clapped with joy, as surprised as the others at the unlikely outcome. He tried to collect his dues from the pirates but received instead a punch in the eye.

'I believe you boys owe the Governor some money,' said Captain Costa to the pirates. 'It's unfortunate. I would have sworn that prize was yours to bag.'

Um Olho puffed his chest, his eyes inflamed. He drew his cutlass to strike the Subedar.

Subedar Khan glared at him, tiger eye to eye.

Um Olho howled in frustration and brought his blade hurtling down onto the red apple instead, splitting it in two.

'I'm terribly sorry, fellows,' said Captain Costa. 'The Subedar won it fair and square. Pay up now. Go on, all of you.'

The pirates grumbled and toyed with clasp knives while reluctantly emptying their pockets. Collectively they mustered a pile of four gold coins, a brass harmonica and a compass. Subedar Khan ceremoniously collected his dues while Amir Dhand gloated.

'Now scram, be gone,' said Captain Costa. 'We are off to the bazaar. See to it that the braces are secure, hurry up or I'll make you walk the plank.'

The irate pirates gyrated back to the ship. The Subedar tossed the gold coins to the local boy and pocketed the harmonica and compass.

'How did you win, Sire?' Madeline gushed.

'Simple, really,' said the Subedar. 'In a fight, the smaller one always tries harder.' He drew the compass from his pocket. Its dial whirred and settled pointing to the true North.

'Monsiour, it was a miracle! Like David and Goliath,' said Madeline. 'You won against all odds!'

'Did you pinch the cock's testicles?' asked Captain Costa.

Subedar Khan smiled.

'Come on, Subedar,' jeered the captain. 'This must have been the tenth time I've seen you do that trick. Is that all you've got?'

'Remember when we bet on hounds in Chatgaon?' said Subedar Khan.

'What did you do to them?' asked the pirate.

'I gave them a whiff of raw meat,' said the Subedar, chuckling.

'Old dog,' said Costa. 'You need some new tricks.'

It seemed to Madeline these two had a history.

For their trip to the Meena Bazaar, Captain Costa, Subedar Khan and Amir Dhand mounted stallions. Madeline was introduced to Didi Ma, an elderly lady who had accompanied them to be her chaperone. They were helped onto a howdah on the back of an elephant.

The beast straightened its hind legs and then its front legs, sending Madeline rocking forward then back. This caused the fontage of her headdress to slip off, leaving the wired framework over her hair in vulgar display. Madeline hastily readjusted her wig and top-knot and placed the fontage upon it once more. The lace trimming had come loose and hung clumsily in front of her face. Riding an elephant felt much like being at sea except the howdah was decorated in silks with tinsels of silver and pearls outlining its edges.

'Bengal is the land of 700 rivers,' said Didi Ma, as they swayed forth. 'This is the Buriganga River. It belongs to Goddess Ganga. Magical herbs grow along its banks. Emperor Akbar drank water from the Ganges daily, had it delivered to him via a string of camels even when he was in Punjab, 200 miles away. Subedar Khan occasionally drinks it too. Some say it is amrita, the nectar of immortality.'

'How old is Subedar Khan?' asked Madeline.

'No one knows,' said Didi Ma mysteriously.

The river was vast. The docks were lined with fishing boats, sail boats, cargo ships and dinghies. Mughal architecture dotted the streets of the city that began as the docks ended. Domes of gold glittered under the tropical sun. Window panes and bolts that were in Paris made of iron were here gold or silver, intricately inlaid with gems. Never before had Madeline seen such opulence.

Vendors and merchants lined the road selling fascinating knick knacks. Children waved at the elephant. Beside them pack-horses laden with sacks of delicate muslin trotted by. Madeline strained to watch the fabric. It was so subtle yet elegant. True haute couture!

'Tell me about Ganga?' asked Madeline.

'Ganga was a female energy who loved the supreme male energy, Shiva. Shiva loved Ganga too because she was divine but his wife was possessive so Ganga could not be with him though she longed to.'

Didi Ma's face took on the same glow Madeline noticed on Abdul when he told a tale. It seemed Bengalis liked to talk.

'One day a fight broke out between the Devil and God,' said Didi Ma, animated. '60,000 people burned on Earth and were strewn as corpses. The smell of rotting flesh permeated the air. The people asked a rishi named Bhagiratha for help.

'Bhagiratha prayed to Shiva for salvation. Shiva asked him to pray to Ganga for she embodied the energy of water needed to heal and cleanse. Bhagiratha did sadhona to Ganga.

'Ganga heard his prayers and agreed to help but her force was too strong. She could not control her immense flow. She would drown Mother Earth. No one but Shiva could temper her vigour.

'Bhagiratha returned to Shiva for help. He was so sincere in his prayer that Shiva listened and let Ganga flow through him to Earth, cooling her without destroying her. So Ganga got what she wanted and was united with her lover forever.' Didi Ma's eyes glazed over as if remembering a past love of her own. 'Ah, here we are!' she said, catching herself. 'The famous Chowk Bazaar built by our Subedar.'

As the elephant and horses were handed to stable boys, Madeline eyed the bazaar. It was more splendid than she had imagined. Its roofs and walls were inlaid with rubies and emeralds. The bamboos structures within the bazaar were wrapped in strands of pearls and precious stones and held up shamianas of crimson velvet bordered with golden embroidery. After admiring a while, red and yellow spots danced before Madeline's eyes.

A cacophony of voices rose above the humid air. Merchants of every caste and creed offered a wide range of gastronomical treats. A man with a basket of fish called in base, 'Eelish maach, rui maach, pangash maaaaaaach.' A puffed rice vendor called out in baritone, 'Moori. Moori. Mooooooooooooori!' A halva maker called in high tenor, 'Lal Mithai. Chom chom. Golap jamunnnnnnnnnnnn.'

To Madeline, the Orient was extravagant and exotic. She had heard of the pomp and splendour of Bengal but her research had not prepared her for this. The sounds, colours, heat, life, everything seemed to be magnified many times over what she was accustomed to. It seemed she had been living life in bland and here it was lived in full flavour, hot and spicy!

Two kinds of Europeans arrived in Hindustan. Those arriving from Kandahar, passing through the Ottoman and Safavid empires, acclimitizing to the Islamic world as they moved in. Then there were those like her, arriving in India from a maritime voyage, with no idea of what to expect.

A rope ladder was lowered from the howdah for Madeline's descent. Dhand offered his strong arms to help her down. The courtyard of the Meena Bazaar was cordoned off with sheets of brocaded silk to ensure women shoppers a modicum of privacy. Didi Ma accompanied Madeline into the tent while the Subedar, Amir and Captain lingered by the periphery.

The Subedar commanded the elite force to wait at the edge of the caravanserai, much to Dhand's flustered opposition.

'It is not suitable for a Subedar to be roaming around without a fleet of bodyguards,' Amir Dhand opined.

'I have you, don't I?' the Subedar replied. He was at ease among people, his royal vestibules hidden.

Madeline stepped into the sequestered garden. Noble women gathered at stalls, haggling with merchants over necklaces modeled by statuesque slave-girls from Abyssinia. Their armed eunuchs and handmaidens busied themselves with a second tier of opportunistic merchants who ferried a cheaper range of goods in wicker baskets.

Women wore muslin, a simple cloth, fluid in form and graceful. Their hair was natural and they had virtually no cosmetic décor on their faces. Their inimitable glamour came from their confidence and dignity, and yes, of course, their jewels, each of which looked like it must have cost a fortune. Like women in France, they too wore their wealth on their bodies but in less cumbersome a manner, as valuable jewels not heaps of cloth.

Madeline became conscious of her own masses of cloth that weighed her down. Perhaps she could have done without the underskirt. Her pile of curls wig made her head look conical and accentuated her physical flaws: high forehead, uneven hairline. No one here wore wigs. Her frilly parasol blocked the scathing sun but made her even more conspicuous on the streets.

Madeline observed the elegant Mughal metropolis as every form of wonder unfolded before her. Parades of snake charmers, monkey dancers, fire spinners, magicians, astrologers, astronomers, yogis, sadhus, rishies, merchants, tailors, seamstresses, jewellers, cobblers crossed her path. Each street she peered into looked like a painting: fine architecture, gurgling fountains and gardens covered in roses, people clad in flowing outfits of sophisticated style.

Here the calls were different. 'Zabarzad, yaqat, ainul hirrat, ilmas…' she heard. 'Emeralds, sapphires, cat's eyes, diamonds…' Every where she looked, stones shined with brilliance. Merchants here had all the trimmings one could desire to adorn the finest of gowns.

A bevy of ladies were gushing and oohing in delight. Madeline stepped closer to investigate.

'Madam,' an atelier called out. 'This way!' With a flourish, he lifted a velvet coverlet to reveal his wares.

Madeline's eyes lit up. Brass trays displayed a rainbow of gems: rubies, emeralds, sapphires, amethysts, citrine and gold. Madeline gazed in awe at a solid gold rose with dewdrops of rubies nestled on a cushion of red satin.

'I have no words to express its beauty,' said Madeline, tears leaking from her eyes.

'The Sun blushes when he looks upon the jewels of this Empire,' said the atelier, his purple turban bobbing as he moved.

Madeline's eyes fell upon a cluster of pearls the size of oranges.

'You will not find pearls like these even if you dive into the seas of Heaven for all of eternity,' he said, following her gaze. 'The pearl fishers of Motijheel can remain underwater for hours without clips on noses or cotton in ears.'

Madeline was about to ask the price when Didi Ma interrupted.

'And that one?' she asked.

The atelier stroked his whiskers. 'That is a talisman to ward off the Evil Eye.' He handed her a turquoise with an onyx.

Didi Ma seemed to consider the item. Madeline was too moved by the sophistication of Mughal fashions to worry about the occult. Bengali women with their silk finery and dazzling jewels seemed to celebrate beauty in a way she had never known and she wanted to join in.

With Didi Ma's help, Madeline tried on several rings and purchased two. She applied henna to her palms and fingertips. She placed a bindi for her forehead. She had her hair braided with flowers. She allowed a perfumer to dab her neck and wrists with a crisp scent of sandalwood and musk.

A magnificent Quran sat on display with calligraphic letters and borders inlaid with gold. Bengal was a place where one could indulge in worldy pleasures or mystical magic. Suddenly the possibility for complete self-transformation loomed before Madeline. Here no one knew who she was. Perhaps here she could start over? She was wondering if she could cut ties with her old life and be free when she caught sight of something spectacular.

'That diamond! Can I see it?'

'Madam,' said the atelier, beaming with pride. 'You have an expert eye. Let me introduce myself, I am Jalal. This is the most precious piece in my collection.' He held it up for her to admire. 'In Hindustan, we prefer rough diamonds to polished ones because a virgin is more desirable than a woman who is not one!'

Didi Ma overheard this and puffing her chest, took a protective stand next to Madeline.

The atelier meant no harm. Besotted with his diamond he chattered on, 'This stone is from Kollur. Hundred and one percent authentic!' He passed it to her.

It was set between two sapphires. Madeline held it to the sun. It shattered light like a crystal prism into a rainbow upon her arm. Seeing a Kollur diamond with her own eyes for the first time gave her a giddy feeling in her stomach. This diamond was probably worth more than the King's crown! And here it was, sitting idly in the shop of a common atelier. She smiled politely and decided to come back later, alone.

CHAPTER 28

While Madeline and Didi Ma shopped, Shayista waited by the Meena Bazaar with Amir Dhand and Captain Costa. A jewellery vendor sauntered past, swinging her hips, a basket of bangles on her heads.

'Sire, I would prefer if we had at least six men with us to protect you from all sides,' Dhand complained. He held his zaghnol out in the open though his sheer size was intimidating enough. It was apparent he could fell trees with bare hands.

'I like to be with my people,' replied the Subedar. 'Not henpecked by guards. And if I must have guards with me, at least let them be of the female variety.'

'Female guards?' Dhand laughed.

'And why not?' said Shayista.

Dhand's cheeks filled with colour. 'Sire, there's something I've been meaning to tell you.' He couldn't bring his eyes to the Subedar's.

'What is it Amir?' Shayista said. 'More bad news?'

'No Sire. Some good news.' Dhand grinned. 'I found myself a wife.'

'You cheeky canker-blossom,' said Costa. 'Congratulations!'

'Yes, congratulations,' said Shayista. 'When did this happen?'

'I met her a year ago but was afraid to inform you. I didn't know how you would take it.'

'Why that's absurd,' said Shayista. 'I am your principal devotee. I shall orchestrate the finest wedding in Bengal. Who is she? A charming girl from your village?'

'No, Sire,' said Dhand sheepishly. 'She's one of the dancers.'

'One of the dancers?' Shayista stiffened.

'Yes, Sire.'

'One of *my* dancers?' he asked.

'Yes.'

'Hmm. You do know cavalry is not allowed into my harem?'

'Sorry, Sire. We're in love.'

'In love?'

Dhand nodded.

Shayista laughed and embraced his friend. 'May you be blessed with joy and happiness!'

'Thank you, Sire,' said Dhand.

'And many sons and daughters!' added Costa, slapping him on the back.

'Yes, especially a daughter,' said Shayista with a sigh.

'Thank you,' said Dhand, tears in his eyes.

'And how is our little one?' asked Costa, reminded of her now. 'How is Pari?'

Shayista looked away and shook his head.

'She is an angel,' said Dhand gently.

'But ... how?' Costa stammered, as he understood what Dhand meant.

'An unfortunate fever,' said Shayista.

'She was the prettiest lady I ever saw,' said Costa.

'A gift from God,' said Dhand.

Shayista nodded.

Costa dug into his pocket and retrieved a golden pendant which he handed to Shayista. Shayista looked at it closely. It said Al-Haq. His face drained of colour. 'You stole my daughter's necklace?' he bellowed.

'I'm a pirate,' explained Costa, anguished.

'It was a protective talisman.' Shayista's temper flared.

'I'm sorry,' said Costa, backing away. 'I'm a kleptomaniac sheep-biting clotpole!'

Shayista punched him, a heavy blow to his stomach.

Costa doubled over in pain, gasping to catch his breath. 'I'm sorry,' he wheezed. 'I'm trying to mend my ways. I'm sorry she's gone. I suffer your pain, amiga.'

Shayista heard the sincerity in his voice. Fighting Costa would not bring Pari back. He sat down with a doleful sigh and wrapped the necklace around his wrist.

Costa looked miserable. 'At least you have a home. I don't have that.'

'Home is not a place, it's a feeling,' said Shayista. 'I too am homeless. I have interred my heart.'

The emotional banter of two grown men feeling sorry for themselves made Dhand uncomfortable. He whistled out of tune and paced restlessly. 'Look around, Sire,' he said, retreating to his obsessive paranoia. 'You're not safe. Bengal isn't secure. There are lunatics among us.'

'Don't worry, Amir,' the captain chuckled. 'No scurvied, lice-infested oaf would attack the Governor in his own province.'

Scarcely had he uttered the words, a black-shafted arrow came tearing at them. Shayista's trained ears heard it whistling through the air in the nick of time. He pulled Dhand to the ground yanking him away from its arc of death. The projectile deprived of its intentional target lodged into the side of the tent.

It was a wooden arrow with a steel head and black feathers. Shayista recognized it as a Maratha weapon. There was no way to pursue the retreating assassin as a commotion erupted inside the tent creating pandemonium. Swarms of women, children, eunuchs, goats and sun-weathered poultry stampeded out.

Wading against the crowd, Shayista entered the tent to find Madeline staring into the beady eyes of a colossal king cobra that had crawled out of a discarded bag. She looked like she was going to faint. The serpent's girth was thicker than her waist and it raised its head to a formidable height of six feet.

The snake hissed its forked tongue. Madeline was standing too close to run, the kiss of death a sliver away. Didi Ma prayed fiercely off to the side, swaying to and fro, rushing her tazbi through her fingers. The others had pulled away leaving a wide circumference around Madeline and the viper.

Shayista leapt over people, pushed Madeline out of the way and brought out his harmonica from his pocket. The sudden movement infuriated the cobra. It snapped towards Shayista and hissed violently, looming up to its full length.

Shayista pressed the harmonica to his lips. Hypnotic notes emerged mesmerizing the snake and onlookers alike. Shayista swayed like a pendulum. The cobra swayed too, spellbound.

Amir Dhand rushed into the tent and gasped when he saw the Subedar in this life-threatening position. Moments later, the cobra slithered out of the tent into the foliaged fringes of the bazaar. The crowd cheered. Amir Dhand clapped. Madeline thanked her saints for the sweet escape.

'Are you alright?' Shayista asked her.

'You saved my life,' she said, her voice shaky.

'Think nothing of it.'

'Sire, you could have died!' scolded Dhand. 'You should have killed it.'

'You know killing snakes brings bad luck?' said Shayista. He was not generally one to harm wild animals.

'How did you do that?' asked Madeline.

'I have a friend from Beder graam,' said Shayista. 'The village of snake charmers. They'll teach you a thing or two if you visit their homes.' He had stayed with a kind family, disguised as a weary traveller, some years ago.

'The cobra was a decoy so the archer could escape,' observed Costa, arriving on the scene with the arrow that had been aimed at the royal insignia on Dhand's cloak.

There were letters carved down the side of the projectile.

'Return Kalinoor or risk eternal damnation.'

It seemed the Marathas were closing in on him. What more could go wrong in one week?

Chapter 29

At the Diwan-i-am the next day, a group of Sunni mullahs arrived as per the summons. Bhopal led them to the stand. Alim Al-Ali, cleric commander, bowed in first.

'Who are you to pass provincial policy?' asked Shayista.

Beads of sweat collected on his forehead. He ran his fingers through his unkept beard and stuttered, 'Your Highness, other provinces in the Empire are passing the same laws with the Emperor's approval.'

'I will never pass a law that prohibits girls from schools.' Shayista could not believe the ulema's gall. Was this yet another outcome of the diamond's curse or did they truly believe the solution to their disillusioned state lay in the exclusion of women?

'Women are like tamarinds,' a mullah piped in. He was young, his beard not fully formed yet. 'When we see them, we are tempted to suck. If they roam among us, can you blame us for desiring them?'

'Hence forth, rape will be punishable by castration,' said Shayista. The man balked.

'Allah has forbidden books by non-Mohammedans,' said another mullah. 'Only the Quran should be taught in schools and only the ulema are qualified to teach it!'

Shayista frowned. 'The density of your ignorance has obscured your view. Allah cannot be known through authoritarian dogma. To find Allah, one must journey into the question, 'Who Am I?''

'We know who we are! We are God-fearing men,' said Alim. 'We follow the rules in the Quran. Music is haram. No more qawalis!'

'Music is the highest form of worship,' said Shayista, though this was not the sort of sapient throng to appreciate esoteric lessons on Sufi secrets. 'I pray that Allah showers you with wisdom to clear your misconceptions.'

'Emperor Aurangzeb has disbanded the Mughal atelier in Delhi and the artists have come to you in search of patronage,' said Alim. 'We advise you not to give them employment in your court.'

'Your understanding of theology is weak,' said Subedar Khan, wondering how they knew this already. 'Your spiritual paucity is appalling.'

'What about jiziya?' said Alim. 'Aurangzeb has reinstated the tax for Hindus.'

There was no end to their intolerance. Their abhorrent desire to create division enraged Shayista. 'Bengal is a secular, liberal and enlightened social sphere. If I hear of any further complaint against women, children, teachers, Hindus, musicians, dancers or artists, there will be severe consequences.' His voice hovered above a lethal whisper. 'This is your final warning.'

What little confidence the mullahs had left dissipated. They dispersed in a hurry, tripping over each other on the way.

Bhopal lingered by the plinth. 'Don't worry, Sire,' he said. 'I have an idea.'

'Shall I send them to the gallows?' said Shayista.

'No.'

'Behead them?'

'No.'

'Musket fire?'

'No.'

'The plank?' offered Shayista. 'Feed them to the crocodiles?'

'NO!' said Bhopal. 'Why not buy the ulema's support? For all their talk of spirituality, they are really after your wealth. With a few lacs, you could build them a mosque like the Seven Domed one you built for the others. Give it eight domes?'

'Bhopal, I am ashamed of you. Would you really have me buy their loyalty? That would only empower them. Radical beliefs will destabilise Bengal if not rooted out. This might be part of the curse!'

'Curse?'

'Don't worry, Bhopal. I will handle it,' reassured Shayista.

'Be careful,' warned Bhopal. 'The Emperor arrives in a few weeks. He has ordered that the ulema be respected. We mustn't anger him.'

Shayista chafed at the advice. Now his chief revenue officer sounded like his wife. With the Nauraz fast approaching, there were bigger things to worry about than his nephew. Kalinoor was out to destroy Bengal. He had to be ready. He completed the public session then retired to his chamber to oil his sword.

CHAPTER 30

The next morning Madeline ventured out on her own to collect clues for her clandestine mission. She wore a pistachio green frock with a matching stomacher and petticoat but skipped the underwire and wig as the heat was unbearable. Finding a mahut to ferry her to the bazaar was uncomplicated. There were hundreds of people milling around the dock to serve the visitors from overseas.

Floating on an elephant along the banks of the Buriganga for the second time, Madeline thought of her precarious situation. From whispers in the salons of Versailles, she had learned of a group of jewel hunters called the Ruby Monkeys who lived in the hinterlands of Chatgaon and could reputedly locate any gem in the East. She had embarked on this journey in the hopes that she would be able to find them and they would help her map the mines. What would happen if things didn't go as she hoped?

At the bazaar, Madeline paid the mahut, straightened her gown and made her way to the meena tent. She walked straight to Jalal who was serenading shoppers. He recognized her and broke into a grin.

'Hello Madam,' he exclaimed. 'Is it my diamond that has brought you back?'

Madeline nodded.

He retrieved the stone from its stand and held it delicately between two gloved fingers. 'It weighs 319½ ratis,' he said with pride.

'How do you know it's from Kollur?' she asked.

'Kollur diamonds have a quality like water.' He held it up to the sun. A river appeared to run through it.

Madeline looked longingly at the specimen. 'How did you procure it?' she asked.

'My son,' the atelier boasted. 'Deccan sultans only allowed the purest souls to descend into the depths of the Kollur mines.' He dropped his voice to a whisper. 'My son has been there! He got this diamond himself but don't tell anyone.'

Madeline nodded, understanding the diamond was stolen.

'He is a fine boy,' said the vendor.

'He knows where the mines are?' Madeline asked with a fabricated nonchalance.

Jalal shook his head fervently. 'No, they blindfolded him, thank God. Such perilous knowledge is bound to corrupt one's soul! Only the Emperor's own men know the whereabouts. And perhaps the Ruby Monkeys.'

'Ruby Monkeys?' Madeline perked up.

'Diamond hunters, the best in the world,' explained Jalal. 'I've asked my son to visit them to get us some new gems but he is depressed.'

'Why?'

'I don't know really. He has no mother.'

'Perhaps I could talk to him?' offered Madeline.

Jalal was touched by her kindness. 'Alright, come back tomorrow?'

'Bien sur!' Madeline agreed.

She left the bazaar feeling elated. How quickly one's fate could turn in the Orient, land of possibility and wonder. She was one step closer to finding the Ruby Monkeys and mapping the Kollur mines! Who said one could not navigate one's destiny? Here she was, charting her way to royalty.

CHAPTER 31

Moonlight poured in through the broken doors of the empty classrooms. Champa arrived at the madrasa to find extremists had vandalized their premises, torn down book shelves, destroyed a map of Persia, stomped on their flower beds and killed their geese.

'Again?' she asked Guru Ma, choking on tears. 'Is this about the dance classes?'

'They were upset. Their meeting with the Subedar went poorly this morning,' explained Guru Ma, trying to restore order to the ransacked room.

'Am I wrong, Guru Ma, to teach the girls to dance?'

'There are as many paths to God as there are people in this world,' said Guru Ma. 'They are fighting for power. The ulema want to control our thoughts so they can control our resources.'

'What's the solution?'

'Dialogue, love, prayer,' said the headmistress.

'Can we really fight violence with love?' asked Champa.

'No but we can fight power with knowledge. The pen is mightier than the sword.'

Champa hugged Guru Ma. The woman who had been her pillar of strength looked fatigued and despondent. Champa couldn't help but feel guilty. Her own father was involved in these heinous acts of vandalism. The mullahs were bigoted and violent, a dangerous combination. She wished she could summon the djinn to frighten them off.

Chapter 32

Casting her fear of assailants aside, Nasim Banu returned to the pir. His outlandish offer to channel the spirit of her son was too tempting to turn down. She didn't expect much of it but then the pir had been so successful with her appearance of youth that she couldn't help but wish.

She had with her a gargantuan emerald necklace, an heirloom from Shayista's mother who received it from Emperor Jahangir when he married Nur Jahan. Set between two rubies, clasped in gold, nonpareil was its beauty. She presented it to Pir Baba, folded within a satin cloth of olive. She hoped it would secure his help.

The pir unfolded the cloth and stared at the gem, surprise superseded by fury. 'What is this?' he bellowed.

'An emerald, Pir Baba,' Nasim stammered, wishing her eunuch had come into the room with her.

'Have you no diamonds?' the pir demanded. Crazed eyes bore into her. 'Dark diamonds? Why didn't you bring me one of those?'

Nasim was perplexed. She had seen a black diamond once. Shayista had given it to Pari on her sixteenth birthday. It was indeed a remarkable stone, caught one's eye from a distance, but Shayista took it back when Pari died. He said he would give it to the daughter of the Persian Shah. 'I have a pink diamond, not a black one.'

'Liar!' fumed the pir, eyes demented with rage. A vein on his forehead throbbed.

Nasim considered running out of the room to escape his startling fury but the thought of Abul Fateh froze her feet. 'I might have a black amethyst, Pir Baba,' she offered.

Zulfiqar studied her face. At last he believed her ignorance. 'Listen carefully. The Subedar has in his possession a very distinct black diamond called Kalinoor. Bring me that diamond if you want to speak to your son.'

'But my Lord husband has given that diamond to the daughter of the Persian Shah,' said Nasim.

'Enough of these wild goose chases!' thundered the pir. 'Your husband planted that lie just as he planted so many others to protect the secret. Kalinoor is in Lal Bagh Fort. Search under every floor panel if you have to. I will not be set back again. Find me the diamond!'

Nasim had never been yelled at before. Too distraught to discuss any further, she excused herself and rushed out with as much composure as she could muster.

CHAPTER 33

The next day, Champa buckled under the pressure of the ulema's threats and decided to visit the Subedar to appeal on behalf of the madrasa. A lengthy line of people waited at the Diwan-i-am but a dwarf at the door ushered her in. Champa took a seat.

'The Amir-ul-Umra, Mughal Viceroy of Emperor Aurangzeb, Governor of Bengal, Subedar Shayista Khan cometh,' announced the dwarf.

Subedar Khan entered looking fierce and decorated. A generously embroidered sword belt held a menacing talwar sheathed in a case of bejewelled leather. His turban was pinned with an emerald broach. He had pearls around his neck. He looked nothing like the cloaked commoner she met in Jannat. Everyone bowed in taslim. Champa followed their lead, wishing she could get a closer look.

Subedar Khan sat upon a gem-adorned dais and gave the signal for the proceedings to begin. The dwarf led the first citizen to the stand from where he presented his woes. The Subedar voiced his verdict with unopposable authority and though he was severe with his punishment, he was not entirely unjust. Champa felt hopeful.

When her turn came, the dwarf led her to the stand and she bowed in taslim as she had seen the others do. Her hands were sweaty, her heart racing, her mouth dry. This was indeed the same man she had met earlier. Though shaven and well-dressed now, he had the same piercing brown eyes.

He recognized her too and did not conceal his surprise. 'You? Here?' he asked.

Afraid of losing courage, she launched into her plea, the way she had heard the others do. 'Your Highness, most just and clement of rulers, I have come to seek your support. I request protection for the girls' madrasa where I teach. Relgious fanatics are pestering us. I appeal to you for help.'

'No,' said the Subedar with finality. High on the pulpit, there was no space for negotiation.

What a brute, thought Champa, though this was not unexpected. A man who killed cats was capable of anything!

The dwarf urged Champa off the stand.

'But Sire, if these girls are denied education, they will grow up in darkness,' she squealed. Raising her voice louder, 'Surely this orphanage has a special place in your heart? It was built by your ...'

'There shall be no discussion,' snapped the Subedar. 'The Emperor has ordered us to respect the ulema.'

The Imperial guards edged towards her. Unable to touch a woman, they hovered by the stand, bewildered.

'But you hate the Emperor!' Champa said just loud enough for the Subedar to hear. She had seen his memories. She had seen the puffed-up Emperor presenting to his father a head on a platter. She had sensed the Subedar's deep despair. It didn't make sense.

'Enough!' thundered Subedar Khan.

Champa looked around the room. The grand durbar, the Persian rugs, the golden chandeliers, the guards in jewelled uniform. The Subedar concealed his beliefs and lied to the Emperor for this position of power. He was dishonest and weak. He would not help her. No one would. She would have to help herself.

CHAPTER 34

Shayista felt a pang in his heart as he watched Champa leave. So she was the new teacher in Pari's madrasa? He had thought she was just a quirky witch who danced occasionally at Jannat. Instead, she was a fiery young lady fighting for the empowerment of women. He regretted that her spark was directed towards him in anger. Was it true what she said? Did he hate his Emperor?

After sitting through a few more petitions, Shayista asked Bhopal to dismiss the court for the day. Hidden under his cloak despite the sun, he made his way to the stables.

He wanted to help Champa but to do so openly would jeopardize the school even further. There was Aurangzeb's spy among them and the ulema and the curse. He couldn't let others know that he cared about this school. All that he cherished perished. Did Kalinoor know about the madrasa already? Was that the next target?

Bageshri was happy to see him. Shayista patted his steed and mounted the jewelled saddle. He realized he was delirious, cogitating the consciousness of an inanimate object. Of course Kalinoor did not know about the madrasa. Of course there was no curse. There were only greedy men who wanted to establish oppressive power structures.

Shayista galloped out towards the madrasa and wondered how it had changed over the year since Pari had died.

Waves crashed along the banks of the Buriganga. Energy was eternal and connected but mortality felt finite and isolated. Beyond his duties, there was nothing he lived for. He was struck by the emptiness of his existence.

Pari had loved the madrasa. To protect her from danger outside the fort, he had tried to discourage her from getting too involved but she was born to love. No cage could hold her in. Finding him unsupportive, she had asked her tutor for help and sold her jewellery for funds. When he saw the strength of her resolution, he relented and financed the establishment. He gave her 1,000 gold coins and five boxes of books for the school library.

Shayista slowed his stallion to a canter as he approached the madrasa. It was apparent the premises had been vandalized. The doors were smashed in, trees hacked, swings torn. Surveying the ruins, his heart broke once again. For all the sophistication of Bengal, there were still so many fools.

Voices in the garden drew his attention. Concealing Bageshri behind bushes, he approached in stealth.

Champa was sitting with a group of girls under the boughs of a krishnachura tree. 'I have a treat for you,' she said. 'Look what I purchased from a hakim at the bazaar today.' She retrieved an object wrapped in silk and passed it to the girls.

'What is it?' asked Marium.

'A magnifying glass,' she said.

'Will we be able to see stars?' asked Rezina.

'It is not a stargazer,' explained Champa. 'It's a magnifying glass. It makes things appear larger than they really are. Look.'

Champa held the magnifying glass over a pile of dried leaves and caught a ray of sunlight. The glass concentrated the light to a pinpoint so fine, it burned a hole through parchment. The girls clapped in delight.

Shayista marvelled at Champa's teaching style. She was confident and bold. He could see the girls adored her. Mullahs with their misplaced understanding of Islam wanted to stop this? They dreamt of virginal houris in the cool pavilions of Paradise and for that reward they would blindly follow their leader without any questions. How could he explain to them that houris were not incarnations of heavenly sluts but symbols of unconditional love? How could he show them that the vilest sin of all was disrespecting life?

Shayista shuddered to think of Bengal under the leadership of men without hearts or imagination. These viruses needed to be exterminated one by one but who would do it? Was it his Destiny to destroy enemies ad infinitum? This was one responsibility he did not want but whom could he hand it over to? Pari was dead. Prince Azam was a deboshed fool.

That Ibrahim fellow had the brain of a barn swallow. Shayista's own sons were already deployed in rural regions, not capable of handling voluminous responsibilities. No competent leader had emerged to take the mantle of command off his shoulders.

Lost in thought, Shayista didn't realize Champa had caught sight of his shadow. Suddenly she was standing before him with a jade-hilted paper knife, coming out to protect her girls from the lurking stranger that she saw him as.

Shayista gently disarmed her with a crouching tiger strike that sent the paper knife hurtling across the garden without hurting her. He lowered his hood. Champa's jaw dropped as she recognized him. She fell to taslim.

'I need to talk to you,' he said.

She nodded and instructed the girls to take a recess. She led Shayista to the inner room where the headmistress was sitting at her desk, deep in study.

'Guru Ma, we have a distinguished guest,' said Champa. 'The Subedar of Bengal. Subedar Khan, this is Saraswathi Rai.'

Guru Ma bowed in taslim, astonished to see him. He bowed back in respect. They greeted each other as old friends, a relationship Champa had forgotten about.

'Why are you here?' Champa asked. 'You already denied us your help. What else could you possibly have to say? Or have you come to shut us down?'

Shayista's face was pained. 'I could not openly support the madrasa. That would make it a target. Your grandfather was right. Everything I cherish perishes.'

Champa's eyes showed that she understood what he said. 'What will you do?'

'I don't know yet. How does one destroy a curse? Perhaps it would be safest to close the madrasa for a while? I fear for your safety.'

'Champa Miss!' called a voice from outside. 'What is this word, come see?'

Called back to task, Champa walked out to assist the girl.

'Closing the school is not what Pari would have wanted,' said Guru Ma, carrying on the conversation.

'The mullahs have been indoctrinated,' said Shayista. 'How do I dissolve their delusions?'

'Your daughter knew the answer.' Guru Ma poured a glass of water for Shayista. 'Princess Pari was passionate about this orphanage.'

'It is dangerous to pursue certain paths,' said Shayista.

'History is shaped by the brave. The brave must take risks. To remain silent is to make space for the militancy of intolerance. One must uphold freedom.'

'As Pari did,' said Shayista, ruefully.

Guru Ma nodded. 'What a brave one she was. When you refused to fund the madrasa, she made arrangements to sell her own jewellery. The invaluable diamond, the ...' She stopped herself short.

'Sell what?' Shayista probed.

'Nothing,' said Guru Ma.

'Kalinoor?' he asked.

Guru Ma nodded.

'She told you about Kalinoor?'

Guru Ma sighed. 'She showed it to me once. She said it was hers to sell if she wanted.'

Shayista was not surprised that Pari didn't think for a moment to sell anything else from the palace, only her own jewels. 'Does anyone else knows about Kalinoor?' he asked.

Swati nodded. 'Only the gem merchant from whom Pari got a quote.'

Suddenly Shayista understood why Kalinoor had become the centre of attention. Word had gotten out. Pari had unintentionally let the secret slip. 'Merchant?'

'A French gentleman.'

Shayista let the bad news sank in. He asked Guru Ma not to tell anyone. For Pari's sake she promised. He left before Champa returned. He had been so careful about the diamond just so this wouldn't happen. Now greed was on the loose.

CHAPTER 35

Later that evening Champa prepared the antechamber for a séance. Dada wanted to summon the djinn to decipher where in Lal Bagh Fort the diamond was hidden. She hadn't told him about her meetings with the Subedar. She didn't like keeping secrets from him but securing help to save her madrasa was not something Dada would approve of. She lit the candles and incense when a frantic knock at the door interrupted her.

'Miss Champa! Come quick!' called a girl.

Champa ran up the stairs to find Marium crying.

'They are burning our books,' she sobbed. 'Guru Ma sent me to get you.'

Champa wrapped herself in a shawl and ran. 'Stay here, Marium!' she called over her shoulder. 'You'll be safe here!'

Champa's feet were moving faster than her mind, taking her somewhere … she realized she was running to the fortress. She was going to the Subedar. He had said he was on their side, right?

She arrived at the gates of the fort out of breath. She informed the sentry that she needed to speak to the Subedar at once. The sentry asked her to wait but she couldn't stand still while the school was burning. She turned and ran towards the orphanage.

Before she knew it, she heard horses' hooves behind her and felt strong arms sweep her up in one fluid motion. She found herself on a horse, powerful arms around her, galloping at full speed towards the madrasa. She knew it was the Subedar when she saw the hand holding the reins and recognized his scent: attar and smoke. He wore chain mail under his cloak and had slung cold, hard swords and axes to his body.

Champa felt a tightening in her heart. 'Don't hurt them,' she said to the Subedar. 'They are misguided.'

The Subedar growled. His eyes were crazed. They saw the flames leaping into the sky well before they reached the madrasa. The Subedar urged his masked horse to accelerate.

'Promise me?' she said.

'No one will destroy Bengal!' he shouted.

She dared not think what would happen next.

As they drew closer, they saw three dozen bearded clerics wreaking havoc. Thick smoke filled the air and the temperature was sharply warmer. In the epicenter of the chaos, was an elephant-sized pile of books consumed in flames, a luminous beacon of hatred.

The Subedar dropped Champa off a safe distance away, telling her to wait there. His soldiers huddled around him as he gave instructions. Champa could not hear him but she was surprised to see a leather-bound Quran in the Subedar's hand.

CHAPTER 36

Shayista stopped his horse at the gates of the school. The night was dry and the flames danced high into the sky. He opened the Quran to the first page and began reading.

> 'Iqra.
> Read in the name of thy Lord,
> Who has created man from a clot,
> Read! Thy Lord is Most Generous,
> He has taught by the pen,
> that which man knew not.'

His words rang through the still night with penetrating force.

'Who goes there?' a mullah called out.

Shayista repeated. 'Read! In the name of thy Lord who has created man.'

'Are you a soldier?' another mullah shouted.

Shayista repeated, 'Iqra. Read in the name of thy Lord.'

There was something eerie about a cloaked stranger reading the Quran by candle light upon a massive steed. The mullahs approached to get a closer look.

Shayista repeated. 'Iqra. Read in the name of thy Lord.'

'What form of demon are you?' cried a mullah.

'Iqra. Read in the name of thy Lord who has created man.'

The mullahs formed a cirle around the batty fakir, for that was what they hoped he was.

'Iqra. Read in the name of thy Lord who has created man.' Shayista held his ground.

Bageshri stamped his feet at the ground as the mullahs closed in on them with flaming torches. Still Shayista waited.

'Iqra. Read in the name of thy Lord.' Shayista read as though the mullahs did not exist.

One mullah grabbed the horse's reins and started drawing him in.

When the mullahs were close enough that he could smell their fear, Shayista shouted, 'IQRA!'

Suddenly, from behind a grove of trees beyond the gate, battle cries erupted, 'IQRA! IQRA! IQRA!' It was as if the forest came to life as Imperial guards swooped out of the foliage and upon the unsuspecting mullahs, tearing at them with swords, spears and axes. Taken by surprise, the mullahs were not able to defend themselves.

Swinging a wicked *Shashbur*, Lung-Tearer, Shayista bludgeoned the two mullahs closest to him. His spiked, sphere-ended mace struck each with such power, it brought their skulls caving down into their ribcages.

An uncontrollable fury rose within Shayista. Overcome by bloodlust, he butchered the unarmed men, yelling his battle cry: 'IQRA!'

Alternating between the shashbur and Azdahar, he decapitated or smashed the heads of mullahs, cracking them open like eggs, spilling their brains on the ground.

Over his shoulder, he saw a juggernaut plowing through. It was Dhand. He rammed his massive body into a group and flattened three mullahs at one go. Dhand's zaghnol came hurtling down on a fourth mullah, hacking off his torso.

Champa screamed. She had defied Shayista's order to wait outside and was now hemmed up against the burning pyre, attacked from two sides. One mullah was trying to fondle her. The other grabbed her choli and yanked it. Her breasts came tumbling out. Crossing her arms over her chest, she hollered for help.

Shayista spurred his steed forward and with two swift blows killed the mullahs who had cornered her.

The battle was over soon after it started. The remaining mullahs turned to run but Dhand closed in on them.

Champa grabbed a shawl from a dead mullah and ran into the school, hands clutched over her mouth. Guru Ma lay on the ground, a bloody cleaver lodged in her back. Champa tried to revive her. Alim cowered behind a table by her side.

Champa turned to him, livid. 'You killed her!'

Alim yelled back, 'It was her fault. She got in the way.' He had a knife in his hand. Before he could fling it at Champa, Shayista jumped to her rescue, bringing his shashbur smashing down on Alim's head.

Alim's body fell shuddering to the ground, the left side of his face obliterated. Champa kneeled by his side.

With difficulty, he said, 'Champa?' choking on his words, 'Am I dying?'

'No! No Baba, please don't die,' she sobbed.

Shayista reeled in surprise. The cleric commander was Champa's father? He thought of Ellora and Shivaji. Was history repeating itself? Was Bengal destined to suffer the same fate over and over again?

Champa tried to prop up Alim's body but he was too heavy for her. He collapsed, body convulsing, dead. Next to him, Champa fainted.

Flames billowed into the air. Swirling eddies of smoke rose to the sky. Shayista ran to the inferno. He retrieved a manuscript of Saadi Shirazi just as flames licked at its precious edges. He leaped to rescue a classic by Jalāl ad-Dīn Rūmī. His cheeks glowed. He was being cooked alive in an oven of books. He managed to rescue an illustrated rendition of Ibn Battuta's travels then noticed a manuscript by Omar Qayyam in the pile. He reached for it but could not grab it, unable to tolerate the scorching heat of its burning embers.

Dhand dragged Shayista away from the blaze. Grievous tears streamed down Shayista's face, his treasures consigned to flames. These were books that he and Pari and Dara had cherished, books that contained the finest thoughts of humanity. Dhand sat behind him silently.

Shayista turned to face the carnage. Three dozen mullahs lay dead in pools of blood, their white robes crimson, heads and limbs ripped off. Champa's words rang in his ears, 'Don't hurt them. They are misguided.'

Shayista wanted to cry. It was his duty as Amir -ul- Umra to put his emotions aside and be objective. He had to protect his people. Still, slaughtering fanatics left a bitter aftertaste.

Shayista stretched his hands out to the mound and shouted, 'O you who died trying to undo knots, you were born in union but you died in isolation. You went to sleep parched on the lip of an ocean. You died indigent on top of a treasure. If only you could see!'

He hated them. He hated their narrow dogmas. He hated their oppressive intentions. He hated their brutal violence. And he hated himself for stooping to their level to fight them. Was there no other way? His head was spinning. His soul was cracking. He wanted to vomit or die.

Then he saw Dhand. When the ground had dissolved into mud below him, when his base was fractured and worms had gnawed through the thin thread of Faith that had anchored him to sanity, when he was unmoored and lost between sorrows and memories, he found himself gently brought down to the humble ground, by his friend. When true love was convoluted, when Death beat its wings above him, when he had to slaughter men to save men and had lived beyond the years of his daughters, one thing could be counted on for sure. That was his friendship with Dhand. Dhand, standing there chewing dried fish, humming some song about love, out of tune. He was real.

The muscles in Shayista's arms and legs hurt. The weight of his chain mail tortured his back but this was nothing compared to the throbbing discomfort in his heart. He lifted Champa's limp body onto his horse and galloped to the fort.

CHAPTER 37

Madeline wore a double-flounced pagoda sleeved gown when she returned to the atelier the next evening. As promised, he had brought his son to meet her. Only a few years older than Madeline, he was a nervous gentleman, shy and bespectacled, nothing like his grinning father. He introduced himself as Mumin.

'I hear from my father that you are a collector of diamonds,' he said politely.

'Ah, well, not exactly. I am here to conduct an empirical enquiry,' Madeline said.

'She wants to know about Kollur diamonds,' Jalal piped in.

Mumin's eyes blazed with excitement. 'What distinguishes Golcondan diamonds from the vast majority of other diamonds is that they are pure carbon, devoid of nitrogen which present in other diamonds, lends stones a slightly yellowish tinge. As a result, diamonds from Golconda have a clear, transparent nature that makes them look like ice cubes. This is not to suggest that Kollur diamonds are always colourless. Occasionally, they are brown or pink, and still rarer are those infused with a delicate blush of blue or gray. They sell at three times the price of diamonds from other mines but really they are priceless.' He blushed. 'I am afraid I have said too much? I must be boring you.'

She had never met anyone as interested in the mineral aspect of diamonds as herself. Despite his unimpressive appearance, this man was learned. Madeline opened her notebook. 'Please, tell me more.'

'There are 23 mines in Golconda, 15 in Bijapur. There is one in Kollur that is special.'

'Have you been to it?' Madeline asked, hanging on to every word. There was something endearing about this man.

'I have been to the secret mine,' he said. 'It lies beyond the Valley of the Moon.'

Goosebumps rose on Madeline's arms. 'Can you show me on a map?'

'No maps mark the whereabouts,' said Mumin cautiously. 'Are you a cartographer?'

'No, a natural philosopher,' she said. 'It is of utmost importance to the medical world that you help me find the mines. The Deccan diamonds have healing properties that I must document for humanity.' Her lies were becoming increasingly outlandish.

Mumin seemed to believe her story. He nodded empathetically. 'The Ruby Monkeys can help you with your noble pursuit but Chatgaon is far from here.'

'What a fortunate coincidence, Chatgaon is where I am headed tomorrow!' said Madeline. Everything was falling into place. Luck was turning in her favour.

Jalal produced two cups of masala serbet.

'Shall I send a pigeon with word ahead then,' offered Mumin. 'Telling them you are on your way and have requested a meeting.'

'Thank you ever so much!' gushed Madeline.

'I travelled with a gem merchant who was a guest of the Emperor himself,' said Mumin. 'We travelled blindfolded. I brought one diamond back.'

Jalal held out the diamond on cue.

Madeline gazed at it lovingly as though it were her first born.

'With the sale of this diamond, I intend to pay for my son's wedding. What say you, Mumin?' Jalal ruffled his son's hair.

Mumin offered a weak smile.

'What's the matter?' asked Madeline politely.

'Nothing,' replied Mumin.

Jalal nudged him to speak up.

Mumin blushed. 'I'm not very charming,' he explained. 'Women find me boring.'

'Not at all! You are lovely,' Madeline blurted out.

Mumin blushed more.

'She said you're lovely!' said Jalal, slapping him on the back.

Madeline blushed too. What had gotten into her? The strangeness in the air had loosened her bearings.

'The finest diamond is not in Golconda,' said Mumin. 'It is right here in Bengal.'

'This one?' asked Madeline, gazing at his precious stone.

Mumin chuckled. 'Much finer than this one,' he said. 'It is known as Kalinoor.' He glanced around. 'Hauntingly beautiful but it brings bad luck to its owners.'

'Who is its owner?' asked Madeline.

'The Subedar of course,' said Jalal.

Madeline was unable to contain her surprise. She chatted a bit longer then thanked Mumin and his father for the serbet and headed back to the ship.

Her poor father had been imprisoned by King Louis for selling him fake pearls that he had meant to present to Madam de Maintenant for their wedding. To secure her father's liberty, Madeline had promised King Louis a map of the secret Kollur mines. France had yet to penetrate the diamond market. Tavernier was the only European with this information but he wasn't sharing it with anyone — especially not the King, now that he had fallen out of favour with the court. There was room for someone with ingenuity to make a name for himself. Or herself, as the case may be.

CHAPTER 38

Champa awoke in a most glorious garden. Around her blazing krishnachuras, shy lilacs, brooding jobas, cheerful hibiscus and elegant dalias vied for attention. A nearby fountain tinkled. Crickets chirped. The night was cool. She could smell rajni gandhas in bloom. Was this Heaven?

'You have been unconscious for three hours,' said a voice. 'Are you alright?'

It was the Subedar. He was not far away. Seated on a tree stump, he rubbed a burnt hand and watched over her. They were alone.

She wiped the soot from her face and stared at him. In his eyes she saw burning books and she remembered all that had transpired. Guru Ma ... Her father ... She began to sob.

'I have asked my guards to give them proper burials,' said the Subedar.

'You cannot quell debate through violence!' Champa lashed out. 'Killing makes you a murderer. Judging them makes you judgmental too. You rule with your false self not your heart.'

'I have made Bengal what it is today, an open and inclusive cosmopolitan of commerce and culture. Look at our growth.'

'Your growth means nothing to me. I live in the Alley among the squalid and forgotten. Your opulence is nauseating, built on the bones of defeated kingdoms. You pursue destruction. You forget that the purpose of life is not division, it is unity.'

The Subedar lowered his head.

'You killed my father!' she shouted.

'This is not what I wanted,' he said, saturated with her reproach. 'I am trying to save Bengal.'

'As if one man can hold back the tides of Destiny. Bengal will rise and fall and rise again, with or without you. Don't delude yourself,' said Champa.

'It is my destiny to destroy.'

'Not your destiny. Your curse.'

'My curse?'

'You were once a Sufi, my Lord. I saw it in your memories. Get rid of Kalinoor. It has cast a shadow on your perspective. Release darkness and let the light of God illuminate. Violence is not the path of Love.'

'Love?'

'Dialogue, education, love.'

'Did you love him very much?' asked Shayista.

Champa nodded. 'Did you love Pari?'

'More than life itself.' He looked lost. 'I built this fort for her.' He began to sob.

This Champa had not expected. The Tiger of Bengal was crying stretched out over a floral tile in his garden? Her anger abated and soon she was crying too.

'Forgive me, Champa,' he said. 'Forgive me.'

She saw the tatters of his separation and the suffering he bore. In the end, he had tried to rescue her and her school. 'No, my Lord, you need not apologize to me.'

'Shayista,' he said. 'I'm Shayista.'

'You are Talib,' she replied. 'Talib.'

'With the blood on my scroll, I can never be Talib again.'

'It is not too late to redeem yourself. Rule not with your sword but your heart. Promise me?' She lowered her eyelashes and opened his eyes.

Shayista nodded solemnly. He handed her a book he had saved from the fire. *The Travels of Ibn Battuta*.

'Marium's favourite,' said Champa.

'I know,' he replied. 'I heard you the other day. Thank you.'

'For what?' said Champa.

'You are right,' he said.

'And Kalinoor?' she said, heavy hearted.

'I will destroy it.'

She nodded, betraying her grandfather whose lifelong quest had been to find the dark diamond.

CHAPTER 39

Shayista's dream was fitful. He saw the mighty treasury of Bengal emptied of its magnificence, one hundred English ships laden with loot. He saw mullahs armed with guns and orthodoxy killing liberty and knowledge. He saw veiled girls dancing behind burning manuscripts. He felt his soul being rattled by a djinn then realized it was Dhand shaking him awake.

He was lying in his garden. The pain in his burnt hand throbbed. Champa was gone, only her shawl on his bench.

'Sire, you have a visitor,' said Dhand. 'It's that Dutch friend of yours. Says it is urgent.'

Shayista rubbed his eyes. His arms and legs ached, his back was sore. His stomach grumbled as he stumbled to the hall.

Van Diemen was waiting, dressed in silk pyjamas and a pink turban with a peacock feather. 'My Lord, I have disturbing news,' he said. 'An English flotilla arrived in Chatgaon today. They intend to form an alliance with the Magh Raja.'

Shayistan could not believe his ears. Was Kalinoor behind this ludicrous reality? He beckoned Dhand. 'I leave the fortress in your capable hands,' he said. 'I am going on a sea excursion.'

'Shall I ready the navy?' asked Dhand.

'No need,' said Shayista. There wasn't time to prepare for war. He would have to outwit the English rather than outfight them. He grabbed Van Diemen's arm. 'Vroomen, we're going on a trip.' Cursed or not, no diamond was going to destroy Bengal. Come what may.

CHAPTER 40

A tangerine sun stretched out its arms and kissed the sky. Morning larks sang tunes of hope. Black-capped kingfishers soared in freedom. Silver hilsa swam in bliss. Pink-headed ducks gathered to gossip. A kingfisher dove into the water and emerged with a hilsa wriggling in its beaks.

Madeline waved goodbye to Dacca as she reviewed her accomplishments. From Mumin she had learned of the Ruby Monkey's whereabouts in Chatgaon but somehow, the local air was starting to change her. She almost didn't care so much for her mission. She almost felt she could abandon her past and be a new person.

Leaning against the rails of Belo Diabo, dressed in a silk choli fringed with pearls, a bindi on her forehead, lapping in the melancholy of waves and fading city din, the options seemed endless. Perhaps she needn't return to France. She could stay, marry Mumin? O Bengal of endless possibilities.

She spotted the Subedar and an effete European man approaching the ship in a skiff. Captain Costa greeted them and soon Madeline learned they were coming along to Chatgaon. There was a diplomatic matter that needed the Subedar's urgent attention. This caused no delay as the Subedar had come with only a small bag carried by a man servant and the European seemed to have no belongings with him whatsoever.

The Subedar greeted her and introduced his scrupulously groomed friend as Vroomen Van Dieman.

Captain Costa hurled profanities at his crew as they skilfully navigated the ship out of the harbour and into the river. Lal Bagh Fort receded like a weeping rose on the riverbank. What once seemed impenetrable now seemed fragile.

Madeline's hat shaded her eyes and allowed her to watch the handsome Subedar unnoticed. He whistled a doleful tune. His European friend and Costa were discussing the journey.

'How long will it take to reach Chatgaon?' she asked. Her emerald bangles clinked as she moved.

'Ten days,' replied Costa. 'Two weeks if weather is rough.'

'What is Chatgaon like?' asked Madeline.

'Green hills, gentle valleys, wild beasts,' said Subedar Khan.

'Wild beasts?' Madeline paled.

'Cheetahs, tigers, elephants, boars,' said Subedar Khan.

'And savages,' said Captain Costa.

'Savages?' said Madeline.

'Maghs from Arakan,' said Costa. 'Yellow livered skunks with Eastern eyes.'

'If they catch you, they'll pierce your palms and pass a cane through the holes and then throw you onto a field to do their tilling,' added Van Dieman.

'Probably cannibals,' said Costa.

'Is it true?' Madeline asked the Subedar.

'Unfortunately, yes,' Subedar Khan nodded. 'They're a simple tribe but violent. No scruples to trouble them.'

'Notorious for slave trade,' said Captain Costa. 'Kidnapped Bengalis to sell to the Dutch East India Company.'

Van Diemen shifted uncomfortably.

'Mon dieux!' said Madeline, nauseous.

'Not any more,' said the Subedar. 'Raja is loyal to us now.'

Madeline noticed the Subedar and the Dutchman exchange an uneasy glance. She wondered if the Ruby Monkeys were Maghs. Would they help her find the mines or simply eat her up for supper?

Abdul appeared with a tray of goblets and a bottle of rum.

Costa poured out goblets for Van Diemen, Shayista and himself. 'To treasure,' he toasted.

'If its treasure you're after, best find yourself a map to the Kollur mines!' said Van Diemen, draining his goblet.

Madeline disliked him immediately. She'd have to keep an eye on this one.

The first couple of days of sailing passed pleasantly enough. Madeline studied her books, Captain Costa and the Dutchman got drunk, the Subedar was lost in thought. No one seemed to notice that she had abandoned her fontage or her wig. No one seemed to care if she wore no cosmetics.

The third evening, after they had anchored, there was something magical in the air: the stillness of the bay, the starlit night, the glimmering waves of the majestic sea. A light breeze swept Madeline's hair. Tranquility caressed her soul.

'How about a swim,' suggested Costa. 'Last of the sweet water. By tomorrow we will be pickled in salt.'

The Subedar agreed.

'A dip in the dark?' asked Van Diemen. 'You must be mad.' With that he pranced back to his cabin for the night.

Shayista and Costa moved to the side of the ship to disrobe. Costa shed his cloak, tunic and breeches. The Subedar removed his weapons, chain mail and clothing, leaving only a slender dagger strapped to his thigh. Madeline's voyeuristic eyes gazed at them from a distance, admiring Bagh Khan's chiselled physique and muscular pectorals. His body was as devastated by scars as his face. Many times he must have faced death.

The men dove into the cold water, yelping. The heat of the day dissolving as the water embraced them.

Madeline longed for cool water on her skin. After a tussle between reason and passion, she decided she would not live as a caged bird. Women too should enjoy a swim now and then. To their surprise, she jumped in, dress and all.

A vigorous current carried them far from the ship. Fresh water washed away their sweat and collected discontents. As they splashed, dusk descended and darkness offered a new intimacy. A space for freedom opened up. Soon they were laughing like children, refreshed, renewed, reborn.

A silent ripple disturbed the water.

Shayista's ears perked up. 'Shhhh.'

In the darkness, another stir.

'Crocodile,' said Shayista.

'Where?' shrieked Madeline.

'Let's swim back,' said Costa.

More ripples as a fearsome snout glided towards them, barely visible in the reflection of the stars.

'Take her back to the ship,' Shayista ordered.

'Let's go together,' said Costa.

'It's too close,' said Shayista. 'I'll hold it back. Take her.'

Madeline bit her lips to keep from screaming.

'I don't know how long I can hold it,' said Shayista, in a sharp whisper. 'Swim in zig-zags. Crocodiles only move straight lines. It'll get confused.'

'How long should I zig before I zag?' said Costa, reluctant to abandon his friend.

'Go!' shouted Shayista.

Costa and Madeline swam towards the ship.

Shayista took out the dagger at his thigh and held it above the water, waiting for the menacing snout. In seconds, the crocodile was on him, mouth open in a display of deadly gnashers. He dodged to avoid its jagged jaws, its hundred sharp teeth, then plunged the entire twelve inches of sharp steel into its head, between its two non-blinking eyes.

The creature reared up above water in maddened pain carrying on its back, Shayista, who held on to the knife with his right hand and the crocodile with his left. Its muscular tail crashed down on Shayista's head, knocking him under the surface. Submerged, he swallowed a gallon of water but did not release his grip on the dagger. The ebony river smothered him but he managed to resurface, gasping for air. The scuffle continued amid thrashing waves.

Madeline screamed.

'Keep going,' ordered Costa, pushing her towards the ship. The current was stronger than it had been earlier. They hadn't noticed how far they had drifted. Madeline panicked and started to cry.

'Come on,' Costa swam, dragging her along.

'I cannot believe this is happening!' she sobbed. She was not a strong swimmer.

The cloudy night closed in on them, obscuring sight of Shayista and the crocodile. Costa pulled Madeline along to the ship and hoisted her up to the rope ladder on the side. Wet clothes clung to her body. Madeline tried to cover her form with her hand.

'Climb,' he barked.

She blushed and clambered up the rope, her pink derriere visible under her skirt. She turned to help him up.

'Get me a blade,' he yelled.

She nodded and ran, calling for the crew and returned seconds later, with a cutlass and two pirates. She passed the weapon to Costa.

'Get the skiff,' he commanded the pirates.

Madeline watched as the pirates guided the skiff towards Shayista, following his voice as the night's darkness obscured their vision.

When they returned to the ship, Madeline embraced Shayista in gratitude.

'Where's the crocodile?' she asked.

'Floating downstream,' replied Shayista. 'Dead.'

CHAPTER 41

Gloomy clouds wrapped dawn in a shroud of grey. The galleon pulled into the harbour of Chatgaon. Shayista gnashed his teeth, expecting to see a row of spiked heads and a chorus of mourners. What he saw instead was worse. There were the usual galleys, cargo ships, noukas and merchant vessels but dwarfing them was a massive English Man-of-War, cannons glaring from its sterns.

'Porto Grande. Here we are! Lower the anchor. Secure the topsails,' Costa ordered.

'How many men aboard that ship?' glowered Shayista.

'Three to four hundred soldiers,' Costa said, sliding out a spy-glass for closer inspection. 'It's a 48-canon warship. What's going on?'

Van Diemen nodded. 'Have I ever given you faulty news, Sire? You can rely on me.'

Shayista cocked an eye brow. 'Can I?'

'Should we send word of your arrival?' asked Costa.

'No,' replied Shayista. 'First let's investigate.'

'I know just the place,' said Van Dieman.

The three men rowed to shore and hired steeds. Reins loose in hand, they galloped into Chatgaon, Van Diemen in the lead. Soon they arrived at a dingy tavern at the edge of town. It was not the only one on the street but the busiest of the lot. They tethered their horses at the gate and walked in, cloaked.

Within the walls of the seedy establishment were intoxicated merchants: Maghs mostly, mingling merrily with pretty whores. The peeling paint and threadbare cushions seemed to have no effect upon the clientele. It was clear from the bustle that the inn keeper did not need to worry about the finer details to secure his business.

A bar girl greeted them. 'Vroomen! Back so soon? Where have you come from?' she asked. She was broad shouldered, rouged lipped, flamboyant, wearing a showy blouse and a gaudy yellow ghagra choli. She was almost as tall as him.

'Here and there,' replied Van Diemen.

The bar girl laughed. It was then that Shayista saw she was actually a *he*, a hijra cross-dresser. Shayista had heard of the transvestites of Chatgaon but he had not met one before. Many had been captured and forced into slavery by the Portugese but a small community continued to exist.

'Tasty wench, get us some wine,' said Van Diemen to her. She strut forth to serve them.

In her absence Vroomen explained that she was a collector of secrets. Shayista realized she was probably the lady spy Van Dieman mentioned earlier in Jannat.

When she returned, she poured for Costa first, leaning in suggestively. 'O Ma, you're a nice one. Muscle-muscle,' she grabbed his biceps. 'Are you a hatman too?'

'Hatman?' asked Costa.

'That's what they call the English,' explained Van Dieman.

'Like the soldier over there.' She pointed to a brawny man with a pink face and freckles. He was sprawled in the far corner of the room, naked. His arms were draped over two whores and his red hat covered his privates.

'Who's that?' asked Shayista.

'I'll tell you but it'll cost you,' said the hijra.

Shayista passed her a coin.

'The Hatman is going to sign a treaty with the Maghs,' said the hijra, slipping the coin into her choli.

'A treaty for what?' asked Shayista.

'I'll tell you but it'll cost you,' said the hijra.

Shayista slipped her another coin.

'For permission to dock in Chatgaon. From there they will amass their forces to invade Dacca.'

'I don't know who to kill first!' said Shayista. 'Dhama Raja or the pesky Company men?'

'Dhama Raja, if you ask me,' offered the hijra, though no one had asked her. 'The English have offered him a diamond and for this he risks the safety of our people.'

'Diamond?' said Costa. 'What diamond?'

'I'll tell you but it will cost you.'

Costa grabbed the hijra's choli and flashed his cutlass.

Van Dieman gasped.

'I believe you've paid enough,' said the hijra, slipping out of his hold. With exaggerated gesticulation, the story was told.

'The noble Candasu Dhama Raja died last year and so ended the golden age of the Arakan court. He was a humble Buddhist and fair to Hindus but he was betrayed by a powerful lord of Laung Krak who had an intimate relationship with his Queen. Together they used black magic to evict him from the throne. When he died, his eldest son, Uggabala, entered monkhood to avoid being killed. The kingdom was without a king till Wara Dhama Raja, opportunist that he is, used his muscles to take the throne.'

Shayista recalled Dara's noble offer to enter monkhood.

'Wara Dhama Raja is neither Buddhist nor Hindu. He is a faithless man who values only money. The English have promised him a jewel from the Subedar's treasury, an ancient diamond that the Tripura Kings believe holds Goddess Kali within it. The Tripura Kings have offered Dhama Raja his weight in gold in exchange for the diamond. For gold, he will sacrifice the glorious kingdom of Arakan! What will happen to us when the nefarious, iniquitous, depraved Bagh Khan finds out?' The hijra looked sincerely frightened.

'Do you have it?' Costa whispered to Shayista.

Shayista groaned. Once a pirate, always a pirate.

'Another drink,' said Van Diemen. The hijra scurried off.

'Sorry she called you nefarious,' said Van Diemen, shifting uncomfortably.

'I'll let it pass,' grumbled Shayista.

'And iniquitous.'

'Hmmm.'

'And de ...'

'Enough!' Shayista watched the two girls attending to the English man. One fanned him with a banana leaf while the other tried to nudge him upright. The man couldn't hold his head straight, slipping in and out of a drunken stupor.

Leaving his friends to their drinks, Shayista walked over to the hatman's whores. 'Is this fellow disturbing you?' he asked.

The first woman had crescent moon eyes, a full moon face and mango bosoms, a typical Magh beauty. 'Hatman won't pay,' she said. Her eyes jolly, despite the problem on her hands. She sized up Shayista and offered him a seductive smile.

'Who is he?' asked Shayista.

'Don't know his name,' said the other whore, running a finger over Shayista's arm.

Shayista grabbed the English man by his shoulders and drew him upright, then punched him twice in the gut. That brought him staggering back to his senses. He fell to the floor and vomitted.

'Hey there, easy now,' said the whore. 'No need to get aggressive.'

Shayista drew his sword. Onlookers hushed, the whores squealed, Costa and Van Diemen watched with amusement. The Englishman looked perplexed.

'Who are you?' Shayista demanded.

The Englishman stuttered something inaudible. Shayista punched his nose. There was a sickening crunch and a howl of pain. The Englishman reeled, blood splattered on the walls. He clasped his hands over his face.

'Who are you?' Shayista repeated.

'William Hedges.'

'Why are you here?' Shayista demanded.

'Who the bloody hell are you?'

Shayista brought his sword hurtling down and chopped off the soldier's thumb.

William screamed, hand over the oozing wound, and reached for his thumb on the ground. Onlookers were horrified.

'Specifics,' said Shayista.

'I'm with Admiral Nicholson. Our orders are to seize and fortify Chatgaon, demand the cession of the surrounding territory, conciliate the zamindars, establish a mint and enter into a treaty with the Magh Raja.' William said it all in one frightened breath.

Shayista's rage towards the Maghs reignited. They had already stolen a precious treasure from the Mughals, Shah Shuja's daughter,

Shayista's own grand-niece. They raped and burned her, despite Mir Jumla's pleas for mercy. And now this?

'Fortify Chatgaon?' Shayista probed.

'Admiral Nicholson was meant to come here with twelve ships, 200 cannons, 200 muskets and 600 men. 400 more would join us from Madras.'

'200 cannons and 200 muskets? Ha! The English don't have enough saltpetre to fire that,' said Costa, joining them.

Costa was right. Shayista had banned the trade of saltpetre. There was reason to doubt this alehouse conspiracy. 'Where's the rest of the fleet?' he asked.

'The other ships didn't make it. Couldn't negotiate the storm. Landed up in Hooghly. They're anchored off the Company's factory waiting for Mr. Charnock and the reinforcements.'

'Why does a small company from a tiny archipelago at the edge of the Atlantic believe it can conquer the world?' asked Shayista, rherotically. Before William could answer, he sliced off his arm.

William screamed in anguish.

'Get on your horse,' Shayista ordered. 'Alert the Raja that the Subedar's contingent will be arriving soon. He is to meet the Subedar at the docks in the morning.'

The Englishman nodded, whoozy from pain and blood loss. Holding his hat in front of his nakedness, he limped out of the tavern.

Shayista wished he'd asked Dhand to send reinforcements but it was too late now. Leaving Vroomen behind, Shayista and Costa rode back to the ship to work out a plan. The English were outfitted with a warship and weapons, the Magh warriors were fierce and on home terrain. Together they had every advantage. How would they get out of this one?

Champa had warned him that violence was not the way. She suggested education, dialogue and love but Shayista felt a vengeful rage rising within him. He would tear apart his enemies bare-handed if necessary before he would let any harm come upon Bengal.

Chapter 42

Confidence is the precursor to victory so Madeline puffed up her chest and marched, chin high despite her tremulous heart. Abdul had rowed her ashore and pointed her in the direction of Magh Bazaar. Her palms were clammy, nipples erect, goosebumps revolted on her arms.

The Ruby Monkeys were to meet her at the bazaar. Mumin had set up the meeting. She wondered what sort of men the Ruby Monkeys were. Would the same rules of negotiation apply? Could all men regardless of their habitas be purchased at a certain price? What currency did the Maghs value? Not human skulls, she hoped.

The crowd at the bazaar was dispersing, the evening's melancholy set in. Magh merchants packed their wares: silver scaled fish, chicken, ducks, leafy greens, turmeric and pineapples. Astonishingly, they were all women and all topless. They wore woven skirts around their waists and hundreds of strings of beads on their necks. The older ladies huddled around bamboo bongs smoking, their crafts packed into sacks next to them. Madeline watched discreetly, too polite to get a good look.

The Maghs were short and slightly built, averaging less than five feet in height. They seemed pleasant enough, not wild or savage. She tried to imagine Magh Bazaar twenty years earlier when it was a slave market. Nothing of that remained. But Madeline knew all too well that history repeated itself and wondered what that meant for Bengal. Would they be selling humans once again, three centuries later? She shuddered. Soon this ordeal would be over and she would have a place in society safe in France.

'Mademoiselle Du Champs?' said a voice.

It must be him, she thought, right where Mumin had said he would be. The Ruby Monkey approached her, eyes darting like stalked prey. Madeline disliked him immediately. He was a stocky man but his movements were contained like a seasoned thief who could come and go without displacing a feather. The thorny problem with thieves of this calibre was that they were as likely to steal from their friends as their enemies.

She tightened her grip on her purse and followed the Ruby Monkey away from the market into the hilly woodland. The night was a symphony of crickets, owls, bullfrogs and tropical monsters creeping around her. She had travelled from France to Bengal with seafaring thugs, timid she was not! But in the throbbing bamboo grove of wild and eerie sounds, she found she regretted her rash idea. She wondered where the Ruby Monkey was taking her. At least he had a lantern.

'Did you come alone?' he asked, as they walked down the hillock.

Madeline nodded.

'Stay close to me,' he said. 'Or be eaten.'

'Tigers?' she asked, anxious. He was shorter than she. Would he be able to protect her?

He showed her a bamboo lute. He put it to his mouth and blew out a pea-sized dart that flew with tremendous force into a tree.

Madeline was doubtful that this bamboo shooter would stop a tiger. It would barely disturb a cat.

'The dart has been dipped in the saliva of a poisonous frog,' he explained. 'It will freeze the tiger's muscles and kill it in less than one minute.'

Poisonous frog saliva? Madeline was intrigued. She would ask for the details later. They walked through a patch of reedy ferns to a row of huts balanced twenty feet above the ground on bamboo stilts. He stopped at the last hut and pointed to the cane ladder.

Madeline's feminine instinct told her not to climb into a secluded hut alone with an unknown man who was armed.

'We build our homes high,' he explained, sensing her hesitation. 'It keeps us safe.'

'From tigers?' she asked, afraid of man-eaters.

'No,' he said. 'Tigers can climb.'

Every inch of her body tightened with fear.

'The height protects us from wolves.'

Aaahooooooo! As if on cue, a haunting howl cut through the night, followed by a choir of canine replies. Madeline crossed herself, whispered a prayer to Saint Anne and hurried up the ladder.

Inside, the hut was spacious, roomier than it appeared from the outside. A single room lit with candles. The floor was of woven cane. Silk cushions were laid out and scattered with flowers. Clay diyas with floating hyacinths fragranced the air.

'Chief will be here shortly,' he announced, dropping his shifty sideways glancing habit. 'I am Diren.'

Madeline forced a polite smile. Soon the ordeal would be over and she would return to Minaloushe and warm baguettes. She could almost hear him purring by her ear, she could almost smell the butter, when THUD, Diren fell to the ground, bowing in respect.

A woman entered: petite, bald, wrinkled and topless. She looked perhaps three hundred years old. She walked to the cushions and sat with her toes pulled up over her thighs, a lotus upon a throne of flowers. Her neck was covered in necklaces. She wore a wreath of yellow leaves. In one hand she held a bell. In her other hand, a small club with spherical heads. Her scent was citronous.

'I present to you our high Priestess, Chief of the Ruby Monkeys,' said Diren.

Madeline's eyes were startled saucers. In Paris and Versailles, they boasted of progress, prided themselves on intellect and liberality, yet they had not celebrated a woman leader. Here, in the backwoods of Bengal, an impish old lady was revered as chief. Stupification transformed into veneration. Madeline bowed as she had seen Diren do.

The Priestess Chief laughed. Her ample bosoms jiggled, sagging down to her belly. She uttered a few sentences. Madeline could not understand a word but she knew what was asked because of her tone and inflections.

'Greetings,' said Madeline. 'I am Madeline Du Champs.'

The Priestess Chief drew Madeline into an embrace, repeating her name gleefully, mispronouncing it as 'Madli' and then sang it in a catchy tune ending with a snap of her fingers. Her cheer was contagious. It was as though they were old friends and this was a wonderful reunion. Madeline felt at ease.

'I am grateful to have been granted your audience. I know you are much sought after,' Madeline said formally.

The Priestess grinned. Diren placed a three-foot bong before her and lit it. It was almost as tall as she. She took a few deep breaths and with each exhale, progressively released the tension in her shoulders and around her eyes. When she was satisfied, she grinned at Madeline, a wide, toothless grin. Her skin glowed like a plum.

'Is it a gem you seek?' asked Diren.

'No,' said Madeline. 'I seek knowledge about the way to the diamond mines.'

Diren translated Madeline's request to the Priestess Chief who continued grinning. She said many things to Diren and gesticulated wildly.

'The Diamond Way is achieved through meditation,' Diren translated at last.

Madeline frowned. 'Meditation? But I don't know how to meditate.'

Diren looked shocked. He turned to the Priestess and translated. She then looked shocked too. Again she launched into a series of animated words.

Diren turned to her and smiled. 'Priestess says the way to the diamond is through the experience of ultimate truth. First you must empty your mind of the five poisons.'

'Poisons?' said Madeline alarmed. 'What poisons?'

'Desire, hatred, delusion, greed, envy.'

'Good heavens, and how shall I do that?'

'With a vajra!' said Diren.

'What is a vajra?' she asked.

'A diamond.'

'Which diamond?'

Diren tried to translate her question to the Priestess. The petite woman giggled and gesticulated as she tried to convey a message.

Diren turned to Madeline, exasperated. 'The vajra is the only diamond of any real spiritual value. It may be used to slice through the Illusion and arrive upon Bliss.'

'But where do I find such a diamond?' said Madeline. 'Is there a map?'

'The map is coded but our Priestess Chief is a Boddhisatva. She can show you the way to Enlightenment.'

This time Madeline laughed. 'No, no, you misunderstood me. I am not looking for Enlightenment, only the diamond mines. Diamonds, you know, like gems, but harder.'

This time Diren's face lit up. 'Gems? All you want are gems? Ha, ha, ha. No problem. Do you like rubies? We have a ruby the size of a sparrow's egg.'

'No!' said Madeline.

'Alright, no rubies. Topaz?'

'I don't want gems. I simply want to make a map.' She felt like crying.

'Map?' asked Diren puzzled. 'You travelled to Bengal from France to make a map?'

Madeline nodded. 'And for freedom.'

The Priestess whispered a few solemn lines and Diren translated, 'If it is liberation you seek, the only map you need is in your heart. Release the paradigms that imprison your spirit to find your true nature.'

This conversation was not going where Madeline expected but it struck a chord. In Bengal, without the prison of identity, routines, obligations, or a past, she felt liberated. She felt free to be herself.

'Priestess says you are beautiful so emeralds will suit you,' said Diren. 'You like emeralds?'

'No, merci,' said Madeline. His words wooed a blush to her pallid cheek. 'Please ask her, would she happen to know the whereabouts of the unchartered territories of Kollur?'

'Kollur?' said the Priestess.

Madeline nodded.

The Priestess took in a drag from the bong and shut her eyes, rocking back and forth in a trance. When she opened her eyes, she motioned Madeline to come closer.

The Priestess ran her wizened fingers through Madeline's hair. Her stroke was calming. Madeline noticed her mottled scalp, beneath her diaphanous silver hair. She smelt of wet leaves and departed lovers and ancient truths and fresh coriander. She emenated grace, elegance and untold strength.

The Priestess passed Madeline the bong and insisted that she take a puff.

'No, no!' Madeline said.

'Don't worry,' said Diren. 'It's herbal.'

Unable to talk her way out of the situation, Madeline arranged her lips around the rim of the bong. She took a tentative puff and erupted in coughs.

The old woman giggled, toying with her hair.

Madeline experienced a tingling sensation and then an inexplicable tenderness for the Priestess Chief and for the natural beauty around her and for life in all its glory. Everything seemed to be infused with love. She felt outrageously mirthful.

'Chief says she does not know the location of the Kollur mine,' said Diren.

From one extreme, Madeline swung to the other. The Ruby Monkeys were not going to help her ... After all she had been through, nothing could be more wretched. Her father would never be released. She would never find a husband of value. Before her stretched the dismal inevitability of poverty and loneliness.

'But,' Diren added, 'She knows someone who does. If she tells you of him, what can you offer in return?'

Finally Madeline was getting somewhere. 'Just name your price,' she said, revealing too early her eagerness.

'Chief wants your hair.' Diren brandished a shiny blade.

Madeline shrank. Had Diren mistranslated? Had she misunderstood? Did they want her HEAD? 'My hair?' she asked, pulling a frizzy coil out to its tip.

'Yes,' said Diren. 'I will cut it, if you permit?'

Madeline mulled over the suggestion. She had never considered her chestnut tresses valuable. Hidden under fashionable wigs, her hair was a bother: hot in the summer, itchy in the winter. Only in the anonymity of Bengal had she discarded the norms of her society and travelled without a manteau.

She saw herself for a moment through the eyes of the Priestess, a sea-born Venus. Hair was only a material halo, superficial and inanimate. The Priestess, without hair, clothes, jewels or youth, was true loveliness. Madeline nodded, ready to discard her distorted ideals of beauty.

The Priestess clapped her hands in delight. With a wide-toothed comb, she ceremoniously combed Madeline's hair down and pleated it with a strand of jasmines. She tied both ends and held it out for Diren to cut.

As the blade snipped through the braid, shortened strands of Madeline's hair bounced below her chin. She swished her bob side to side and took in a deep breath of freedom. She was more than flesh or bones or hair. She was more than her past or her present. But what was she? Who was she? Had she travelled across the world to lose herself or find herself?

The Priestess rubbed the braid against her cheek, cooing softly as though it were a sparrow perhaps or a kitten in her hand.

'Priestess says one man can help you. His name is Tavaji,' said Diren.

'Where can I find him?' asked Madeline.

'He lives in the hut under the pomegranate tree at the edge of the bazaar,' said Diren. 'Beware. What you desire and what you need are not always the same.'

Madeline thanked them for their help and made her way back to the beach to find Abdul and the rowboat. It was too dark to search out Tavaji's hut. She would return in the morning.

CHAPTER 43

'I will not tolerate subverters,' said Shayista when the Magh Raja arrived at the docks the next morning.

Wara Dhamma Raja, a squat, slovenly man, fell to the floor in taslim. With him were William Hedges, arm in a sling, and a bespectacled Company representative, presumably, Admiral Nicholson.

Van Diemen, slightly sobered, arrived in tandem, wondering what was going on. Shayista was happy to see him there, news would spread quickly.

'Your Highness,' stuttered the Magh Raja. 'O, Brightest Sun of the Mughal Empire, we were not expecting you. We have not had time to prepare a proper peshkash. Forgive me. As a token of my goodwill, I present to you these three elephants and golden howdahs laden with pineapple, guava and banana. Do you like fruits?'

Shayista glared at him.

The Raja shrank like a child. His eyes were fearful, his chin defensive. His body language revealed the jarring discord between his words and the truth.

Shayista fingered the hilt of his sword and contemplated a quick execution of the Raja. Or perhaps he should sew him up in the carcass of a dead jackass. 'What business do the English have here?'

A torrential sweat broke out on the Raja's forehead, a pained smile on his face. Admiral Nicholson adjusted his spectacles thoughtfully, twiddling his nervous thumbs. William Hedges was pale as a ghost.

Shayista called William forth. The man bowed before him. Shayista grabbed him by a fistful of hair and with one strong swipe, relieved him of his troublesome head.

'This is what will happen to you!' he said to Admiral Nicholson, holding the head out for him to see. Blood dripped down the severed neck and onto his sleeve. 'Will anyone dare steal from Bengal? Anyone? ANYONE?'

A moment of stunned silence followed.

Shayista wondered if they would cower before him or assassinate him right then and there. He had no reinforcements on the way, only his bluff. He hoped they would not notice the beads of perspiration on his brow.

Raja Wara Dhama threw himself at Shayista's feat, grovelling for mercy, promising to pay indemnities, swearing to never entertain English guests again.

Shayista kicked the recreant aside and turned to Admiral Nicholson. 'And you?' he asked.

The Company man's face drained of pallor, his voice trembled. 'We shall return to England at once. This is an utterly inhospitable place infested with mosquitoes, snakes and tigers.'

True to his word, the admiral led his men to Hooghly, and from there, retreated as fast as he could, across Ispahan, Shiraz, Basra and Mashhad, across Aleppo and back to England, putting as much distance as possible between himself and the diabolical Viceroy of Bengal.

Shayista, Costa, Van Diemen and the crew rejoiced at the fortuitious victory.

CHAPTER 44

As she ripped through the bramble in the morning, Madeline wondered what was happening to her. The flimsy foundation of her beliefs was crumbling. She came to Bengal to map Kollur as a last attempt to clear her father's tarnished name so she could find a suitable husband who would secure her a place in aristocracy but now she wasn't sure if that was what she wanted.

She had left Abdul and the rowboat at the water's edge and was making her way to the bazaar to find the pomegranate tree. What an absurd predicament she was in. She had voyaged to Bengal to negotiate her freedom and what she found instead was an exotic new perspective. Now Paris seemed dull. Marriage seemed dreary. The rigid social structures of France seemed drab. Her insipid dream had lost its charm.

In Hindustan, with the startling loss of familiarity, Madeline found a space to be uncensored. She could embrace topless strangers, experiment with novel coiffeurs, consume hallucinogens and swim in rivers. Ensconced in obscurity, she found the courage to be her natural self: no expectations to conform to, no norms defined.

The pomegranate tree was just where the Priestess had said it would be and next to it was a well-maintained hut. She knocked at the door but there was no answer. She wondered what Tavaji would be like and poked her head in.

A portly man in a white kurta and a turban wrapped with pearls was busy at a desk, his back to the door. Madeline coughed politely to announce her presence.

The man whipped around, his lips around a bamboo shooter, pointing a poisonous dart at her. She reeled in shock.

He put the weapon down. 'Madeline Du Champs? I have been expecting you,' he said with an expansive smile and bow.

'Mon dieux! Jean-Baptiste, you nearly gave me a heart attack.'

The florid Frenchman had gone local. He was dressed in full Mughal attire. He wore an embroidered vest and gemstones on all his fingers, a golden cummerbund and string of pearls. Sapphires twinkled in his turban knot. Even in his outlandish costume he looked impeccable. She was suddenly conscious of her coif.

'And you, in Hindustan, mais pourquoi?' she asked, though she knew perfectly well the answer to her question.

Jean-Baptiste Tavernier was a notorious hedonist and a spy who romanced princesses from Persia and wrote obscure travel books. He was not only a diamond merchant, he was the pioneer of the diamond trade with Hindustan. If he was in town, there could be only one sparkling reason why.

'Nothing like a bit of tropical air to keep a man young,' he said. 'Besides, I do prefer the brightness of a copper faced lady to the pallid hue of the European damsels. Looks like you've gotten some sun. What brings you out this far?'

'I have come for herbs,' stammered Madeline, with a sinking feeling in her gut. Tavaji was not going to help her at all. She was chasing a chimera.

'Isn't destiny splendid?' Tavernier laughed. 'I was wondering how I would reach you, and voila, here you are at my door step! Incroyable, n'est pas?'

With a heavily bejewelled hand on her shoulder, he propped himself up and leaned on his walking stick, a polished piece of mahogany with a golden handle the shape of a serpent. He walked over to a stand with a decanter and two glasses. 'This tribal region is titilating, is it not? Have you tasted their rice wine?'

Madeline shook her head. His slurs suggested that he most certainly had.

'Would you like some?' he asked, waving his stick. It was about four feet long and delicate, with intricate designs chiselled on the serpent, ornate gold inlays and encrusted jewels.

She shook her head. Her hair was light and bouncy.

'Liquid jollity is my raison d'etre.' He smiled indulgently at his big belly and poured himself another glass. 'As a connoisseur, I do say, these simple folks have perfected their brew.'

He walked back to Madeline, tapping his stick with each step. Tap, tap, tap, tap. 'There's a proper matriarchy here. In my 180,000 miles of travel, I've never come across anything quite as quaint.'

What was he getting at? What did he want from her?

'While Bengal flourishes, look at us?' Tavernier cleared his throat. 'France is being taken over by narrow-minded zealots.' He paused to polish the golden snake hilt of his staff with his handkerchief. Its eyes were made of red rubies. Its teeth were sparkling diamonds.

'*Code Noir?*' He spat out his words. 'King Louis is a fascist slave trader!'

Madeline shrank back.

'Do you know he has evicted Protestants from the country?' Tavernier's eyes were raving with hatred. 'He's a pig! Un conchon! Un CONCHON!'

'Where are your manners, Monsieur?' said Madeline, scared.

'Don't pretend to be so honourrrrable.' He stumbled towards her. 'I know why you are here.' He caressed a strand of her hair. 'Trying to weasel your way into my diamond outfit?' He was so close, his speech sprayed on her face.

She pushed him away.

'Mademoiselle, such arrogance when you know nothing? You must really gather more intelligence if you plan to succeed. You see, I know everything about you.'

'No you don't.'

Tavernier raised a cocky eye brow. 'Your father was caught selling fake pearls to Madam Maintainant for her wedding and now you are trying to win back his freedom.'

Madeline froze.

'Don't look so surprised. It's not much of a secret anymore. Everyone in Versailles knows you supplied those pearls to your father. He sold you out! He is grovelling at King Louis' feet. Now it is your own freedom you must earn, not his.'

Madeline glared at Tavernier. There was nobody she detested more. Could it be true? Her own father had betrayed her?

'I could kill you right now,' said Tavernier. 'And no one would ever know.'

Madeline disguised her fear. To show fear would be to lose the battle. 'I am not here alone. If I go missing...'

He drew a skinny, straight sword out of his walking stick. It looked more like an accessory than a weapon but its tip could surely poke a hole through her dress.

'I could kill you,' said the intoxicated Frenchman. 'But I won't. Not if you agree to help me.'

'Help you?' asked Madeline. 'But how?'

He waved the blade at her face clumsily. 'I sold my chateau to finance this odessy.' He traced her figure with the tip of the blade. A storm clouded his countenance. He grabbed her by the shoulders and shook her. 'I want that diamond.'

'Diamond?' Madeline could not conceal her shock. She thought they were talking about maps.

'Sacre bleu, do you take me for a fool? I'll kill you,' he shouted.

'Talk business rather than threatening me. We may both have something to gain.' She spoke with an even voice though fear knocked her entrails. She glanced out the window and wished she had brought Abdul along with her. There was no one to call to for help. Later, she would pay Costa to stick a dagger in this fool's derriere.

Tavernier resumed his seat. 'You have access to the Subedar?'

Madeline nodded. 'He is an extraordinary gentleman.'

'Here is the plan. It's simple really. Purchase Kalinoor then hand it over to me.'

'Since you want it, I assume it will cost a fortune,' replied Madeline, her heart racing. 'I don't have that kind of money.'

'I will take care of that. Your only task is to convince the Viceroy to part with his bijoux.'

'Why don't you buy it yourself?' she said.

'The Viceroy and I have our ... differences.'

Madeline raised an eye brow.

'As a young soldier, Khan fought with Aurangzeb to overthrow the Deccan Empire. Their campaign was successful and Khan came into possession of the treasury of Qutb Adl Shah of Golconda.

'Khan was rich before but after that he became one of the richest men in the Empire. Within his collection were several unique specimens. Diamonds of immense size and power, unusual colours: pink, yellow, blue.'

'Blue?'

'Deep-blue like the ocean,' said Tavernier, nostalgically. 'Glows in the dark. Cool to the touch. Never have I seen anything as exquisite.' His eyes sparkled with pure adoration.

'You stole it?' said Madeline.

'Stole is an unflattering word,' said Tavernier. 'I appropriated it from Khan just as he appropriated it from the Deccan.'

'It is an ancient gem,' said Madeline, recalling words she had heard earlier. 'It belongs to these people.'

'Khan offered 300,000 rupees for the return of the French Bleu. I sold it to King Louis for a whopping 450,000 rupees instead!'

Enough to purchase a castle, thought Madeline, but not class.

'I am an afficionado of art and fine gems, same as you,' said Tavernier. 'But let me warn you, you cannot pull off this heist on your own. You need me. Without me, you're nothing. Bring me the diamond and we can both make it big. You can return to France *alive* and purchase all the posh friends you dream of.'

Madeline narrowed her gaze. 'Why would the Subedar give me the diamond?'

Tavernier glared. 'Don't be daft!' His spit sprayed all over her face. 'How does a woman persuade a man of anything?'

Madeline scowled at the impropriety of his words. 'If I can obtain Kalinoor,' she said cautiously, 'How will I find you?'

Tavernier smiled. 'I'm coming with you.'

CHAPTER 45

That night after the warship departed, Shayista fell asleep and dreamt of enemies. They strolled through his slumber, plundering his fortress: Company men, Marathas, zamindars, elitists, fanatics, bigots and more. He tried to fight them but they kept emerging: the shamefully narrow, the disgracefully greedy, the slothful, the arrogant and the weary. Fortunately his uncomfortable sleep was disturbed by an urgent banging at the door.

He rubbed his eyes and opened the door. It was Champa, windswept hair rippling like the Ganges. Her eyes blazed with yearning. She wore a crimson cloak that hung to the ground, murmuring as she moved towards him. Confused, he asked how she had gotten there.

'My Lord, I thirst for your lips,' she whispered, closing the door behind her. She traced his lips with her finger. 'I crave you just here.' She nuzzled her cheek into the space between his clavicle and shoulder. Her energy was different: confident, seductive, bold. Her smell was infused with a tantalizing mix of cinnamon, musk and ... was it sulphur?

'This neck, how I have longed to kiss it!' She pressed her wet lips against the nape of his neck and sucked his skin.

'Champa, you're acting odd,' he said but didn't push her away.

'Is it odd for a woman to have desires?' she asked. She lifted her arms to the sky. The cloak slipped off her chocolate shoulders and fluttered to the ground. She stood before him naked, her smooth skin glowing. She invited him to kiss her.

Shayista could not be sure if he was awake or dreaming.

She wrapped her arms around his neck, her thighs around his body. The warmth of her breath revived long abandoned feelings. Her ankle chains jingled. 'Deny me not,' she commanded, tearing away his clothes.

Inflamed to vagary, deny he did not! In their naked glory, he dove into her valley and scaled her mountains, licked up her sorrows and drowned in her seas. She was full and soft. Their bodies merged. She moaned and meowed, once a purring kitten, once a growling tigress. He galloped on her like a thunderstorm. With salt and star dust on his lips, he was conquered by her lust. He pushed her against the bed, threw her onto the floor, banged her against the wall.

Then a knock at the door.

'You wrestling a croc in there?' asked Costa.

Champa warned Shayista not to mention her appearance.

'I'm fine, just doing some yoga,' said Shayista.

The captain went away and now Shayista was sure that Champa was real. With savage devotion, he plunged his tongue deep into her ravenous depths. Her juices ran down his cheeks and elbows and collected in puddles on the floor. She was the Buriganga pouring into his mouth, love and destruction smashing through the embankments drowning the firmament. She was the choir in the cathedral, the bird in flight, the parting rain clouds. It was a night of transformations and rapture, a night of unadulterated passion and unbearable lightness. He held her to him tenderly and felt their hearts beat in sync, in rhythm with the universe.

'I love you despite your disappointments, your scars, your flaws. I love you,' said Champa.

There was something aching and noble in her. Shayista realized he loved her too but it was not love he dwelt on for long. Love made him think of loss. A vision of Pari's cold corpse drifted through his mind. Poor Pari, poor little Pari Bibi, wrapped in a daffon cloth of white.

'My Lord, where is the diamond of Bengal?' said Champa.

Pari, his most precious treasure, lay beneath the gaudy mausoleum. The loss was so raw. He could not come to terms with his grief. He could not accept Pari's death.

'Where is the diamond?'

'In the Lal Bagh mausoleum, there my diamond is buried,' he mumbled.

Suddenly Champa vanished. Shayista rubbed his eyes, dazed. Did that just happen? In the moonlight through the cabin window he saw Madeline returning to the ship in a rowboat with the kitchen hand and a portly sailor.

CHAPTER 46

Nasim greeted the pir in the private audience chamber of her fort. Dressed as usual in black garbs with a tight black turban, his eyes only were different, lit with fervour. She had received a message from him earlier that day. He claimed to know where the Kalinoor was hidden and he wanted to help her unearth it quite immediately. Now here he was, seated before her.

'We must use the cannon,' said Pir Zulfiqar. His rapacious demands were startling.

'What ever for?' asked Nasim Banu.

'I had a vision. Kalinoor is hidden well below the earth. We will need the cannon.'

'I beg your parden, Pir Baba, we cannot blast the cannon at will. It is only for battle.'

'Nevertheless, your Highness,' said the pir.

She could tell from his posture, he was bent on having his way. Ultimately, how much damage would it cause apart from provoking her husband? 'Alright,' she said at last. 'We shall fire ONE cannon ball. Not more.'

'Fine. Point it at the mausoleum.'

'Mausoleum?' Nasim repeated. 'Pari Bibi's mausoleum?'

'Yes!' barked the pir. 'That's where he hid it!'

Nasim pondered the plausibility of this claim. Could Shayista have chosen such a macabre location to hide his jewel? Of all places, a sepulchre? Why not behind a false wall or in a hidden vault?

'Ready your guards,' barked the pir.

'Wait,' said Nasim. 'I spent two lakh rupees building that mausoleum. Can't we excavate the diamond with a shovel? I would hate to ruin the expensive craftsmanship.' Besides, what would Shayista say if he found out she had fired the cannon at his daughter's tomb?

'It must be done!' said Pir Zulfiqar.

'Shall I call the Amir-i-akhur?' Ambar offered.

'Can this wait till after the Emperor's visit?' said Nasim.

'There is no time to waste,' said the holy man.

Nasim nodded, feeling faint. The mausoleum was her masterpiece. She had brought in black basalt from Rajmahal for the walls, sandalwood from China for the trimmings, fretted marble screens for the windows.

Amir Dhand was summoned.

'Your Highness?' he said, bowing low.

'Amir, ready the cannon,' she said, concealing her misgivings.

'Pardon?' he said, taken aback. He eyed the holy man.

'Ready the cannon, I need to blast it.'

'Your Highness, at whom?' he asked. He shot a dirty look at the pir, ready to grind him to a pulp if her Highness requested. 'If this man is bothering you...'

'No, not at all! Dear me, no!' said Nasim, glanced apologetically at the revered holy man. 'Please point the canon at Pari mausoleum!'

This time Dhand gave her a bemused look. 'At that goliath you have been building for over a year?' The irony of her capricious whim was not lost upon him.

'Yes,' said Nasim, burning with humiliation.

'As you wish,' said the Amir.

He stepped out of the garden with Nasim Banu, Ambar Khajah and the pir following him. Two elephants dragged the cannon onto the lawn and pointed it towards the spectacular crypt, a cannon ball in its mouth.

The heat sweltered. Beads of sweat trickled down Nasim's back. She mopped her forehead with her dupatta and asked the artists to dismantle their work and preserve as much as possible. They wept when they heard she was going to destroy the tomb.

A crate with black powder was carried forth. 'What is it?' Nasim asked Dhand.

'Saltpetre,' he explained, brimming with pride. 'The world's largest supply is ours.'

'Yes, yes, I heard,' said Nasim, impatiently. 'Zamindar Shobha mentioned trade was booming. The English are a peculiar race. They seem to prefer saltpetre to muslin!'

'Zamindar Shobha Singh?' repeated the Amir.

'Oh, I know, I know. I have heard of the zamindar's spat with my Lord husband but really, Amir Dhand, he has been such a staunch supporter of the Empire, I feel Shayista is being too harsh.'

Amir Dhand's face showed no reaction to her words so Nasim quickly dismissed the subject and moved on to the task at hand.

The cannon was ready. Nasim nodded her assent. The Amir advised her to plug her ears.

'On my command,' said the Amir. 'Ready, aim, FIRE!'

The shot burst through the air. Never had Nasim Banu heard anything so loud. It sounded like the trumpet of Judgment Day, shaking her intestines, stopping her heart. In seconds, the magnificent mausoleum came crumbling to the ground, smashed to pieces. Fragments of rock, stone, marble, brick lay strewn across the lawn.

Nasim ordered her servants to turn up the earth and search for a silver jewellery box. They did as they were told but three hours later, with no rock left unturned, there was still no diamond to be found.

On the verge of tears, Nasim dismissed the Amir, the soldiers and the servants, and retired to her private audience chamber with her eunuch and the pir. Given that he was wrong about his prediction, Nasim felt she should be the angry one but to her surprise, it was the pir who was incensed.

'I don't understand,' he thundered. 'The diamond of Bengal is buried with Pari. He said it loud and clear. I WANT that diamond!'

Sensing the pir's escalating fury, Ambar intervened. 'Pir Baba, once we commune with Abul Fateh, it is our duty to return the diamond to its rightful owner.'

'Rightful owner?' asked Nasim.

'Why the Emperor, of course!' said Ambar. 'Such a valuable Deccan jewel, it belongs to the Emperor not the Subedar of Bengal, and definitely not some provincial holy man.'

Pir Zulfiqar glared at Ambar. His eyes took on an inhuman glow. 'How dare you speak to me like that?'

Nasim Banu shrank with an erstwhile unknown fear. 'Pir Baba, my eunuch meant no offence...' she stammered.

'He is a SPY!' bellowed the pir. 'Planted by the Emperor.'

'Maybe I am!' Ambar shouted back, to Nasim's surprise.

'Khajah, what are you saying?' she said, horrified.

'Yes, it was the Emperor who sent me here to find out where Kalinoor is hidden but not out of ill will to you or the Subedar. Only for the good of the Empire...'

Suddenly he gagged as though choking. He scratched at his neck to pry open the constricting grip that was not there. The pir's shadow loomed collosal behind him, asphyxiating him.

Nasim wanted to help him but then again, he had betrayed her. Perhaps he deserved a moderate punishment.

Ambar's body was thrown onto the wall by the mysterious force. He fell to the floor and was lifted up again, as if by magic, his feet dangling off the ground.

A diabolical grin spread on the pir's face. He poked his finger into the air. Ambar yelled and brought his hands to his eye, as if he had felt it there.

To Nasim's shock, his punctured eye oozed with blood. 'Stop!' she screamed, unable to tolerate the gore.

Pir Baba ignored her and poked his finger into the air again. Ambar howled in pain, cupping his hands over his other eye.

'Noooo!' she screamed.

Gone were his eyes. A few more blows against the floor, and finally, he fell silent.

Nasim froze in terror. The pir left without a word. When he was a safe distance away, she rushed to the limp body of her eunuch. To her surprise the blood was gone, there were no signs of harm on his eyes or body but he was dead.

Chapter 47

Unable to swallow her grief, Champa sat with her grandfather in the antechamber, watching as he groomed his falcon. Dada had been in a foul mood since he returned from an errand. Champa wondered when he would regain his calm. She needed to ask him for help.

'Why are we such an unkind species?' she began.

She had spent the morning cleaning the madrasa. The girls had been temporarily shifted to a house provided by the Subedar while the premise was repaired. Only a few books were left unburnt, one was a book of verses by Hafez. The poet had been her father's favourite. Champa wondered if it was he who had saved the book. Perhaps there was still a trace of goodness in him.

'Humanity is lost,' said the pir. 'We will die of greed.'

'There must be a solution, Dada?'

'Beggars and kings, the wise and the foolish, they are all the same. God gives us resources in abundance but we spit in His eye. We pollute, we deplete, we destroy. But there is hope.'

'What hope?'

'Kalinoor can absorb solar energy and focus it into a single point of clarity hot enough to burn a porthole through the fabric of illusion. Through this gateway, I shall summon the most powerful djinn in the universe.'

'And what will you command it to do, Dada?'

'Eliminate mankind through floods. The time has come for forty days of torrential rain to cleanse the world once again. The land will belong to flora and fauna! Tigers, cobras, cheetahs, chimps. Mother Nature shall flourish as God intended.'

'Dada, that sounds a bit destructive. Surely there must be some other way?'

'There is no other way.'

Champa mulled over her grandfather's words. He and the Subedar were not so different. Both were delusional and violent and neither would stop at anything. Men! What would become of Bengal?

CHAPTER 48

As the pirate ship pulled into Dacca's harbour, Shayista wondered how he would get rid of the curse. Adamantine was indestructible but perhaps if he threw Kalinoor into the Buriganga, water would drown out its power. Or would the stone continue to damn him from the bottom of the river?

He bid his friends farewell, having elicited from them a promise to join him for supper, and made his way back to the fortress on horseback. He was puzzling over his dilemma when he detected a sound. He pressed his ear to the ground and ascertained ten horses bearing soldiers in armour, fast approaching.

Swoooooooooosh. An arrow cut across the sky. It whizzed by his ear. He was not in the mood to take on enemies alone. He had the diamond to worry about. His mind raced to the Chowk Bazaar gates, the closest Imperial guard post. His adrenal reflexes catapulted him into action.

Shayista leapt with his horse over shanties, scaled the walls and darted through busy avenues, upheaving carts, knocking over pack horses, frightening children, scattering goats. Ducks and chicken flapped out of his way. Passersby gathered to watch. Soon the assassins were in sight: orange-turbaned Marathas.

A few more leaps and Shayista reached the Imperial post where soldiers were stationed. 'Under attack!' he shouted.

Imperial officers sprang into action, mounting steeds and drawing weapons. Plumes of dust, sweat and battle cries rang through the air. Musketeers took aim.

'It's too dangerous,' shouted Shayista, stopping them. 'Too many people around. We must fight close combat.'

The Marathas were not prepared for the ambush. They pulled back to regroup.

Shayista drew Azdahar and charged after them. Another arrow whistled past and impaled one of his soldiers. Then another and another.

Shayista looked up to see a most glorious form silhouetted before the moon: Arjun drawing a bowstring from the rooftop of the Bazaar. He was mounted on a white horse and he had on a black scarf over his face. A leather godhu protected his arm from the bow string on its return. His quiver, red velvet and embroidered in gold, was larger than he was. He gripped the bow in a classic *Changal-i-baz*, Hawk's Claw, holding the arrow still, his advanced foot forward for balance. His aim was precise. It was evident he was a master.

The faultlessly executed arrow sailed towards Shayista who watched it, mesmerized. It traced a perfect path towards him and lodged in his turban. Soldiers shot at the archer but he eluded them, only to reappear and resume his projectile assault a few yards away.

'Cover me,' Shayista shouted to his guards. Swords and spears clashed above his head as he charged.

When near enough, he stood upon his saddle and leapt onto the roof. The archer saw him and tried to withdraw. Shayista threw a rock at him, knocking him off his steed. The archer fell to the ground. Shayista lunged at him with his sword.

The archer jerked back avoiding the blade which snagged on his scarf and tore part of it off, revealing an astonishing sight: a head full of hair. This Maratha marauder was a woman.

In a moment of confusion, Shayista lost his advantage. The Maratha parried Shayista's blade with a shield and drew an arrow from her quiver.

'Give me the Kalinoor and you can ride away with your life,' she said, her bow taut, arrow aimed at his Adam's apple.

Shayista didn't want to hurt her. She sounded young. He whistled, diverted her attention and knocked the bow out of her hand with his steel forearm guard. She grimaced and yelled. He grabbed her wrist and drew her into a gentle bind.

'The dark diamond is cursed,' he said.

'Unhand me, you barbarian!' she demanded.

'Why do you want Kalinoor?' he asked.

'It belongs to me.'

'Didn't you hear me?' said Shayista. 'It is cursed.'

'As if I'd believe you, you liar. You killed my mother and now I will kill you!' She struggled to escape his hold. In the tussle, her scarf fell, revealing her face. It was a conglomeration of loveliness.

Shayista reeled, dumbfound. She was the spitting image of Pari. His knees buckled, he released his grip.

'Do not pity me because I am a woman. I am as powerful as any man. I am the granddaughter of Shivaji Chattapatri of the Bhonsle clan. You have something that belongs to me. You stole it from my mother. I want it back.'

Shayista could find no words to respond. Could this possibly be his long-lost daughter Miri? Alive? He wanted to hold her in his arms and tell her many things but she jumped onto a horse and escaped. He stared after her in wonder.

CHAPTER 49

Below deck in the Belo Diabo, Madeline was waiting for the pirates to disembark so she could lead Tavernier off the ship without being seen. She was grateful that Abdul had not informed Captain Costa of their stowaway, the strange foreigner she had picked up in Chatgaon and kept hidden in her cabin for the week. He must have assumed the elderly man was her lover and even if he could not understand her taste, at least he honoured her secret.

Madeline struggled to come to terms with her failure. How could her own father have betrayed her? After all she was doing for him? Even if she managed to map the Kollur Mines and get hold of Kalinoor, would they let her back into high society? And what would she do about Tavernier?

She decided to test one of the potions in her spell book. The effect of this tonic was apparently to loosen one's tongue. Perhaps she could gather some information about the Kollur mines. It was worth a try.

She offered Tavernier the drink and wondered if he would smell the danger, as the Subedar had once done. To her surprise, he swallowed the whole mug in one gulp. The spell had warned of overdose but she had doubled the quantity nonetheless. Now she feared perhaps she had overdone it. Inquisitively she watched as her experiment unfolded.

At first Tavernier stared at her, eyes spinning. She could see his dizziness. He wobbled off balance then sat heavily into a chair and began talking. 'Like you, I was born with my head wrapped in maps,' he said. 'Son of a cartographer, my dreams were of faraway kingdoms. At sixteen, I embarked on my first expedition, an errand boy on an uncle's ship. By the time I was twenty, I had seen Italy, Switzerland, Germany, Poland and Hungary. I spoke the principal languages of these places well enough to buy a meal or woo a lady.'

The concoction seemed to be working!

'I travelled to Constantinople, Tokat, Erzerum, Erivan and Persia,' he continued. 'I made it as far as Isfahan before I returned by Baghdad, Aleppo, Alexandretta, Malta, Italy, back to Paris. Then Hindustan, a journey that changed me forever. Here sensuality and opulence are the lay of the land. Trade, commerce, grand parties, attractive women, gargantuan jewels. It has everything.' He was sweating heavily and his face had taken a pinkish hue.

'I visited the court of the Grand Emperor Shah Jahan,' he continued. 'It was then that I first visited the mines of Golconda, as his guest. I began trading and soon enough, my charm propelled me into success. I became a merchant, trading in costly jewels and precious wares with elite customers, princes of the East.

'On one of my voyages, I came to acquire an immaculate diamond, the French Blue. I sold it to King Louis and with the money I purchased the Barony of Aubonne near Geneva and married the daughter of a Parisian jeweller, but alas, the tides turned.'

Tavernier tugged at the collar of his kurta, visibly uncomfortable. His face was beet red, his neck swollen. She feared he might burst.

'What happened?' Madeline asked.

'I was double crossed. Dutch East India Company sent agents to kill me.' He displayed his missing ear. 'Louis turned on me. Times are not favourable for Protestants in France. The Elector of Bradenburg is my only friend. He wants me as his ambassador to India for his own Company. He expects from me a hefty investment. He believes I am stupendously wealthy though really I am flat out bankrupt.'

Such a confession from Tavernier? The potion was potent. Madeline wondered which other spells she should test.

'And ... Kollur?' she asked. 'What about the mines?' Would he spill his secrets?

'I'm warning you, Mademoiselle,' said Tavernier, suddeny apopleptic. He grabbed her elbow hard. 'You have until tomorrow to get me Kalinoor. If you fail, you will go back to France penniless, with nothing but your ruined reputation.'

With that, Tavernier began coughing and wheezing, tottering off balance, then collapsed on the floor, unconscious.

Madeline shuddered. She and he whom she hated were not so different. They were both exiles trying to buy back their reputations. Kalinoor and Kollur could change everything for them, transform their destinies like alchemy.

CHAPTER 50

Returning home after the Chatgaon jaunt, quelling the Magh-Company uprising, fighting off the Marathas and discovering that his daughter was still alive, Shayista felt dishevelled. He hoped to stretch out on a silk cushion with a pipe to reflect on the events but such luxury was not his. The fortress was bustling with guests. A cluster of elephants, saddled horses and turbaned soldiers idled by the gates. His guards explained there was a celebration underway.

The courtyard was lavishly dressed for a party. An elegant pavilion had been constructed. The evening's theme was red roses. A shamiana of brocaded silk canopied a structure of bamboo wrapped in golden thread. Along the edges, cane trellises supported vines of roses. Strands of rose buds fell from silk clutches pinned on top. Candles in clay bowls dotted the walkways. A zephyr carried the pleasing fragrance of hasna henas and incense.

'What's this about?' Shayista asked.

'Sire,' said Dhand. 'Her Ladyship has invited guests.'

A mammoth eunuch dressed in a starched white kurta and red cummerbund offered Shayista and Dhand a drink. Shayista accepted. Dhand declined. A bearer with spiced kebabs and fried pakoras had his interest. A tray of figs and dried apricots made its way around. Shayista could smell mutton on the grill. The sharab quenched his thirst. He needed another glass to subdue the battled body aches.

'There you are, Jahanapana,' said Nasim, peeking out from behind a brocaded purdah. Her heavily embroidered golden churidaar murmured on the grass. Her ankle bells jingled. Her earrings tinkled. Her bangles jangled. Her nose ring glittered.

'My Lord, please wear this,' she said, thrusting a white turban into his hands. A huge heron feather secured with a sapphire jewel flapped in his face, its height symbolic of his status in the Mughal hierarchy.

'No, thanks,' said Shayista.

Nasim pouted. 'You haven't worn it in forty years. I gave it to you when Abul Fateh was born.'

'How kind you are,' said Shayista, compelled to don the headgear.

'Try this.' She shoved a halva towards him.

He tried to say 'no thanks' but she took the parting of his lips as an opportunity to stuff the sweet into his mouth. It tasted sickeningly syrupy.

After swanning about for a while, Nasim fluttered off.

Shayista lifted his chin high and greeted his guests. Sycophantic noblemen scrambled to taslim when they saw him. After a round of obligatory mingling, Shayista asked the Mir-e-Tazuk to commence the festivities.

The musicians climbed onto the dais and sat upon Persian carpets, each with an instrument mastered to perfection: a bashi, a tabla, a sitar and a voice. Behind them, the dancers came on stage. Shayista settled down to enjoy the performance when Dhand called him aside.

'Sire, I must warn you,' he said. 'There is a traitor among us.'

'You told me.'

'No, I mean, now. Right here, at this lively gathering. Zamindar Shobha Singh.'

Shayista raised his eyebrow.

'He sells saltpetre to the English.'

Shayista glowered. Selling *his* gunpowder to arm *his* enemies? Rage fired through his veins.

'Her Ladyship invited him,' said Dhand.

Shayista ground his teeth, ready to rip the zamindar apart.

Dhand placed a restraining hand on his chest. 'Sire, he has eaten your salt.'

Shayista snarled but he could not disregard the rules of hospitality. He would not kill a guest in his own home. Instead, he marched over to the loathsome renegade and demanded, 'Shobha Singh, why are you here?'

The dirty double-crosser lay reclined on a cushion, sipping tamarind serbet. 'Subedar, salaam. How lovely to see you,' he said languidly, no intention to bow.

'You are not welcome here,' said Shayista. 'Leave.'

Nasim Banu fluttered to the scene to interfere but Shayista would have none of it.

Shobha bristled. 'Would you slight me twice?'

'Leave!' Shayista thundered.

Shobha rose to his feat, a frosty coat of indignity wrapped around his anger, and walked out, much to Nasim Banu's dismay. Outside, his retinue of mercenaries waited.

As soon as they left, Shayista excused himself from the party. He donned chain mail, armed himself and summoned fifty of his elite guards. They gathered around a mound of earth next to the South Gate of the fortress.

When the mound was shovelled aside, a rusty door was revealed. The guards gasped and cleared the entrance of debris. The door was pried open to unveil a deep tunnel.

The tunnel was a carefully guarded secret that ran for nearly a mile below the Buriganga and emerged on the other side of the river. It was built as an escape route.

With lanterns, walking single file, Shayista marched his men into the the gaping mouth of uncertainty. It was damp but well dug out. There was room to stand and walk. They could hear the mighty river above. They were grateful for the darkness which concealed the primordial creatures slithering in the subterranean earth around them.

The soldiers reached the opening at the far end of the river an hour later and waited to waylay the zamindar.

'Not before my signal!' whispered Shayista. He was eager to attack. The warning was as much for his men as himself. A methodical exercise of draconian force was necessary to run an empire. Shobha had gone too far and Shayista was keen to make an example of him. 'Leave the zamindar to me!'

The mansabdars stilled their hearts in preparation for battle. Shobha and his men approached noisily in the distance, careless, unaware of the danger.

Shayista waited, patiently manipulating his breath to prime his body. He felt the combustible energy escalating within him. When he could see Shobha's eyes, he gave the command. 'Attack!'

Hacking, slicing, smashing like a madman, Shayista ploughed into the zamindar's force. The insurgents were trained Afghani mercenaries, armed with spears, pikes, karuds and chaqus. They fought with ferocious desperation but they were caught by surprise. The charging demon that bore into them, caring little about whether they lived or died, had killed half of them before they even registered the trouble.

Within minutes, the mercenaries' ranks broke and the Mughals were among them, a solid phalanx of deadly soldiers disciplined with thousands of hours of battle training. The carnage that followed did not last long.

The zamindar was left sprawled in the middle of the fallen mercenaries. His horse had bolted throwing him on the ground. He stood up groaning under the weight of the weapons he was armed with as Shayista approached.

'Sire, don't kill me! It is not my fault. I was born to this Destiny,' he said. He watched Shayista to see his reaction.

'Give me one reason why I should let you live?' thundered Shayista.

'Because you have a heart that is not made of steel?' said Shobha. His lips stretched in cunning exultation.

The words stung. Shayista recalled his promise to Champa. He set aside his urge to take the zamindar's head off with one swing of Azdahar. 'I will let you fight for your life,' he said. 'A duel to death.'

A malicious grin lit Shobha's face. He felt sure he could take his opponent. He had been training hard.

Shobha launched his garhiya javelin for an early kill. It sliced through the air expertly but Shayista deflected it with his shield. Shobha yanked the gurz from his belt and swung it over his head in a circle three times before throwing the spiked-ball at Shayista. Launched with such force, if this struck it would be sure to kill.

Shayista ducked the ball and entwined its chain around his katara. The gurz was heavy and though Shobha was strong, Shayista managed to use its impetus to fling him to the ground, wrenching it out of his grip.

Two weapons down, Shobha did not waste a second. Slung over his back was a vicious battle axe. Double headed, on one side a broad blade, on the other, a lethal point: a classic Tabar Zaghnol. With a battle cry, Shobha swung it at Shayista.

Shayista leapt out of the way and thrust his katara into Shobha's arm. He screamed and dropped the zaghnol. He recoiled and drew a seven-bladed sword with a thick center blade, six jagged blades branching off it.

Shayista deflected the savage potential of its first swipe and circled in towards Shobha. When close enough, Shayista lunged, thrusting Azdahar at Shobha's midsection. The lunging foot landed on warm horse dung and Shayista slipped. He landed on his right knee to stop from losing balance. The zamindar stepped back with alacrity. Shayista's blade grazed his chain mail without injuring him and arced away.

This was an opportunity for the zamindar to deal a killing blow. Gripping the seven-bladed sword with both hands, he swung as far back as he could and lashed out. The extra second he took to gain momentum gave Shayista time to position himself.

Shayista felt the clanging blow on his shield. His left arm went numb but the shield did not break in half. Held at an angle, balanced on his knee, the shield warded off the blow and sent the heavy sword sliding away across it.

Shayista jumped to his feet and struck with Azdahar, a slashing blow that cut across the zamindar's chest.

'I surrender!' the zamindar squealed, gripping his wound, falling to the ground.

Shayista stepped close. 'If I ever see you again, I will kill you. Now run.'

CHAPTER 51

Leaving the pile of dead assassins on the road, Shayista's soldiers preferred to charter a ride across the river to return to the fortress. By the time they arrived at the South Gate of Lal Bagh Fort, it was near dawn. No sooner did they enter the gates, a dreadful thunder storm attacked.

Sheets of rain plummeted down, wrecking the shamiana. White muslin and red silk lay in tatters on the ground. Guards rushed to take shelter as bolts of lightning struck at them. One bolt hit a soldier, killing him instantly.

Shayista saw a shadow lurking in his garden. It was the old pir beneath the bougainvilleas, his hair stretched out to its ends, fiery filaments of hellish fury. Olive light radiated from his eyes. The lightning appeared to emanate from his fingers.

'Where is Kalinoor?' the pir demanded as Shayista approached.

'Stop this destruction at once!' shouted Shayista.

'People are polluting Earth, wounding the majestic kingdom of God, destroying beloved Bengal. Join me, Subedar. Together we can put an end to the mindless snivelling of human beings. Come, let us eradicate mankind once and for all!'

'Never!' shouted Shayista. 'Guards, seize him!'

Soldiers rushed to the pir but he was encircled by a ball of energy that prevented them from getting close. From his protected sphere, Pir Zulfiqar hurled one bolt after another, striking down soldiers like they were toys.

'Stop!' Shayista shouted. He ran towards the pir, when something came crashing into him and brought him hurtling to the ground. It was Bhopal.

'I've been hit,' gasped the dwarf, thunderstruck. He had jumped in front, taking a bolt meant for Shayista. Bhopal squinted in pain, lips pursed, hands gripping a ghastly wound. Blood oozed through his charred flesh.

Shayista scooped Bhopal into his arms. 'What kind of fool are you?' he scolded, gulping his tears. 'Why did you have to be so brave?'

Bhopal coughed feebly, eyes full of love.

'Farewell my giant friend,' said Shayista. He whispered a prayer and laid Bhopal on the ground.

A shadow loomed above Shayista. Its cold fingers gripped his throat. He felt a tightening then he could no longer breathe.

The magician smiled diabolically, hands poised like a vice, asphyxiating him from a distance with mind tricks.

'Where is Kalinoor?' Pir Zulfiqar demanded.

Shayista gasped for air and fell to the ground. The shadow lifted him and banged his head against the trunk of a tree, once, twice, three times. Pain seared through his body. Blood dripped into his eyes. The world was afloat a sea of crimson.

Nasim ran into the garden. She had seen this kind of magic before. It left her eunuch dead. 'Stop!' she screamed at the pir.

Shayista fell from the stranglehold to the ground. In the haze, he saw Dhand trying to break into the pir sphere with his zaghnol. The invisible wall repelled his attempts. The Imperial Tir-Andaz who rarely missed their target shot a chain of barbed arrows at the sorcerer but deflected by the forcefield, these fell to the ground like discarded matchsticks.

Desperate to save Shayista, Dhand yelled, 'Here is the diamond!' He kicked over the floral tile under the bougainvilleas. There within the ground was the silver jewellery box he had hidden one year ago when Pari died. 'Forgive me, Sire,' said Dhand, kneeling by him. 'It's just a stone.'

In a rush of magic, the box flew out of the mortar and into the pir's hands. With a snap of his finger, the pir cracked the lock and opened the box. Inside, the diamond sat like a final judgment, irreversibly determining the sorry fate of those who loved it. The pir cupped the diamond in his palms, cackling. 'At last!' he said. 'At long last!'

A buzzing sound, a faint hum of rising pitch, emenated from the depths of the stone: a baby crying, a mother weeping, a wounded soldier, a wailing widow, a malignant muezzin, the whip of injustice, the breath of treachery, the crescendo of commerce, the groan of an Empire staggering to its death. The pir lifted the diamond up to the sky and began chanting.

Shayista could not hold up his injured head but he saw from the corner of his eyes, Champa tugging at her grandfather's sleeve.

'Restrain yourself!' thundered the pir, shoving her to the ground.

Champa waved her hand to stir the wind but the pir stopped it with a fist in the air.

'You cannot use my wisdom against me,' he bellowed. 'Don't try to stop me or you will die!'

Shayista floudered to his feet. 'I will fight you, whatever you are,' he shouted. 'Leave her out of this. Just you and I.'

The necromancer said, 'I accept.'

'No!' shouted Champa to Shayista. 'Don't hurt him! He is all I have!'

'What is your weapon of choice?' shouted Shayista.

Zulfiqar tapped his temple.

Shayista sheathed his talwar and sat cross-legged in front of the pir, head pounding. 'I accept.'

'Very well.' The wizard waved his hand and the world around Shayista disappeared. The fortress, the garden, Champa, Dhand, Costa, all vanished.

'You won't need those,' said the pir.

Shayista's sword and shield fell out of his hands.

The magician brought the diamond to his third eye.

Next thing Shayista knew, he was shackled to a brick wall. Violet mind-altering smoke rose from the ground like steam, enveloping him, sapping him of energy. His muscles slackened, his vision blurred. A dullness weighed his senses. The magician was toying with him.

He was dizzy, spinning, twisting. His soul, wrung out of his flesh, drifted upwards to the sky. An icy breeze chilled him. An acrid smell of sulphur permeated the air.

'Salaam,' boomed a woman's voice inside his head. It was raspy, deep and anguished, as if struggling out of a forgotten tomb, from the shadows behind the manifestation of Now, from the moment before God said 'Let there be light', from the cusp of existence, she emerged. She was old: one hundred, two hundred, perhaps a thousand years old.

'Walaikum assalam,' said Shayista at last, goosebumps on his arms. He couldn't see her but he could feel her presence. *Where are you?* he thought.

'You see this green field?' she replied.

Suddenly Shayista was in a vibrant field of pistachio green. The sun warmed his back and parakeets twittered.

Yes, said Shayista.

'You see the fields of paddy?' said the djinn.

A stretch of paddy loomed ahead. The sky was a startling blue. The air crisp.

'You see that mango tree by the hill?'

He saw a grove of mango trees ahead. The tangy smell enwrapped him.

'Upon the leaf, do you see a dew drop?'

Her power of suggestion was nonpareil. Shayista saw exactly what she said: a trembling leaf, a dew drop sparkling immaculate. Within it, the delicate universe spun alive.

'That is where I live,' she said.

Shayista wanted to stand up and open his eyes but he could do neither. The physical plane no longer existed, only the astral plane was real and here she was real too. Confronted by something he had never believed in, Shayista felt humbled. There were perhaps many worlds, dimensions and ideas that existed beyond his comprehension.

He found he was standing in Agra Palace, in the elephant ring, in the fighting pit. Only it wasn't him, it was his spirit animal, a Royal Bengal tiger made of glowing white light.

From the other end of the ring came a blood-thirsty howl. It was the djinn, incarnated as a dragon-scaled demoness with eight arms. As she approached, the ground shook.

Shayista was frightened, more frightened than he had ever been. Never had he fought djinn, if such a battle were even possible. How did one fight a creature of smokeless fire?

Through the violet mist, Shayista saw his fortress garden far below, his physical body slumped on the ground. Costa and Dhand had penetrated the pir's forcefield. Costa had ensnared Zulfiqar's bony wrist with his whip and Dhand lunged at him with a flying side kick. It landed on his shoulder and sent him flying through the air. He lost of hold of the diamond.

Shayista's attention was drawn back to the ring. The djinn dragon was racing towards him. Alarmed, he tried to embody the tiger. He stepped cautiously, testing his limbs, one paw then the other. His tread was solid, his paws silent but strong. His shoulder blades commanded acceleration. With each step he was moving faster, gaining momentum. Soon he was running. The demoness was running too. When she was close enough, Shayista leapt on her, biting into her shoulder with his powerful feline jaws.

The djinn reeled in pain. 'It was you who killed Arjumand,' she screeched.

Shayista's mind flooded with self-lacerating thoughts. He had failed to save his sister, failed to protect her sons.

The djinn struck him in the stomach and sent him hurtling through the air, crashing into the wall. He landed in a cloud of dust.

Barely had he landed, he had to leap out of the way as the djinn swooped down on him.

He ran. His sleek tiger body effortlessly picked up speed but there was nowhere to escape. He turned to charge at the djinn again. He swiped at her with razor claws, tearing off a chunk of her head. Curdled blood gushed out.

The djinn shrieked and slowed her pursuit.

Shayista licked clean his wound and watched.

Bit by bit, she revived, invigorated with fury. 'Ellora died for loving you,' she said.

Shayista felt his body freeze. Ellora whom he loved, Ellora whom he failed to save.

Two grotesque cobra heads rose out of the djinn's split skull. The Devil himself could not create a more hateful beast.

Shayista felt a tremor of uncertainty.

The spirit of smokeless fire expanded, drawing herself up to double his size, a black vortex swirling towards him.

Using the massive muscles of his hind legs, he leapt at her, plunging his teeth into her neck.

The djinn howled, 'You let Huzur die,' she shouted. 'You let Pari die.'

Shayista started losing grip of her neck. He felt weak, unable to hold on.

The demoness was growing in size. She grabbed him by the neck and threw him off.

Shayista landed hard on the ground and whimpered.

Her dark energy grew strong as his light faded.

He saw below, Zulfiqar had cornered Dhand and Costa. They were losing their battle.

The djinn laughed. 'Your friends will die.'

'No!' roared Shayista. He leapt at the djinn. By now she was an immense force. His bite did nothing to her. The djinn shook him off as if he were a gnat.

She began throttling the life out of him. His head spun. His white light flickered. The world was losing shape.

As the last flutter of his spirit threatened to extinguish, Pari's amulet wrapped around his paw-wrist tingled.

Help me, Shayista prayed.

Inside his mind, the spirit of his venerable Huzur appeared. 'Only through love can we break free of our limitations,' he said. 'Tear down the boundaries. Let love flow.'

Love is rough and tyrannous, thought Shayista.

'You cannot close your heart. Open yourself to love.'

But how? thought Shayista.

'You have so many questions. There is only one answer, one Truth.'

Shayista remembered a lesson he had learned as a child when Huzur had left him by a rock. He had prayed and prayed in earnest and at one point he felt the boundary of his ego melt away and he connected to God. The Truth he experienced was Divine Unity. It was an ephemeral Truth that mostly he forgot to remember as he stumbled through the rolling solitude of life.

'A Sufi's force is from Love,' said Huzur. 'The Love that comes with practice and discipline and surrender, the Love that allows the spirit to fly out of the cage of rationality, the Love that dwells in perfect union, the undying Love of the soul, the soul which is connected to all souls, eternal and infinite, the Soul of God. That

Love is strong in you, Talib. Embrace it. Forgive yourself and embrace love.'

Glowing Huzur light in Shayista's mind's eye disappeared.

Shayista realized he could not fight the djinn with hatred. His anger made her stronger. He had to accept his mistakes. He had to suffer his pain. And then, crushed by it all, he had to affirm life and let love in. Only positive energy could counter the curse.

Shayista tried to recreate the sensation he had experienced in youth when he had connected to the cosmos. His light flickered hopefully. He found that he could breathe again. He gulped in air and clung to the feeling, channelling his energy. The deeper he breathed, the brighter he glowed. His energy whirled like a dervish, spinning faster and faster. His heart expanded. He placed a paw on the djinn's chest and gently pushed her away.

'Do not fight me,' he said. 'You want freedom. The pir is your enemy, not I. I grant you your freedom. With love, I release you from this prison.'

The djinn hissed and erupted into blisters oozing with pus under Shayista's paws.

'Have you been enslaved so long that you have forgotten what it means to be free?' asked Shayista. 'I grant you freedom. You are no longer chained to this world.'

The djinn convulsed and began disintegrating.

Shayista's white light grew brighter and within his tiger body his heart beat red like a blazing fire. He found himself forgiving God for the Destiny he was granted. Love flooded into him. He started to glow. He forgave his father and radiated brighter, light emenating to the sky. He forgave himself and the entire cosmos was lit brilliant.

Shayista climbed upon the shrinking djinn and squeezed it into a compact ball that he could contain within his paws. He pressed his paws together till there no space left for darkness. The djinn became a wisp of smoke and vanished.

In the distance Shayista heard the roar of the Buriganga and the song of a nightingale. He felt the warmth of sun on his back and the kiss of a misty winter morning. He recalled the wind of Bengal Bay and the melancholy of monsoon rains. He remembered laughter shared with friends and mornings when he awoke in his lover's arms. The tiny yet immeasurable space within his heart expanded into infinite tenderness. How precious life was, how unbearably precious.

Thank you, he said to God. *Subhanallah!*

He opened his eyes and was back in the physical world. Near by, he saw the pir had drawn a silver dagger and was thrusting it at Dhand. Dhand stepped back just in time and caught the pir's wrist, redirecting the weapon. It pierced through the black garbs and into the pir's heart. The last thing Shayista saw was the pir fall to the ground. At the same time, he collapsed too.

CHAPTER 52

When Shayista awoke, he was lying in his garden in the flesh cage of his human body. The metaphysical battle with the djinn had not manifested its wounds on his physical body but it had brought about an astonishing change. It made him age. He became an 84 year old in an 84 year old body. His muscles felt feeble, his skin soft and wrinkled.

The black diamond rested in its silver box next to him. He noticed Champa seated at a distance, staring at him in horror. The corpse of the pir lay by her feet, shrouded in her shawl.

'They killed him,' she said, her voice scarce above a whisper. 'He was a pious man who helped people and they killed him.'

'I'm sorry, Champa. He wanted to destroy Bengal.'

'They didn't have to kill him,' she said.

Shayista regretted that it was his friends who killed the pir. It should have been him. He should have sewn the pir into a donkey's pelt.

'You cannot save Bengal from its enemies,' said Champa. 'You are not God. Light and darkness both exist within us. You are so busy trying to extinguish the darkness in others that you don't see the beast you are unleashing within yourself. All this killing is making you evil.'

Shayista felt like she had slapped him with the Truth.

'Power corrupts completely. If you want power, you have to play by power's rules: you have to play from the head not the heart. Release the desire for power. Desire is from the ego.'

Her words struck a chord. Somewhere along the journey, he had lost the plot. Though he had forgiven himself only minutes ago, now again he was filled with self-loathing.

'Leaders should lead with love,' she said.

Shayista hung his head. 'I'm a failure. I'm worthless.'

Champa frowned and wiped a film of sweat off his forehead.

He saw in her eyes that she cared for him tremendously. What had he done to deserve her affection? He felt wretched. Azdahar had spilt the blood of so many sons and fathers. With arrogant vigour he had crushed entire clans to hold power. The facade of purpose he had built came crumbling down. He thought of the stormy victory in 1630 when half his men died by his side. They had won but for what?

Shayista held the diamond in his palm. This malignant beauty had destroyed the lives of hundreds before him and would destroy hundreds more. He had to get rid of it.

Shayista ran out of the garden, rushing through the walkways of the fortress, racing to the main gates as if possessed, sprinting past the guards and out into the open night.

The diamond howled, clamouring in his ears, weeping, screaming, screeching as he ran to the river and flung himself in. The mighty Buriganga beat against him, furious currents carrying shipwrecked hearts and drowned sorrows. The machinations of time and mutinies of friends hung heavy above him, he was waist deep in roaring waves.

With vicious force he had decimated his opposition. The truth of it hit him hard and he staggered to stay afloat. He raised his arm to fling the wretched curse into the fathomless river when a faint sound from behind stopped him.

'Shayista, don't!' It was Champa, calling from the shore, her body a meagre outline of black in the distance.

Her voice carried clear across the water and now the howling of the diamond and roaring of the waves and pounding of blood in the temples of his head receded. Resigned, he waded back to the shore and to Champa.

'Do you know the story of Kali?' she asked.

Shayista shook his head.

'Kali was born out of Durga's forehead to fight the buffalo-demon. Once born, the black goddess turned feral and ate all the demons she came across and drank their blood. Their heads she strung on a chain around her neck. It seemed impossible to tranquilize her fury. Her attacks began expanding to include any and all wrongdoers. But everyone does wrong sometimes.'

'What happened?'

'Mighty Shiva stopped Kali's destructive rampage by lying down in her path. When the goddess realized just who she was standing on, she finally calmed down.'

'Are you telling me to calm down?'

'Extreme destruction is not the way. Ma Kali is also Shakti. She is unconditional love. Her blackness is a symbol of eternal darkness which has the potential to both destroy and create. Love is more powerful than hatred. Look within, Talib,' said Champa. She handed him a book. 'I came to give you this.'

It was a book of verses by Hafez. He opened it to a page that had been folded in.

'I wish I could show you
when you are lonely or in darkness,
the astonishing light of your own being.'

CHAPTER 53

The Emperor arrived a few days later upon a golden howdah. He had travelled by land, the rivers were not yet swollen with the rains of Srabon. Caparisoned elephants marched before him. Behind him, a retinue of horses, camels, musketeers and columns of infantry.

The entire imperial army of Dacca stood in formation to receive him. Shayista welcomed him with a fleet of dhols, trumpets and a statue made of gold. Nasim Banu had a velvet carpet two miles long laid out across the walkway leading up to the fortress with flowers planted along both sides.

That night, the Emperor, his family, attendants and soldiers feasted heartily on spit-roasted chicken with herbs, koftas and kebebs, lamb cooked in the tandooor, Persian pulao, and then retired to luxurious tents set up for slumber.

The next morning, Shayista greeted the Emperor in the Durbar Hall. Aurangzeb was dressed in a starched kurta, rigid and austere. By his side were his Vizier, his Amir-i-Akhur, his Diwan-i-Baksh and an Englishman introduced as Governor of the East India Company. To Shayista's surprise, the Emperor was accompanied by Madeline. She was wearing a wide-skirted gown and a wig of curls. She avoided his gaze and shuffled behind the Englishman.

Shayista had not seen his nephew in over two years and they had much to discuss. He was not pleased to have so many outsiders present. He had not even allowed Dhand to attend the meeting.

'Uncle,' began Aurangzeb, 'Thank you for this grand reception.'

'Emperor Aurangzeb Alamgir this is but a humble offering compared to what you deserve,' said Shayista, bowing.

'I am grateful to you for bringing cultivation and commerce to the far eastern stretches of the Empire. Revenues have never been higher. Rice has never been cheaper.'

Shayista bowed humbly.

'You have brought about an epic transformation in Bengal. For this, all of posterity should salute you.'

'It was my duty,' said Shayista, bowing again.

'Mostly you have done well but I have a few concerns.' He stroked his beard thoughtfully.

'Yes, your Highness?' said Shayista.

'You reprimanded a Hindu zamindar for trade with the English?' said Aurangzeb.

Shayista didn't blink.

'We need the jiziya to pay for our battles,' said Aurangzeb.

Shayista resisted the temptation to tell him it was wrong to divide people by religion to extort advantages from one group in favour of the other. People of all faiths should be treated with dignity and respect. Diversity was to be celebrated not used to create hierarchies.

Aurangzeb continued. 'I have been informed of an incident in which thirty members of the ulema were killed accidentally by your mansabdars.' His voice was arctic.

Aurangzeb had always been narrow-minded. It was Dara who had absorbed the words of their Sufi Huzur. Shayista masked his anger.

'Most disturbing of all ...' Aurangzeb shook his head in disapproval. 'Rumours suggest you and your friends killed a revered pir. There are riots in Indur Goli. This is not what I expected when I removed Azzam and posted you back here.'

The snide remark dug at Shayista. How dare Aurangzeb compare him to his whimsical son? Still Shayista maintained a stoic veneer.

The Englishman leaned to the Emperor's ear and whispered.

'Ah yes,' said Aurangzeb. 'One more thing. I hear you have a diamond from the Kollur mines, a diamond that rivals the Kohinoor?'

Shayista could not believe his eyes. Aurangzeb was taking counsel from the Englishman? This was too much to bear.

'I want that diamond,' said Aurangzeb. 'It belongs to the Empire.'

'Your Highness, it is cursed,' said Shayista.

'Hang on a minute,' interrupted the Englishman. 'Did you say, cursed? You see, Sire, the old Viceroy is trying to hood-wink you! Cursed, my ar...'

'It's alright,' said Aurangzeb. 'It's alright, Uncle, I have deciphered the cause of your strange behaviour. You are under a spell of black magic. Fortunately I am here to rescue you. Guards,' he shouted. 'Bring the witch.'

The gates of the durbar opened and two soldiers marched in carrying a rough spun cloth parcel that they laid at Shayista's feet. The bundle unravelled to reveal a livid Champa within, tied and gagged at the mouth.

'What is the meaning of this?' said Shayista, jumping to ungag her and remove her bonds. 'If you have hurt her, you will pay.'

'Step aside, Uncle,' said Aurangzeb. 'She has poisoned your mind and made you kill her father and grandfather. She has tricked you but fear not, tomorrow she will hang.'

'NO!' shouted Shayista. He could no longer uphold the construction of the Empire. The illusion had cracked.

The room was brighter, the path clearer. He felt a transformation beginning. Success was not defined by externals, what he earned, what he built, what he accomplished, who he killed, but how deeply he loved.

'I will not let you hurt her. And I will not kill for you again.' Shayista threw Azdahar to the ground before the Emperor. It fell with a minatory clatter.

Aurangzeb gasped in shock.

'How dare you address the Emperor in such a manner!' said the Englishman.

Aurangzeb glared at Shayista. 'Give me the diamond and the witch can live.'

Shayista lowered himself to his knees before Champa, her bruises flashing before him, her eyes pained. His meager offering he lay before her: the diamond.

'Champa, I bring to your feet all my failures and my life's most precious possession. If you can forgive me or look at me with compassion even for a moment then all my wasted efforts I will bury and begin anew.'

Champa's eyes glazed over with tears. 'I forgive you, Talib,' she said. 'Let it go.'

Shayista turned to the Emperor. 'You want it? This cursed diamond? Take it then.' He tossed it to the Emperor who had murdered Dara and Huzur. He deserved the curse.

Aurangzeb caught the dark diamond, his eyes expanding at the sight of its fantastical proportions.

'All that you cherish will perish,' Shayista warned, laughing.

Aurangzeb turned abruptly and stormed out. With him marched the Englishman followed by Madeline, his Vizier, his Amir-i-Akhur, his Diwan-i-Baksh and his guards.

The trajectory of the cursed diamond was a mystery to Shayista: Delhi, London, Paris. What did it matter? So long as he stayed positive, he was free from its curse. He would love again and Bengal would thrive.

CHAPTER 54

'Are you alright?' Shayista asked.

Champa nodded. Her eyes twinkled with love.

Dhand approached with a captive: the Maratha warrior princess. Her fugitive spirit, her passionate animosity, even her snarl was a canvas of perfection. Dhand had not bound her but he had confiscated her weapons.

'Sire, she was found scaling the fortress walls,' said Dhand, stupefied by the lady's remarkable resemblance to Pari.

'I only came for what belongs to me,' she said.

Shayista saw in her eyes a defiant young girl. He wept inside for the childhood he had missed: the lullabies he had not sung, the nightmares he had not chased away. 'First tell me this,' he said. 'How did you learn about Kalinoor? I have kept it hidden for twenty years, almost your entire life.'

The truth spilled out. She told him everything. 'Every Maratha knows you captured my mother and kept her imprisoned in Lal Mahal. When my grandfather attacked to reclaim his fort, he found her there. She was wearing a dark diamond of unspeakable beauty that you gave her to mark her as your chattel. Since I was a child, I have dreamt of fighting you to avenge my mother. I will take back the diamond that was hers.'

'And what would you do with it?' asked Shayista.

Miri's face softened. 'My people are tired of being oppressed by Mughals. The diamond will buy us a truce so we can live in harmony in Hindustan.'

Shayista understood the noble efforts of his daughter. His heart warmed. 'The diamond will not bring harmony to Hindustan,' he explained. 'The Emperor wants to sell it to the English to finance the Deccan wars.'

The princess frowned. 'Why should I believe you? You killed my mother.'

'No. I loved her,' said Shayista. 'More than life itself. She gave my life purpose till she was snatched away from me. It was Kalinoor that killed your mother. The dark diamond is cursed.'

'I don't believe you.'

'History is not objective,' he said. 'Facts are changed, truths are lost. It doesn't matter. Your mother taught me how to love. This bougainvillea I planted for her. This one I planted for you. This one, for your twin.'

Miri looked at the bougainvilleas and then at him, stunned.

'Miri,' said Shayista gently, 'For that is what your mother and I named you ... I am your father.' His eyes glistened.

To show her the truth, Champa read Miri's palm and revealed some long-forgotten memories. Miri's face underwent a series of transformations, from anger to shock to denial to acceptance. Caught in a maelstrom of emotion, she began to sob.

'I promise to tell you about your mother someday,' said Shayista. 'And your sister. Keep this. It was hers.' He handed her the protective amulet.

'My sister?' asked Miri.

'She died last year,' said Shayista.

Miri was shaking with grief. Shayista offered her a chamber to rest in and watched her retreat from the durbar.

CHAPTER 55

Madeline ran as fast as she could till her lungs wheezed and her legs threatened to collapse. Unable to continue, she hid under a leafy neem to catch her breath. There were no signs of pursuit. Not yet.

She had to get to the docks before they realized the treasure was missing. They would send soldiers after her. And hunting hounds. Costa would be tracking her. Tavernier too. And the Emperor. She had to find a ship of European origin and pay her way home. She hadn't thought this through. She hadn't planned the escape. An opportunity came up and she grabbed it.

She had kept an eye on the diamond from the moment Shayista gave it to the Emperor. Through the day, there seemed no hope but finally a chance came when the Emperor gave it to his bakshi for safe-keeping.

The bakshi was an elderly man and easily seduced. Madeline charmed him in the privacy of his room then sedated him with some poisonous frog saliva tincture she had picked up in Chatgaon. Confiscating the diamond was then as easy as stealing bonbons from a sleeping baby.

Gazing upon Kalinoor for the first time brought tears to Madeline's eyes. Flawless divine beauty.

Leaving the fortress was no challenge. The guards had seen her entering as the Emperor's own guest earlier and suspected nothing of her. The real problems began once she was beyond the walls of the temporary garrison erected for Aurangzeb. Paranoia began creeping in. She thought someone was following her.

She avoided the bazaar and the main road, walking close to the forest's edge. She would rather face wolves than a tavern of nosy thieves. In the morning she would charter a ride out of Dacca. She thought of visiting Mumin one last time but it was too risky.

Exhausted, she lay against a branch and retrieved the diamond from her purse. It glittered in her hands. Ominous and malevolent. She felt a thrill, such enormous wealth in her palms. Finally, freedom was hers! She was so transfixed by its beauty that she didn't hear the beast approaching until it was too late.

A deep growl rumbled the earth and reverberated within her gut. She swung around in time to see a Royal Bengal tiger, its eyes burning bright.

Madeline scrambled to her feet, backing away slowly. The feline pulled back on its haunches then pounced on her. With one clean swipe, it broke her spine, killing her instantly. It devoured her over the next few days.

Princess Miri witnessed it with her own eyes. Unable to accept such an exact end to what had been her life-long mission and her last connection to her mother, Miri too had kept a watch on the diamond. She saw the Emperor give it to his bakshi and saw Madeline steal it from him shortly after. As Madeline escaped from the fortress with the stone, Miri followed her.

When the tiger attacked Madeline, Miri did not intervene but it occurred to her that Subedar Khan was telling the truth. The diamond was cursed. It brought the downfall of whosoever possessed it. This truth convinced Miri that the Subedar's other words were true too, and heavy-hearted, she left the tiger to its feasting, returning to Lal Bagh fort to make peace with her father.

CHAPTER 56

Nasim Banu lay in the hammam the next day contemplating the latest turn of events. With the Pir of Lal Bagh dead, there was no hope of speaking to Abul Fateh but at least the Emperor had relented to her pleas and promoted Iradat. This boon he granted her despite being entirely furious that Kalinoor had slipped out of his hands. Thank God it was stolen under his watch and not Shayista's. There was nothing he could do to hold that against her.

Imperial troops were sent out to search for the diamond and when they found the bones of the French jewel thief, they then tracked down the creature that had eaten her. The tiger's stomach was torn open but there were no traces of the diamond. The Emperor and his retinue left a few days later and Nasim was glad to be rid of them.

Overall, she couldn't complain. She had hired a new eunuch who was even more attentive than Ambar Khajah had been. Iradat was over the moon with his promotion. Shayista was happy to have found his long-lost daughter. And she had a new hobby. The jar of youth serum the pir had given her had worked wonders so she established a laboratory and employed a team of fifty experts to replicate it.

CHAPTER 57

Shayista called for his musicians to play a cheerful tune as Champa danced. Her shimmies were in perfect sync with the universe. Shayista smoked a hookah and recalled the morning only a month ago when he first met her at Jannat. Since then, his priorities had shifted completely.

He let out a round of meandering smoke rings. Over the next few months he would help Miri erase her pain, help Champa with her madrasa, help Costa with his hunt for the Emerald Tablet and help Dhand marry the woman he loved. He would live for his friends. He would live for love.

Destiny would have its way. If one accepted it rather than resist, one could ride it to incredible heights. A journey was charted for him the day he was born, the day two angels were sent to his mother's womb to write his Fate, and having written it, the mighty pen moved on. Surrendering to the grander design felt like an immense relief. For the first time, Shayista felt free. He opened his heart so Destiny could be fulfilled.

~

'Though Destiny a hundred times waylays you,
in the end it pitches a tent for you in Heaven.
It is God's loving kindness to give you darkness,
in order for you to see the light.'

— Jalal ad-Din Rumi

Author's Note

Dear Readers,

As a social psychologist and writer living in Dacca, I was hungry to learn about Bengal's ancient history. My grandmother's house in Lal Bagh triggered a lingering curiosity. As I began to explore, I discovered Subedar Shayista Khan: a poet, warrior, Sufi and visionary. Though Bengal flourished under his rule, he occupies only a few dry paragraphs in history text books. Thus I set out to give him some flesh (albeit, scarred flesh) so my children and others could know our hero. My kids are 5 and 7 and I daresay, Shayista's biggest fans.

Very little is written about the Mughal experience in Bengal, even less about the women of the time. Shayista Khan, Shobha Singh, Shivaji, Admiral Nicholson, William Hedges and Wara Dhamaraja are all real characters. Nasim Banu, Champa and Pari Bibi are real too but there is scarce evidence of them. What I did find was that Champa is buried at Lal Bagh Fort and rumors suggest she might have been Shayista's late mistress. Legends claim Pari's ghost haunts the fortress still and she may not have been Shayista's biological daughter but rather, war booty, a princess from Assam. These conjectures led me to play with her origin, to bring Ellora into the story. Ellora is the only character completely constructed by my imagination though who is to say our handsome Subedar did not have a few princesses on the side? As for the diamond, certainly my readers have heard of Kohinoor, the French Blue and the Pink Diamond, all of which are said to have magical powers. Perchance then readers have also heard whispers of a dark diamond?

Here are some of the books I read to write this: William Dalrymple's White Mughal and The Last Mughal, Richard Eaton's The Rise of Islam and the Bengal Frontier, John Richards' The Mughal Empire, Tapan Raychaudhuri's Bengal Under Akbar and Jahangir, Fergus

Nicoll's Shah Jahan, Joshua Ivinson's Diamonds and East India Company, Seema Mohanty's Book of Kali, Alex Rutherford's Empire of the Moghuls, Hafez's The Gift, Dr. Aye Chan's An Arakanese from Myanmar, Abraham Eraly's The Mughal Throne, Indu Sundaresan's The Twentieth Wife, Richard Wise's The French Blue, Niall Ferguson's The Empire, Susan Ronald's Sancy Blood Diamond, Richard Zaqcks' The Pirate Hunter, Sun Tzu's The Art of War, Nitish Sengupta's Land of Two Rivers: A History of Bengal, and others. I also gleaned some juicy facts from a PhD titled 'Life and times of Shaista Khan' by Noopur Sharan of Allahabad, 2005, that was not available in print, for which I had the opportunity to visit the marvelous British Library.

What I find sad is how history repeats itself. In Bangladesh and the world today we are threatened by many of the enemies Shayista Khan fought back in the 1680s. Does this mean we are not taking the lessons of history to heart? Or is this our predestined journey?

I hope you enjoy the adventure. Thanks for reading.

Yours,
Shazia

Shazia Omar is a social psychologist. She completed her undergrad at Dartmouth, USA, and her Masters at LSE, UK. She has written a novel, *Like a Diamond in the Sky* (Penguin 2009), a play, *Karma Coffee* (2014), and a mind-body-spirit book, *Intentional Smile* (Bloomsbury 2016). She teaches yoga, works for the poorest and enjoys being a mom.

www.shaziaomar.com